BOOK 2

Rebuilding

BY J.D. CRIST

Copyright © 2025 by Pumpkin Head

Publishing

All rights reserved.

No portion of this book may be

reproduced or used in AI in any form

without written permission from the

publisher or author, except as permitted by

U.S. copyright law.

Dedication

To my family, who continue to support and encourage me in this process. It is your love and support that keep me going. Without all of you, Emily and Marley's story would still be untold.

Trigger Warnings

This book explores several themes and topics that may be uncomfortable for some readers. These include:

Death

Zombies

Killing

Blood

Attempted Rape

Abuse of Women and Children

Strong Language

If you are unable to continue, I understand. But if you are, welcome back to the world of The Dead Flash.

Chapter 1

Much had changed since Hope was born, and Sanctuary was coming to life. Emily stood at the top of the wall, looking out over the town with Hope on her back. The sun was barely up, but movement was happening everywhere. Emily knew Jacob was working hard on the farm, and Terra was trying to finish her morning chores before school. Emily went to the farm some mornings to help and was amazed at their accomplishments over the past four months. The animals were healthy, and half of the cows were pregnant. Jacob had cleared the dead crops from the fields, and a sea of green now stood in each.

Even high up on the wall, Emily could smell that Julia was already baking the bread for the day. Julia made a fresh loaf of bread for each household every day. While Emily had told her that this was unnecessary, Julia insisted. Sam was already walking the streets, doing his morning checks on each person. Derick was going to the construction building to work on his project for the day. Howard and June would enjoy their morning coffee and prepare to head to school.

Jessica would be in the grocery store. She spent most of her time there, as it was the most used store. They had gotten the credit system online, and she worked to ensure everyone used it correctly. Sarah would be down in the communications building. It was an office building, but Emily had Derick convert it earlier this month. Sarah had plans to set up a system outside the wall to help people find Sanctuary and help them to communicate while they were out.

Marley would be back any moment; he ran the wall each morning to look for Shawn while Emily waited. Shawn always took the two-to-six wall shift so everyone else could rest. Emily had no idea when he found time to sleep with as many shifts as he took. Their numbers were still so few that they couldn't have a proper watch duty. Emily was pulled back from her thoughts by the sound of playful barking. She looked to her right to see Shawn and Marley walking toward her.

"Everything quiet?" she asked.

"A few dead in the distance, but nothing to worry about," Shawn smiled back at her.

"Who's taking the next shift?" Emily asked while walking toward him.

"Howard is this morning," Shawn replied after thinking for a moment.

"Howard?" Emily asked, confused. "Doesn't he normally do the after-school shift with June?"

"Normally, but Bobby has been doing well with his school work and has been asked to do a shift with his dad. So, Howard switched with Sam so they could do it after school."

"That was nice of him."

"Yeah, except June told him he could make dinner tonight since he didn't have to work," Shawn laughed.

"Oh, she is brave to let him cook," Emily mused. "You know, he told me one time that he burned water."

Hope giggled from her perch on Emily's back.

"She is growing fast," Shawn remarked as he reached and tickled Hope under her chin. "Already holding her head up enough for the backpack."

"I know it," Emily smiled. "I feel like I'm going to wake up tomorrow, and she will be full grown."

"Yeah, I heard that's how it works. But you are doing it right, you know?" Shawn stepped back and looked at Emily once more.

"What do you mean?" Emily asked.

"You take her with you everywhere. You spend every possible moment you can with her. Most moms in your position would have hired a nanny or something to watch after the kid while they worked."

"Yeah," Emily laughed. "That's not going to happen. I hate asking someone to watch her."

Emily remembered seeing these types of moms before. Some of them were so busy with their careers that they forgot their kids' names.

"Oh, we know it," Shawn laughed.

Emily loved it when he laughed. It made her feel safe, almost as if he felt comfortable laughing, nothing in the world could be wrong.

"So, any idea what Derick is working on today?"

Emily hoped that Derick would be finishing the quarantine zone soon. Doc had said it would be safer if Derick built some huts separated by walls for newcomers. The cabins would give them a chance to ensure that none of them were infected or give them a safe place to say their goodbyes if they were. Derick had disagreed, saying they should kill anyone suspected of being infected.

Emily had to put her foot down on the issue. She had been bitten and was immune. While rare, there could be others like her, and she would not kill them. He had been drawing out the project to show his protest, and Emily was frustrated.

"He's working with Sarah today. She had something she needed his help with."

"Another delay with the quarantine zone," Emily sighed.

"Did he not tell you?" Emily turned to look at Shawn. "Of course, he didn't. He finished those yesterday. I checked it out, and it's good work."

Emily could not help but let out a little squeal. Finally, Derick had finished, and she could stop asking about it daily.

"I have to see this," Emily replied while heading for the stairs. Marley began to follow as she ran down.

"I'll be down as soon as Howard arrives," Shawn called to her.

Emily hurried down the metal steps and towards the gate. She left the inner gate open a little to allow Derick to get in and out with the construction supplies. To the right was where they parked the cars they used for runs. They tried to keep them inside, but there was too much clutter. A wall was built in front of the cars with a wooden door. Emily knew that behind it was the graveyard where Ronald was buried. She turned her attention to the left and saw a small building attached to a wall that spanned the area between the metal plates.

There was enough distance between the building and the gate to give them room to drive vehicles in and turn around. Emily opened the door to the small building and saw that the building was set up with everything Doc had requested. There was an exam area with a table, a closet where clean clothes would be stored, and plenty of space for medical supplies. Emily headed through the door on the wall and found herself with the metal plate on her right and more wooden walls on her left.

She opened the first door on her left and found a small one-bedroom cabin-like structure. It had four built-in bunks and a washing station in each. In front of each was a small fire pit with seating. Emily continued down the wall and found six areas in total, exactly what she requested. Nothing fancy about them, but they had plenty of comforts to get folks through a couple of days. They would have to bring bedding and food to each as they came, but that would be no issue. Emily headed back through the wooden wall and out of the gate.

"So, does it meet your standards, your highness?" Emily could hear the hatred in Derick's face as he spoke.

"They are perfect!" Emily tried to pretend he was not trying to instigate a fight. "Thank you so much for doing that."

"Not much of a choice," Derick spat back at her. "If it wasn't you bitching at me, it was that criminal."

"Derick, I wasn't trying to…." Emily tried to explain she wasn't a nag, but Derick was not in the mood.

Derick turned and headed into the communications building to meet with Sarah. At this moment, Emily realized she had no idea what

Sarah's project was. Emily started to follow Derick to speak with Sarah about it.

"I wouldn't do that if I were you," Shawn called out from the steps.

"Why not?" Emily asked.

"Two reasons," Shawn replied as he walked towards her. "One, she said it was a surprise. Two, you don't want to be a witness if she kills that bastard, do you?"

"Oh, when you put it that way, I have something else to do way over there," Emily laughed back at him.

"I thought you might. Do you mind if I walk with you?" Shawn asked.

"Of course not." Emily turned and began to walk back up the main street with Shawn and Marley.

"We should plan another run soon," Shawn stated as they walked.

"Are we out of something?" Emily couldn't help but sound concerned. Robert had filled Sanctuary with so many supplies that it was hard to believe that they could be gone so soon.

"Lumber is starting to run a bit lower than I would like. Derick is already trying to use it as an excuse not to do projects."

"Robert had a delivery of lumber that was supposed to come in before the flash. It's probably sitting in town still."

"That was my thought. If we're lucky, it may already be on a trailer just waiting to be brought in."

"Fingers crossed," Emily smiled back. "You and I can head out on Monday to check it out."

"Sounds like a plan, boss lady." They had reached the end of the main street, and Emily stopped.

"I should probably check in with Doc or Jessica to see how things are going."

"You may want to start with Jessica. She was pretty angry last night, but said she would only talk to you."

"Well, that sounds like fun." Emily rolled her eyes and headed for the grocery store. The small bell that Jessica had installed rang out as she opened the door.
"I swear to God you will not get any more, no matter how much you scream!" Jessica yelled from the back of the store.

"Okay, but just so I know, what am I not getting?!" Emily yelled back. Jessica came running to the front, and Emily could tell Jessica was visibly shaken. "What happened?" Emily asked.

"It was Derick. He has already gone over the weekly alcohol limit. I know I shouldn't have let him go over at all, but I just wanted him to go away," Jessica explained. "He came in last night to get more and didn't have enough credits. I told him I couldn't give it to him, and he lost it. He threw the bottle at my head and started screaming at me."

"He did what?!" Emily couldn't help the anger she felt growing inside her.

"He said he wasn't going to let a child tell him what to do and grabbed another and walked out," Jessica continued. "I locked up the rest of the bottles in the back. He returned this morning to get more, and I refused him again. I have spent the past hour cleaning up his mess, looking for more. He told me to have his bottle ready tonight, or there would be hell to pay."

"You did the right thing." Emily tried hard to steady herself. "Next time, though, come tell me right away. Don't wait."
"I didn't want to bother you because I know Hope was in bed already." Emily could tell that Jessica was embarrassed.

"I appreciate that, but you could have been hurt," Emily explained. "Does it cause any issues for the alcohol to be locked up in the back from now on?"

"No, no one else gets it. Shawn and Sam occasionally do, and I think June and Julia each have taken a bottle of wine."

"Let's keep it locked up then, and if you don't mind, people can only have it by request. I want you to charge the credits for the broken bottle and the one he took to Derick's account."

"I can do that, but it's not going to stop him from coming in and throwing a fit." Jessica was visibly scared of a repeat encounter with Derick.

"I'll take care of that. We need to list people and specific goods they are no longer allowed to have."

"Are you saying he's never allowed to have alcohol again?"

"At least not for a very long time." Emily could see that Jessica had a new fear. "Don't worry, I'll tell him, and I'll make sure that someone is close by when he's done with work for the day. I won't let you deal with him alone again." Emily could see that Jessica relaxed.

"Are you going to tell him now?" Jessica asked.

"I'll head straight over as soon as I leave here. Unless you need something else?"

"Maybe Hope should stay with me?" Jessica looked at the ground as she spoke. "I would feel awful if he went into another fit and she got hurt."

Emily smiled and turned her back to Jessica. Jessica quickly removed Hope from the backpack and began talking to the baby.

"I'll be back in a little bit. Don't you two go causing too much trouble," Emily smiled as she left.

Jessica helped Hope by waving goodbye and then headed back into the store. Emily could see Shawn talking to Sam across the street. Part of her thought of going to him and asking for his help in breaking the news to Derick. However, she forced herself not to and continued walking. Derick had no respect for her as it was, and if she kept asking Shawn to help her in these situations, it would only get worse. Emily continued to talk to herself as she walked. She had faced down a gang of rapists and walked out the winner. She had Marley with her, after all. What else did she need?

Emily reached the communications building and saw Sarah and Derick standing at a table. Sarah looked annoyed and explained to Derick that she was asking for a simple design and would not change it. Emily entered the building and waved to Sarah.

"Thank goodness," Sarah breathed. "I wanted it to be a surprise, but apparently, there are not enough supplies to get it done."

"So, you need me to approve my surprise?" Emily smiled.

"Yes," Sarah sneered as Emily walked towards the table. Emily looked down at the drawings. "They're communication stations for outside the wall. I will need four of them to put up to the east, west, north, and south. Each will hold water, a little food, a map, and a solar-powered walkie. The stations will allow us to find people and help them get to Sanctuary."

"Seems like an efficient design," Emily commented. "What's the problem?"

"The problem is that the lumber is almost gone," Derick replied. "I can do this if you want, but then I will be out of work until you get more."

"Go ahead and get these done." Emily smiled back at him. "How long do you think they will take?"

"I don't know, a week, maybe two?" Emily knew that the project shouldn't have taken more than a day or two, but wouldn't argue it with him. "Great, we should have the lumber delivery here before you finish these."

Emily could see Sarah smiling at the irritated look on Derick's face.

"We'll see." Derick gathered the papers from the table and headed for the door.

"Wait up," Emily called to him. "I have something else to talk to you about."

"If it's another project, I'm not discussing it until you get more lumber."

Derick walked out the door without looking back. Emily walked quickly to chase after him and caught up with him on the street outside.

"It's about what happened in the store with Jessica," Emily started as she reached him.

"Oh, lord," Derick exclaimed. "If that little cunt can't handle an angry customer, she is in the wrong line of work. Just tell her that the customer is always right and to give me my damn drink!" Derick began to walk away.

"I'm here to tell you that you cannot purchase alcohol anymore."

Emily watched as he froze mid-step. Even from behind, she could see his ears turning red and imagined that his face was the same red shade.

"What?!" Derick yelled as he turned and began to make his way toward Emily.

His yell had gotten the attention of others on the street. Everyone had now turned to see what was going on. Marley moved to stand between Emily and Derick, a growl escaping his throat.

"You are blocked from all alcohol purchases until further notice," Emily explained. "This decision is based on...."

"Bullshit!" Derick was not calming down, and Marley's growl grew louder. "This decision is based on bullshit! You cannot take away my basic right to drinking!"

"You cannot threaten Jessica and throw a temper tantrum," Emily heard herself yell back. "This decision is final!"

Everything seemed to be moving in slow motion. Emily watched as Derick dropped the papers to the ground. He closed his fist and began to draw it back. He stepped forward and began to draw his fist forward. Suddenly, Derick let out a scream that sped the world back up. Emily saw that Marley had attached himself to Derick's arm, stopping the fist from coming at Emily. The red blood was already dripping from Marley's jowls and splashing on the pavement.

"Enough," Emily yelled out, and Marley released Derick's arm.

"I'm going to kill that fucking dog," Derick screamed while holding his bloody arm.

Emily drew back her fist and hit Derick as hard as she could. She was surprised to see the man fall to the ground. Emily saw Shawn running towards the scene, but stopped a few steps away. The smile on his face could have been seen from the top of the wall.

"Could you help him get to Doc's to get stitched up and then get him back to work?" Emily asked as casually as she could.

"Yes, ma'am." Shawn pulled Derick to his feet and began to walk him to the clinic.

Emily could still see some of Derick's blood on Marley's face. Just then, Sarah came out of the communication building with a glass of water, laughing.

"I'll get Marley cleaned up, and if it's okay, I think I would like to donate a steak to his dinner tonight." Marley began to wag his tail, but sat as Sarah ran the cool water over his face.

"I didn't understand everything going on, but I know Derick deserved what he just got," Sarah continued. "Thank you so much for allowing me to see it happen."

Sarah had finished washing Marley's face and turned to face Emily.

"I was afraid you might be upset that

Marley bit him or that I punched him afterward."
Emily had a hard time believing that Sarah would
find this funny.

"Marley warned him that day we all agreed
to stay, and Derick chose to push him. That is all
Derick's fault as far as I'm concerned. And the
punch, he didn't learn from the bite. He deserved
that, too. So, you were just driving the lesson
home." With that, Sarah headed back inside the
building.

Emily could see that Shawn had Derick in
the clinic and couldn't help but smile when Sam
and Howard began to clap and cheer. She walked
back up the street with Marley and went back into
the store. She explained to Jessica that the
situation was handled, and Jessica helped Hope
back into her riding position.

When she headed back out, she saw Shawn
leaning against the clinic, having a cigarette.
Seeing her walking towards him, Shawn knocked
the cherry off and slid the remaining part into his
pocket.

"Doc said it wouldn't take him long to stitch
Derick up. He did want me to ask if Marley got a
rabies shot before the flash."

"Yeah, I think it was a two-year dose."
Emily tried hard to remember.

"Damn, I guess Derick won't need that
treatment."

"Is he still going to be able to work?"

"Oh yeah. Derick told Doc what happened
and was trying to get some painkillers. Don't
worry." Shawn saw the look of concern on her
face. "Doc told him no."

Emily breathed a sigh of relief.

"I think Derick's more upset by the nose than the bite," Shawn laughed.

"What happened to his nose?" Emily asked.

"You broke it!" Shawn laughed even harder.

"Didn't see it until I got him halfway here that it was bent and bleeding like hell. I don't think he will take another swing at you anytime soon."

Chapter 2

The next day, everyone heard about what happened to Derick, and Emily didn't want to defend her or Marley's actions. It was Saturday, so the school would be closed. Terra and Bobby usually took Marley to the farm to play. Emily did not know how he would react if they feared him. Emily found her courage and opened the front door. A smile spread across her face as she saw Terra and Bobby waiting in front of the house. Marley rushed out the door to join them, and Emily watched as they ran towards the farm together.

Emily closed the front door and headed to the main street. Jessica waved from the store window, and Sarah was waiting for her by the wall. Emily relaxed as she waved back at Jessica and made her way to Sarah.

"Hey there, slugger," Sarah teased as she approached.

"Hey there yourself," Emily replied.

Sarah smiled and then handed a walkie to Emily.

"I got them all working last night," she explained. I've got everyone on channel three. They are solar-powered, so they should charge while you are outside, but just come to me if you have a problem. I have batteries if needed."

"Wow, no more running or yelling to get each other's attention," Emily mused.

"It will be extra important if we find new people," Sarah continued. "I got the radio working in the COM room, so I'll always be reachable, and

I put one in the control room for whoever's on wall duty. I also have one for Doc, Sam, Shawn, and Jacob."

"Sounds efficient," Emily remarked as she attached the walkie to her waist.

"I also have four we can put on the stations once they are ready. I'd better get the rest of these delivered."

"Don't let me stop you." Emily motioned for Sarah to go on her way as she headed up to the wall. Shawn would be on duty again, but she stood and watched the town from above until he arrived.

"You're not going to throw me off the wall, are you?" Shawn called out when he saw her.

"Why would I do that?" Emily smiled back at him.

"According to Derick, your act of violence last night showed that you are willing to kill us all for no reason." Shawn continued to walk toward her with a big grin on his face.

"Oh, well, if Derick says it's true, you'd better watch out."

Emily had expected Derick to try to say both she and Marley were crazy and maybe even bloodthirsty.

"I'll take my chances," Shawn replied as he walked beside her. "Did you get your walkie?"

"Sure did," Emily patted the walkie on her waist.

"Sarah said we're all on channel three, and the ones outside will be on channel two. I figure you and I could use channel one just in case of a security issue."

"Sounds like a plan," Emily replied.

Emily did not know what kind of security issue they could have. However, knowing she had a way to reach Shawn was comforting.

"Um, Emily, it's Doc." Doc's voice erupted from both of their walkies at once.

Emily grabbed her walkie from her hip and pressed the button.

"Go ahead, Doc," Emily said in her most official voice.

"I need you to come by the clinic as soon as you can…. over." Emily could not help but laugh, and could hear Shawn doing the same.

"I'm on my way."

Emily also thought about saying it over, but feared Doc would hear her laugh.

"Duty calls." Emily looked at Shawn as she spoke.

"You'd better hurry over." Shawn laughed back at her.

Emily went down the stairs and back up the road to the clinic. Doc had not changed much in here since he arrived. The only noticeable difference was the playpen set up in the corner. On occasion, Doc would babysit Hope while Emily was on a run. Emily scanned the office but found that Doc was not there.

"Doc!" she called out.

The irony of her saying they would no longer have to scream for each other was not lost on her. Within moments, Doc came into the room with a smile on his face.

"I thought you would be upset about the stitches and broken nose yesterday?" Emily asked.

"Oh, my no," Doc replied. "It was a pleasure to patch Derick up, deny him pain meds, and send him back to work."

"Glad to hear it," Emily smiled. "You needed to see me for something?"

"Yes, I was wondering if I could get a blood sample from you and Hope?"

"Any particular reason?" Emily asked.

"I guess I should explain," Doc began. "I want to see if I can identify the marker in you that makes you immune. Then I can check to see if Hope has it as well."

"That would be amazing."

Emily had wondered if there was a way to tell if Hope was immune. The only test she knew of was if Hope got bitten, not something Emily was willing to do. Emily began to remove Hope from her back. This process usually took two people, but Emily had mastered doing it alone.

"I think it's logical that I explain everything before taking your blood," Doc said.

"There's more?" Emily asked as she held Hope.

"Yes, see, after I identify the marker, I want to try to use it to make an antidote or vaccine that could help those without it."

"Do you think that's possible?"

Emily couldn't hide the excitement in her voice. If Doc could do what he said, that would be a big step in getting the world back on track.

"I believe so. I worked a little with an experimental medicine, so it will take a while, but eventually, I think I can do it. I will ask everyone in Sanctuary for a blood sample to test."

"You can tell them all I approve," Emily smiled at him. She expected Doc to take them to a room to do the blood draw, but he stood still. "Is there more?" Emily asked.

"Unfortunately, yes. To do the proper tests and experiments, I will also need the blood of the dead ones," Doc explained. "I will need to study it to find out how it works and mix it with live blood to see if my trials may reverse it."

"I don't think we have any of that in here," Emily replied. Doc looked down at the ground as if he were ashamed of his request. "Shawn and I are heading out on the run on Monday. We are sure to find a dead one while we are out. Do you just want us to bring the whole body back?" Emily felt like someone else was talking as she casually suggested they bring a corpse home.

"Yes, that would give me plenty of subject matter to work with." Doc could not hide his excitement.

"I do have a question, Doc."

"Of course," Doc replied as he waited.

"Why all the secrecy? You only wanted me to know what you're working on."

"I don't care who knows; I'm working on a cure, but I feel it would be safer if they didn't know I was using your blood to do it," Doc explained. "I fear that if certain people find out, they will do something stupid. Like kill you and drink your blood to become immune."

"Would it work?" Emily asked.

"Of course not, but then they may turn to Hope to do the same thing. People can be stupid when driven by fear."

"I understand and agree with you," Emily replied. "I will have to tell Shawn at least part of it. How else will I explain wanting to bring a corpse back to town?"

"Good point," Doc smiled. "Why don't you guys come back to the exam room? It's time for Hope's next round of vaccines anyway."

Emily followed Doc back to the exam room. She held Hope as Doc inserted the needle into her arm and took a few vials of blood. Once he was done, it was Hope's turn. Emily held Hope on her lap, and Doc started with the blood sample. He feared Emily would change her mind on the blood sample if Hope threw a fit during the vaccinations.

Emily braced herself to hear Hope cry and scream as the needle entered her arm. However, Hope sat silent as Doc continued and took a vial of blood. Doc bandaged Hope's arm and proceeded with the vaccinations. Again, Hope remained quiet and still for each one.

"She is the bravest baby I have ever seen," Doc remarked as he finished.

"She is a trooper." Emily tickled Hope and watched as the baby laughed.

"I will get started on these samples and let you know the results as soon as possible."

"I appreciate it, Doc," Emily replied. Emily left the exam room and headed back into the lobby. Within a few minutes, she had Hope strapped to her back and was headed outside. She could see Shawn leaning against the wall as she opened the door.

"Everything good?" he asked as soon as he saw her.

"Yeah, Hope needed some more shots, and Doc needed a blood sample from us."

"Blood sample? What for?" Shawn looked concerned, like something might be wrong with them.

"He's trying to find the marker in my blood that makes me immune and is going to check Hope for it as well," Emily explained.

"Oh, that makes sense." Emily could see the relief on Shawn's face.

"He also asked a favor, and I need your help with it," Emily began. Shawn raised an eyebrow as he looked at her. "He wants to develop a vaccine to either cure someone who is bitten or make everyone immune. But to do it, he needs a zombie's blood for the trials."

"You want me to go grab a jar from the store?" Shawn teased, motioning at the grocery store.

"Of course not," Emily laughed. "When we go out, we always find a few dead ones. If you could help me bring one of the corpses back, that would be all he needs."

"Bring it back, brain-dead, right?" Shawn raised his eyebrow once more.

"Yes, brain dead," Emily laughed.

"I see no problem with it. Everyone will be glad to know that we may have a shot at a cure."

Emily bit her lip as he spoke. "I'd rather keep this quiet for now."

"Why?" Shawn asked. "You are always looking for ways to show them that the living stand a chance in this world. This would go a long way to doing that."

"Doc is going to use my blood to make the vaccine," Emily explained. "People can do crazy things when they are afraid. If they find out that my blood may hold the cure, they may kill me or Hope to take it." Emily felt her tears welling as she explained this. Though she had heard Doc say it, it made it more real when she said it herself.

"Oh shit, I didn't think of that," Shawn remarked. "Top secret then," he reassured her.

"He did say he would need a sample from everyone. Maybe you could head in and give yours now?"

"But I'm afraid of needles," Shawn tried his best to look scared.

"Get in there, you big baby. Hope did it and didn't even flinch!"

"Well," Shawn straightened himself, "I refuse to be shown up by someone so small."

With that, Shawn headed inside to give his blood sample. Emily shook her head, laughing as she walked back into the street.

"Emily, could you come to the COM building?" Sarah's voice rang out.

"I'm on my way," Emily replied.

She returned the walkie to her hip once more. She had only had this thing for a few hours, and already, people were blowing her up. She laughed, remembering the day Chad repeatedly called her cell phone. These calls she wouldn't ignore because they were from people who needed and cared about her. In a few minutes, Emily reached the COM room and was surprised to see wooden structures leaning against it. Emily headed inside to find Sarah and Derick waiting in silence.

"I wanted your approval before I took off work to heal." Derick motioned to his arm, but Emily could not help but stare at the bruise on his face. "They are exactly what she asked for."

Emily looked at Sarah, who nodded in agreement.

"If Sarah says they are what she needs, that is good enough for me. Please take the rest of the weekend to rest."

"I can't risk wasting any more lumber until I have more," Derick grumbled.

"We will have your delivery on Monday," Emily reassured him. She expected Derick to leave, but he stood there staring at her. "Is there something else?" Emily asked.

"I hurt like hell, and Doc says I can't have pain killers. I need something to dull the pain. May I please have one bottle due to my condition?"

Emily was shocked to hear him say Please. She knew that Doc denied him painkillers for the same reason she had cut him off from alcohol.

"I'm sorry, but no," Emily responded. "However, you can take some ibuprofen to help dull the pain."

Emily could tell he was angry at this response. However, he simply pushed past her and left.

"Oh," Sarah complained. "I was hoping for round two."

"Stop it," Emily jokingly scolded her.

"Fine," Sarah agreed. "So, I need your approval with Jessica to make the station's food and water packs. I should be able to get everything ready by Monday if you guys want to take them with you."

Emily suddenly felt like all of the air had been sucked out of the room. With everything that had to be done, she thought it would take longer to set up things to bring in new people. She was beginning to panic as Hope squirmed on her back. Emily had gotten lucky with the first group, with only one bad apple. But he could be kept in line. Emily could not guarantee she would be that lucky again. The world was full of bad people before there were any laws.

"Are you okay?" Sarah asked, pulling Emily back from her thoughts.

"Are you sure this is a good idea?" Emily asked.

"Of course, the radios will work fine."

"Not the radios. Do you think letting more people in is a good idea?" Emily hated herself as soon as she said it, and the look on Sarah's face made her feel worse. They had been talking about this for months, but now that it was time, Emily could not help but be scared.

"We have to try," Sarah said, almost pleadingly.

"I know," Emily replied. "I'm just...scared."

Emily felt like she was going to choke on the last word. She hated admitting she was scared these days.

"We all are," Sarah comforted her. "But if you had let that fear control you, we wouldn't be here. Hope wouldn't be here."

"You're right," Emily replied. "I'll let Jessica know you have my okay to make the supply packs." Emily could still hear the uncertainty in her voice as she spoke.

"Thank you," Sarah replied. "I promise that we are all in this together, no matter what. We won't let anything happen to Hope."

Emily nodded and headed back outside. Usually, the fresh air would comfort her, but today, her head was just too full. She walked back up the road and found Jessica. She explained the packs that Sarah wanted to make, and they agreed on what would be in each one. Emily left Jessica still feeling like she was in a daze. Emily didn't want to worry everyone with her uncertainty, but knew she had to talk to someone.

Hope was fast asleep on her back in her regular milk lunch nap. Emily would typically stay out and allow Hope to sleep in the carrier, but turned towards their home today. She was happy to see Marley asleep on the porch. He woke as she walked up the stairs and stretched. He was tired after a playful morning. Usually, he would have rested here and come to find her after his nap. Emily stepped past him and opened the front door. Once inside, she took Hope upstairs and laid her in the crib as Marley curled up under it. Emily left the room and allowed them to enjoy their nap.

Once back downstairs, Emily felt the house's emptiness begin to weigh down on her. She sat on the couch and allowed her mind to run wild. She saw images of Jeff finding the walkies and getting in the gate. She saw Hope being taken by some unknown stranger. She saw the people who lived in Sanctuary crying, and everything they worked for was being taken away.

Emily was pulled from her thoughts by a knock at the door. She composed herself as best she could and answered it. She was relieved to see Shawn standing on the other side. She stepped aside and allowed him to enter before closing the door again.

"Sarah just told me about the stations. I guess we are going to have a full day on Monday," Shawn smiled as he followed her into the living room.

"I guess," Emily muttered.

"She also told me about you having second thoughts. What's going on?" Shawn asked as he sat down on the couch.

Emily felt the tears she was holding back escape as she told Shawn everything, collapsing on the couch beside him. She told him how scared she was that they would let someone in that would hurt them and how their luck would have to run out sooner or later. Emily had no idea how long she talked, but Shawn sat and listened without interrupting. When she finally finished, she waited for him to tell her what an idiot she was. Instead, he simply pulled her close to him and wrapped her in a hug. Emily allowed herself to lie against his chest. She let the tears run until they came to a stop on their own. Shawn remained quiet, and Emily remained still.

"You know, channel one was not really for security emergencies." Emily forced herself to pull away and look up at Shawn. "Everyone needs someone to talk to, especially if they have as much pressure on them as you. I hoped you understood that if you needed to talk, that's how you could always find me." Shawn smiled down at her.

"Well, apparently, I missed that," Emily laughed.

"Apparently," he replied. "I know you're scared. You would be a fool not to be. But we need more help to keep this place around for years. I can't promise that no bad people will find us. But I can promise that if they do, we will stand together. We are a family now, all of us. We will throw them off the wall together if the bad get in."

Emily searched for the feelings that drove her insane just a few minutes ago, but couldn't find them. Shawn was right. They were a family now. Derick even filled the role of the mean drunk uncle that no one likes but tolerates because he's family. Emily nodded back at him and allowed herself to be swallowed by his embrace once more. Shawn leaned back on the couch, and the two sat until Hope began to fuss.

Emily had no clue how long they had been sitting. She knew Hope was the only person who could get her to move. Emily slowly lifted her head and looked at Shawn. He rubbed her on the back, and Emily stood and headed for the stairs. Emily could not help but smile as she climbed the stairs, remembering the comfort she had found after all this time. She would have never imagined that Shawn would be the source of it, but now she can't imagine it being anyone else.

Emily opened the door to Hope's room and found the baby trying to crawl in her crib. Marley was awake as well and sat by the crib watching. Emily walked over and picked up Hope, embracing her in a hug. She then gave Hope a quick diaper change and headed back downstairs. She felt like a teenage girl at the thought of seeing

Shawn again. Though she had only been gone a few minutes, she was excited to see him.

As Emily reached the bottom of the stairs, she looked towards the couch to find it empty. She quickly scanned the rest of the room and couldn't help but feel disappointed that he was gone. Emily walked back to the couch and sat down with Hope. She then noticed the piece of paper on the table. Emily picked it up and read the words like a note passed to her in class.

I had to go to another wall shift. Sorry to leave without saying goodbye. I'm still here. Remember, Channel 1.

Shawn

Emily placed the piece of paper back down on the table with a smile on her face. Hope began to fidget in her arms once more. Emily pushed the table towards the television and placed Hope on the area rug. She watched as the baby tried her best to crawl, and Marley encouraged her every movement. Like most babies, Emily waited for Hope to get frustrated and give up, but Hope refused. She continued for hours until her body grew tired and she fell asleep.

Chapter 3

Emily spent Sunday at home with Hope. She checked in with everyone by walkie and explained that she was taking a vacation day. Everyone seemed to understand and even be proud of her for making this decision. She explained that she was available if there was an emergency, though she knew none of them would be calling her. Emily spent the morning reading to and playing with Hope. She felt like she was alone in her world with Hope and Marley. They had just finished a book when Emily heard the radio spring to life.

"Emily, security channel, please," Shawn's voice rang. Emily clicked her walkie over to channel one.

"Is there a problem?" Emily stated after pressing the button.

"I just wanted to make sure you are okay. I haven't seen you since I left yesterday." Emily smiled at the memory of lying against his chest while he held her.

"Everything is great. I wanted to spend the day with Hope before heading out tomorrow."

"So, our date is still on for tomorrow?" Shawn asked.

"I'm not going to stand you up," Emily laughed. "I promise."

"If you need anything, just let me know. You guys have fun, and I'll see you in the morning."

"Will do," Emily responded and turned the radio back to channel three.

"What the hell is a security channel, you guys?" Sarah's voice rang out.

"I'll explain," Shawn responded. Emily placed the walkie back on her waist and took Hope upstairs for her nap.

Once Hope and Marley were tucked in for their nap, Emily headed back downstairs. She took the time to clean up the house and do some dusting that she had neglected. Once she finished, she sat on the couch and thought for a while.

The peacefulness she felt during this time was more than she could explain. Hope was getting to sleep in her bed, and Emily had time to keep house. Emily had been so focused on the town and making sure it ran smoothly that she was robbing her family of these moments. When Emily heard Hope begin to fuss to get out of bed, Emily decided that she would make this their new daily routine. Hope was no longer going to take her naps in the backpack but in her bed.

Emily opened Hope's door to find her and Marley awake and Hope trying to crawl again. Emily picked up Hope and soon had her changed for the afternoon. Once they were back downstairs, Emily placed Hope back on the floor for another crawling lesson. Hope was so close to getting it, and Emily didn't want to miss it while she was gone tomorrow.

Hope rocked back and forth on her belly for a long time. Still, she never grew frustrated or angry. Her little face looked determined as Marley moved to lie next to her. Hope looked at Marley as he began to do a dog version of an army crawl. Emily could swear it looked like Hope was studying him. Once Marley finished, he turned and faced Hope on the carpet. It took only a few minutes, and Hope began to pull herself forward towards Marley.

As Hope reached Marley, Emily clapped and cheered while the two celebrated. Emily tussled Marley's ears as Hope let out joyful squeals. Emily could not believe what she had just seen. Marley had seen what Hope wanted to do and taught her how to crawl. Once the celebration was over, Hope was on the move once more. She seemed determined to investigate every corner of the room. Emily remained seated and watched as Marley followed Hope. If Hope crawled too close to the table or wall, Marley lay in front of it. Hope would become agitated when he blocked her path, but soon would turn and go in a new direction.

Emily always knew that Marley was a fantastic dog. He had protected, comforted, and guided her in more ways than she could count. However, she could never have dreamed that he would have this much insight regarding a baby. Emily continued to sit, watching her small family walk around the room several times. Hope began slowing down, and Emily realized it was supper time.

Emily made Hope a bottle and fed her while Marley went into the backyard. Marley came in just as Hope finished eating and began to eat his dinner. Emily took Hope upstairs and gave her a quick bath before dressing her for bed. When Emily entered Hope's room, she found Marley lying under the crib. She knew he would stay here until she was ready for bed herself.

Emily tucked Hope in for the night and headed back downstairs to feed herself. After supper, Emily headed upstairs for a long, hot shower. This was the most relaxing and rewarding day she could remember in a long time. Once Emily was dressed for bed, she went to check on Hope once more. As Emily opened the door and headed for the master bedroom, Marley came out. Emily looked at the sleeping baby for a few moments and then followed. She crawled into the bed next to Marley and wrapped her arm over the massive dog. It did not take long before both she and Marley were fast asleep.

Emily woke early the next day and quickly moved through the routine. Soon, the three of them were headed out the door into the town. Emily headed to the bakery, where she could smell the fresh bread. She saw that Julia was waiting for her as she entered the door.

"Anything I should know?" Julia asked as she took Hope from Emily's arms.

"Well, she's mobile now," Emily smiled.

"Wow, she's starting young," Julia remarked while holding Hope.

"With Marley as a teacher, nothing is holding her back," Emily laughed. However, she noticed Julia's face turned more serious.

"Something wrong?" Emily asked.

"I know you can let yourself in, but what if?" Julia stopped her sentence short.

"What if we don't make it back?" Emily finished for her.

"I've worried about it every time you leave," Julia confessed.

"I've left behind the key to the gate each time," Emily smiled at her.

"Where?" Julia asked with confusion.

"Bobby knows he just doesn't realize it," Emily smiled back. "If I'm gone for more than a week, just tell Bobby that Hope needs a little luck. He will bring it to you."

"I don't understand," Julia replied.

"That's the point. I trust you with the clue because I know you won't ask him for it unless you truly believe I'm gone." Emily smiled at her friend as she turned and headed out the door.

Emily found Shawn waiting for her by the gate. He already had the stations loaded up in the bed of the pickup.

"Figured we would do these first and work our way around to the lumber yard."

"Sounds good to me," Emily replied. She walked upstairs and entered the code to open the outer gate.

She watched as Shawn drove the truck with Marley in the bed out of the gate. She walked down the stairs and through the gate. Once outside, she opened the outer control panel and entered the code again to close the gate. She then joined Shawn in the cab of the truck. Once she was in, Shawn began to drive down the logging road.

Emily watched ahead in silence, almost holding her breath. She hated passing by the old SUV every time she left. It reminded her of Jeff and how she destroyed the SUV to escape him. It wasn't long before they passed by the SUV. Emily stared at it as they passed.

"Maybe we should push it off the road," Shawn commented a few moments later.

"No, one day I'll be able to let the pain of it go," Emily replied. "I won't know when that happens if it's gone."

Shawn nodded in understanding and then focused on the road once more. They drove for a while until they reached the main road. The logging road was easy to miss as trees on either side blocked it. Unless you were looking for it, you would pass it without even realizing it. Shawn slowed the truck to a stop. This was one of the locations that Sarah had decided on for the stations.

Shawn climbed out of the truck and took a shovel from the back. He set to work digging holes for the ground post on the stations. Emily gripped her crowbar and climbed out to join him. Marley jumped out of the bed of the truck and stood beside her. Emily kept watching the wood line while Shawn worked. It didn't take him long before he finished.

"You mind giving me a hand?" he asked while walking back to the truck.

Emily laid her crowbar on the truck seat and helped Shawn pull one of the stations out of the truck's bed. Once the ground posts were in the holes, Emily held the station while Shawn packed in the dirt around them. Emily then returned to the truck and grabbed one of Sarah's packs. She removed the walkie and hung it on one hook and the bag of supplies on the other. Across the top of the station, Derick had painted "Sanctuary – A Place to Live Among the Living."

Emily felt the butterflies begin in her stomach as she looked at the station. Letting strangers in still scared her, but she knew it was the right thing to do. Emily felt a hand on her shoulder, turning to Shawn behind her.

"It's going to be fine," he said in a comforting voice.

"I know," Emily smiled back at him.

She squeezed his hand and headed back to the truck. Marley jumped back in the bed, and soon they were on their way to the next location. They repeated the process three more times without incident. Soon, all the stations were done, and they were ready to head to the lumber yard. The day was already half gone, and they would need to move fast to make it home by dark.

"Any other time, we would have seen a dozen of those bastards by now," Shawn commented as he started the truck. "But want one, and you don't see any."

"I'm sure we will find more than we want in town." Emily felt confident in her statement. Shawn nodded in agreement and began the drive into town. Emily hoped he was right that the lumber would be loaded and waiting for them.

As they made their way down the road, Emily spotted some people walking toward them. She turned to point it out to Shawn, but could tell that he saw them as well. As they grew closer, Emily could tell the person was shambling, not walking. Shawn slowed the truck to a stop, and Emily could see the cloudy white eyes from a distance.

"It will be easier here than in town," Shawn stated as he climbed out of the truck. Emily reached for her door handle to follow.

"I got this; you just wait there." Shawn shut the truck door and walked toward the zombie.

The zombie was a well-dressed man and appeared to have been killed by the flash. Emily didn't see any tears or bites from where she was. She tried to imagine what this man could have been doing before it happened. Was he just passing through on business? Was he on his way to the Sanctuary?

Emily's thoughts ended as Shawn hit the man in the skull with a small knife. Shawn left the knife and picked up the corpse from the ground. He carried it back to the truck and placed it in the bed. He then covered it with a tarp and climbed back inside. Shawn put the truck back into drive and started back towards the town.

Emily watched the road as they continued down. She felt the knot twist in her stomach as she saw the edge of town. She immediately started flashing back to the memories of Jeff and his gang blocking the streets. Then she saw herself in the cellar, standing in a group of men cheering as Jeff tried to force her into being his slave.

Emily was pulled back to the present as Shawn took her hand. She turned to look at him and could tell he knew what she was thinking. She allowed her fingers to intertwine with his and found strength in his touch. They passed by the dealership, and Emily managed to keep her composure.

After a few more minutes, Emily saw that they were approaching the lumber yard. Shawn pulled in front of the building and stopped the truck. Emily felt Shawn release her hand as he climbed out. Emily joined him, her crowbar in hand.

"We should check around back to see if there is a trailer," Shawn stated after looking at the parking lot for a few minutes.

"I'll follow you," Emily replied.

Emily followed Shawn around the back of the building, and Marley followed right behind her. Emily gripped her crowbar, the same one that Joe had given her long ago. As they rounded the corner, Emily saw three trailers were back there. She followed Shawn to each one and felt defeated as each of them proved empty.

"So much for luck," Shawn breathed as he looked at the last empty trailer.

"There are tons of supplies back here. Let's load up one and get back on the road." Emily motioned to the rows of lumber in the yard.

"I'll get the truck, so we can back the trailer closer. No need to work harder than we have to."

With that, Shawn headed towards the front of the building. As Shawn pulled the truck around, Emily was waiting for him by the trailer. Emily helped him back up the truck to the trailer as she had helped her father many times. Soon, they had the trailer backed up and were working together to load it.

"We can't take everything, but at least we know where we can come for more," Shawn commented.

"We will just take what we can today and come back if we need to," Emily agreed.

They continued to work for a few more hours until the trailer was nearly full.

"That is plenty for now," Shawn said after loading another two-by-four. "If we want to get back before dark, we should get going."

Emily looked down at Marley, who sat beside the trailer watching for danger.

"Are you ready to go home, boy?" Emily asked. Marley began to wag his tail and jumped around excitedly.

"I'm sure he's exhausted from all the work he's done today," Shawn teased. Marley didn't seem to mind as he ran and jumped into the truck's bed.

"I'm glad we found that one on the road," Emily replied as she looked around. "I expected there to be more dead here."

"I think someone was through here recently," Shawn replied. "The windows on the pawnshop were busted in when we drove by."

"We probably shouldn't stay here after dark then." Emily couldn't help but look around.

"They may still be around here, and Jeff seemed pretty comfortable here last time I saw him."

"Let's load up then. It will take us about an hour to get back."

Emily nodded in agreement as she walked back to the truck. She heard Shawn close the trailer on the truck and watched as he climbed into the cab a few moments later. The truck roared to life, and soon they were back on the road. Emily could feel her muscles already becoming sore from loading the lumber. She rubbed her arms as she leaned back against the seat.

"Feel free to close your eyes. I'll get you home safe and sound." Emily couldn't help herself as she allowed her eyes to close. Soon, the sound of the road faded away, and Emily drifted off to sleep.

The sleep was not dreamless. Emily was back in her house and was watching Chad paint the nursery. Emily rubbed her bulging stomach, where she knew a baby was growing. The scene changed fast, and Hope was lying in the crib in front of her. She looked down at Hope as Chad entered and put his arm around her shoulder. Emily screamed at herself not to fall for it, not to let him near Hope. Dream Emily did not listen and instead lay her head on Chad's shoulder. Chad kissed her on top of the head.

"Until death do us part, babe," Chad whispered to her.

Emily shot awake with a gasp. She looked around to see that they were approaching the gate at Sanctuary.

"You alright?" Shawn asked her from the driver's seat as the truck stopped.

"Just a bad dream," Emily replied as she got out of the truck to enter the gate code.

The sun was nearly set, and they had barely made it back in time. Emily entered the code and watched as the gates began to move. Shawn pulled the truck closer, and Emily climbed back in. Once they were inside, Emily hurried to the control room. She looked back to see Shawn driving toward the clinic. She hoped that they would be able to get the corpse in without anyone noticing.

Emily reached the control room and quickly entered the code to close the gate. She heard the gates close beneath her. Emily headed back downstairs and made her way to Julia's house. Marley joined her once again on her walk. She knocked on the door and waited for Julia to answer. She felt warmth in her heart as Julia answered the door with Hope in her arms. Emily pulled Hope close to her and thanked Julia for babysitting. Julia insisted that it was no trouble. Emily turned and headed home with Hope.

As she reached the house, she saw that the corpse had been unloaded, and Shawn was leaning against the front of the truck, smoking a cigarette. Emily waved at him as she headed inside. She closed the door behind Marley and felt herself start to cry. She pushed the tears back as she carried Hope upstairs and put her to bed. Emily closed the door as Marley was lying down and went to take her shower. Emily allowed the tears to flow freely as the warm water ran over her. She kept hearing Chad's words over and over in her mind.

"Until death do us part." She had always taken her vows seriously, though Chad had not. Due to the flash, she could not end her marriage to Chad. She felt her vows were still in place, betraying herself and everything she stood for. She was doing it every time she took comfort in Shawn's touch. She did it every time she allowed herself to grow closer to him.

Emily finished washing and got dressed. She had slowed the tears by the time she opened Hope's door. She walked over to the crib and looked down at Hope. One day, she would have to explain Chad to her. She would have to teach Hope how important it was to keep it when she made a promise. How could she do those two things if she did not find a way to release herself from her wedding vows before moving on?

Emily kissed Hope on the forehead and walked out of the room with Marley. She closed the door softly behind her as she went. Once back inside her room, she climbed into bed with Marley. She thought back on the events of the past few days. She heard Shawn's heartbeat under her head as she lay on his chest. She felt the comfort in his touch as he held her hand in the truck.

Emily felt a few more tears roll down her cheek and hit the pillow below her head. She took a deep breath and steadied herself. She didn't know what was going to happen with Shawn. She only knew that she couldn't let it grow into anything serious right now. She was promised to Chad. She had made that promise. She would need to figure out how to let go of that before moving on and trying again. It wasn't fair to Shawn or Hope to let anything happen before she did. Emily lay in the dark a long time before sleep finally won out.

Chapter 4

"I need Emily, Shawn, Sam, and Doc to report to the control room."

Emily woke to Sarah's voice through the walkie on her nightstand. Emily opened her eyes to see that morning was already well underway. This was the first morning she had overslept since everyone came inside. Emily reached over and grabbed the walkie.

"I'll be there in ten," she replied.

"Can you make it faster?" Sarah asked in an anxious tone.

"I still have to get Hope dressed and make her breakfast. Is everything alright?"

"A group just made contact. They are about ten minutes out from the gate." Emily stared at the walkie, trying to process the words.

"I can come to care for Hope," Julia's voice rang out. She must have been with Sam and heard the conversation.

"That would be great. I don't want her with me when I greet the newcomers."
"I'm headed your way. I'll be there in just a minute."

The line went dead, and Emily jumped out of bed and quickly dressed for the day. She had just finished putting her hair up when she heard the front door open and close.

"Emily?!" Julia's voice rang out.

"Upstairs!" Emily replied. She opened her door as Julia reached the top of the stairs. "She's still in bed. Thank you again for watching her."

"It's no problem. I'll get her dressed and take her to my place for the day."

With that, Julia headed towards Hope's room, and Emily headed out with Marley. Marley was confused as Emily opened the front door and stopped in the front yard. Emily turned back to him as he looked at her with pleading eyes.

"Go ahead," Emily told him. "Just find me when you're done."

Marley took off towards the backyard without hesitation. Emily turned and ran towards the COM building. She reached the door and found that everyone else had already arrived.

"Sorry, I'm late. How far out are they?" Emily asked, slightly out of breath.
"We see the wall, but the gates are closed. Are you still there?"

Everyone looked to Emily as the voice cut out. Emily nodded to them all and began the runup to the control building. She reached it and entered the code to open the gate. She watched as five vehicles drove through and shut the gate behind them. She then opened the inner gate just enough for them to walk around. Emily then ran down the stairs and felt relieved seeing Marley waiting for her. Emily walked towards the opening in the gate and could hear that Shawn and the others were already inside.

"Our leader will be here in a minute," Shawn was explaining.

"You mean you're not in charge?" a man's voice asked in a shaky tone.

"No," Shawn replied.

Emily took a deep breath and entered through the opening with Marley. She could see

Shawn smile as she did and hoped that her entrance looked as strong as she intended.

"Welcome to Sanctuary," she said to a group of unfamiliar faces. "My name is Emily."

Emily looked at the group, trying to take in the faces that stared back at her. There was a Hispanic-looking man with one arm around a woman and the other around a small boy, probably about Bobby's age. An older couple also looked to be in their late sixties or early seventies. The woman was clinging to the man's arm. Emily could tell she was having trouble standing independently and needed him to stabilize her.

Emily looked to the next set of faces and saw a young red-headed woman standing next to a young teenage boy. The boy seemed to be trying extra hard to ensure that he looked braver than he felt at the moment. Emily moved her eyes to the next group. A dark woman stood there with a man, whom Emily assumed was her husband, and a set of twin girls, maybe ten years old. Emily then turned to the last man and stared to ensure she saw right. He was an older man with a white beard. Emily could not help but notice that he dressed like a priest.

"I'm sure you all have questions," Emily continued. "I will gladly answer them once we get you all inside."

"What's the price of admission?" the Hispanic man asked pointedly.

"A physical exam," Emily replied, and motioned for Doc to step forward. "Doc will examine each of you to ensure that none are at risk of infection."

"So, he will tell you which of us can work to your standards and which cannot," the Hispanic man continued. "Then he claims the unneeded ones are sick, and you stick a knife in their brains."

"We would never." Emily could not help but sound appalled at the suggestion of her motives. "Through that door, we have quarantine areas set up. If Doc sees anything suspicious, we will invite you to stay there. We will supply you with food and other needs. If you develop a fever, then Doc will discuss the next steps with you."

"You are trying to tell us that if you see an obvious bite, you will just put us up and not kill us," the red-headed woman asked.

"That's what I'm saying," Emily replied. "We know that not everyone who gets a bite turns into one of the dead." Emily looked around at each of their faces.

"What do you mean?" the Hispanic man asked.

"I know from experience that very few people are immune to the bites and scratches."

"What personal experience?"

The man was not taking her broad answers to the questions. He was looking for specific examples. Emily looked back at her friends for guidance on handling the situation.

"We've seen it," Shawn spoke up. "That's the best we can tell you for now."

The man seemed not as willing to question Shawn and asked no further questions.

"I don't know how long I can stand," the older woman said. "Would anyone mind if I went first?"

Everyone stood silent, and Emily watched as the gentleman helped the woman walk forward. Emily offered help as they came near her, and the woman grabbed her arm.

"Thank you, dear," the woman said. "My name is Margaret, and this is my husband, Ben."

"It's a pleasure to meet you both," Emily replied.

She helped Ben walk Margaret into Doc's exam room and came back outside. It wasn't long before they came back out, each clutching a cold water bottle.

"Next!" Doc called out.

Emily couldn't help but smile at how he acted like this was just a typical waiting room of patients. Emily turned to see Sam coming back through the gate with a chair. It looked like one out of the COM room. He set the chair near Margaret, who gladly sat down.

Emily, the group entered the exam room one at a time and returned with a water bottle. After finishing with the priest, Doc rejoined them by the gate.

"Everyone is cleared," Doc reported. "Nothing suspicious on any of them."

"If all of you would like to follow me, I'll show you our town, get you some clean clothes, and fresh food."

Emily turned and walked back through the gate opening. She glanced back only once to ensure that the group was following. She knew that the walk would be challenging for Margaret and made sure to slow her pace so Margaret would not have to struggle to keep up.

"All shops are located here on the main street," Emily explained. "We have a system where everyone works, gets paid in credits, and then uses the credits to buy the goods they want."

"I assume your wage is the highest," the Hispanic man spat at her.

"Everyone receives the same pay regardless of their job. Parents receive a set amount for each child. An extra payment is received for shifts taken on the wall, but everyone must take at least one a day. That may change as our numbers grow, but that is our current situation." Emily continued her way down the street.

"If you choose to stay, you will be given a house based on your family size and a job based on your skills and abilities. Until you make that decision, I will invite you all to stay with me." Emily motioned towards her home as they approached. "Jessica will see that you each get two changes of clothes. You will then be welcome to clean up. There is hot water, but you must take turns in the bathrooms." Emily listened to the murmurs about hot water and waited a few moments before she continued.

"Once you are all cleaned up, I will have lunch ready and answer any questions you may have." Emily reached her front door as she finished. "Jessica will be here in a moment to take each family one at a time to pick out some clothing. If you will, please come in and relax until it is your turn."

Emily opened her door and watched as everyone walked into the air-conditioned home. She led them into the living room and motioned for them to sit. Jessica arrived a few moments later. She took the Hispanic family first. Everyone waited in silence until they returned. Jessica took the next group. This process continued, and everyone began to work their way through the showers. Emily headed to the kitchen and prepared sandwiches and iced tea for everyone. Emily set everything in the dining room just as everyone started to file into the room.

"Is this bread real?" Margaret asked as she sat.

"It is," Emily smiled. "It's baked fresh every day by Sam's wife, Julia."

Emily watched as they began to dig in, and their voices filled the room. Emily excused herself to the living room, where Shawn and Sam waited.

"What do you think?" Sam asked as she entered.

"Trust issues, but who can blame them?" Emily explained. "I think they could be a real asset to what we are trying to do here."

"Do you think you can get them to trust you enough to stay?" Shawn asked.

"I have an idea," Emily replied. "Would you two stay here while I run out for a moment?"

"Oh, I'm staying here as long as they are."

Shawn's look told Emily that he was not changing his mind. Emily nodded in understanding and headed out the door with Marley. It didn't take her long to find Julia to pick up Hope.

"So, what are you thinking of them?" Julia asked as Emily approached her.

"The older couple seems nice," Emily replied. "The others are still too scared to figure it out."

"I would be surprised if they weren't scared." Julia handed Hope to Emily. "Plan on using this little angel to gain some trust?"

"She's good at getting people to open up," Emily smiled back.

"If you need anything, just let us know." Julia smiled at Emily as Emily turned to head back to the house.

"I will," Emily called back to her.

It only took a few minutes for Emily to return home. She could hear the voices in the dining room and saw Shawn leaning against the wall. The look on his face told her he wasn't happy about her decision to bring Hope in so soon. Emily continued past him and into the dining room. The voices all went silent as Emily entered.

"How old is she?" the red-headed woman finally spoke.

"Just over four months," Emily replied. "She was born inside the wall."

Emily watched as they all looked at each other. Emily wanted to start telling her story, of explaining everything to them, but forced herself to wait. Emily knew that saying too much too soon would put too much pressure on them. Instead, Emily walked to her chair at the head of the table and sat with Hope. Shawn had followed her into the room and now stood silently behind her.

"You have a beautiful daughter," Ben said, looking at Shawn.

"I'm not her father," Shawn replied.

Emily could hear in his voice how much this statement hurt him. She knew he loved Hope as if he were her father.

"Her father was my husband before the flash," Emily explained. "But those who live here are our family now."

"Did you guys build this place?" the Hispanic man asked.

"No, I found it Christmas last year," Emily began. "It was built by a man named Robert."

"Is Robert here?" the man asked.

"No, he killed himself before I arrived," Emily explained. "He had plans to make this place a community safe from the virus."

"So, he prepared this place before the flash?" the red-headed woman asked. "How could he know this was going to happen?"

"He was part of the team that was tricked into creating it," Emily explained. "I have Robert's journal where he explains what happened. I can loan it to anyone who would like to read it."
"I would if you don't mind," the priest said.

Emily nodded and planned to grab it once they were finished.

"So, you and your group found this place, and now you are just welcoming people in?" the darker-skinned woman asked.

Emily felt like she may have been of Pacific descent.

"I found it when I was pregnant." Marley looked up at her from the floor. "Well, my dog Marley and I. We lived here alone until March. I went into labor just as Shawn and his group arrived. Doc saved my life and delivered Hope. They were the first people I agreed to let stay, and they became our family."

"I understand you all have many questions, but if it's not too much trouble, I have one of my own. Other than Margaret and Ben, I haven't heard any of your names."

"I'm Cara, and this is my son Aiden," the red-headed woman said.

"I'm Isabella, my husband Jose, and our son Martin," the Hispanic woman said next.

"Alec, my wife Samara, and our daughters Natalia and Talia," the dark-skinned man spoke next.

"I'm Father Nathan," the priest said.

"It's a pleasure to meet you all," Emily smiled.

"You are the leader. Is that correct?" Jose asked.

"Yes," Emily smiled. "The first group decided I would lead as I found this place and cleared it."

"No offense," Alec spoke, "But are you strong enough to lead? Especially since you plan for this place to grow. I mean, are we all expected to protect you if someone attacks?"

"I am capable of protecting myself," Emily replied.

"I can introduce you to our construction guy if you need to see for yourself," Shawn laughed. "Marley gave him a bite he won't forget, and she broke his nose. The guy didn't get one shot in."

"A mother protecting her child's home is stronger and tougher than an army of men," Ben stated.

No one seemed willing to argue this with him.

"Do we get to choose if we stay or not?" Cara asked.

"Of course," Emily replied. "You are not prisoners. You are welcome to stay the night and take your time deciding. If you choose this is not for you, that is fine. We will give you some supplies and let you go on your way."

"You have given us a lot to think about," Ben smiled.

"I understand," Emily replied. "I will get the journal and leave you all to talk. I will be around if you have any questions."

Emily carried Hope into the study and grabbed Robert's journal. She returned to the dining room long enough to give Father Nathan the journal and inform them that the children were welcome to watch the television if they wanted.

Emily then headed to the kitchen to make Hope's lunch. Hope quickly ate and began rubbing her eyes. Emily knew that Hope was ready for her nap. Emily carried her upstairs and laid her down as Marley took his position under the crib. Emily left the room, closing the door behind her.

"You trust these people enough to leave her alone?" Shawn's voice made her jump with fear.

"I trust them as much as I trusted all of you that first day," Emily smiled. She watched as Shawn smiled back at her. "And what do you mean by alone? Marley is in there."

"She might as well have a tank guarding her as she sleeps," Shawn laughed.

Emily began to walk past him, but Shawn put his arm out to stop her.

"I just wanted to make sure you know I'm staying here tonight."

"I figured that," Emily replied, resisting the urge to look at him.

"I just thought I should have asked if that's okay. With everything going on between…."

"Of course, it's okay," Emily replied, still not looking at him. "Especially with Hope here, it would make me feel safer."

Shawn lowered his arm, and Emily made her way downstairs. She could hear Shawn following her down. Emily quickly went to the bathroom and locked the door behind her. Emily sat on the tub's edge and dropped her head into her hands. She knew what Shawn was talking about upstairs. He was talking about what was going on between the two of them. The almost romance she didn't know how to tell him would never happen. It wasn't that she didn't care about him or that she didn't want to see what their feelings could grow into one day.

Emily did care for Shawn, but couldn't get her dream out of her mind. She couldn't imagine her life without him, but didn't see how to end her marriage vows. Even though Chad wasn't here, he still had control over her life. Emily sat for a long time, trying to push her feelings back down and figure out how to tell Shawn.

"Emily?" Julia's voice called out from the other side of the door. "Emily, is everything all right?"

Emily forced herself to stand and put on her brave face. She opened the door to see Julia standing there with a worried look.

"Sorry." Emily tried not to let the turmoil she felt inside show in her voice. "I just needed a moment to gather my thoughts."

"Shawn says you've been in there for almost two hours."

Julia knew that Emily was dealing with more than she was saying.

"He got Hope up and radioed asking for help with dinner for the new group."

"Has it been that long?" Emily truly didn't realize how much time had passed.

"I only came because Marley is starting to get irritated. It's almost like he believes the new group did something to you."

"I'm sorry." Emily started to move to walk out the door, but Julia did not move.

"If you need to talk, I'm always here," Julia offered.

"I know, but I don't think you can help with this." Emily couldn't help but sound ashamed.

"Try me." Julia used her mom's told as she spoke.

"I'm sorry, Julia. Unless you know a way to release wedding vows in a world where divorce isn't a thing, you can't help."

Emily pushed her way past Julia, and Marley ran towards her. Emily reached down and ran her hand over his fur. She watched as he visibly relaxed. Emily could hear the sounds of people in the kitchen. From the sounds, everyone had answered the call for help with dinner. Emily started to walk towards the kitchen as Hope crawled out of the doorway. Emily instead sat on the floor and allowed Hope to crawl toward her. Emily decided to let the others handle dinner now and take this time with Hope. Marley lay on the ground with them and allowed Hope to crawl on him, happy to be part of the game.

Emily could see that Shawn had followed Hope into the room, but she resisted the urge to look up at him. Shawn watched them play for a while and then went back into the kitchen. Emily knew that he was probably confused by how she was acting. But she didn't have the strength to deal with that right now.

"Dinners ready," Bobby chimed as he entered the living room.

"We are on our way," Emily replied with a smile.

Emily picked up Hope and headed toward the dining room. The dining room was packed with many people standing.

"We won't be staying," Howard spoke. "We just wanted a chance to introduce ourselves and tell them what it's like here." With that, everyone from the original group left except for Shawn, and Emily took her seat at the table.

"Let's eat," Emily smiled at everyone.

Chapter 5

Emily woke the following day and looked in the bassinet beside her bed. Hope was still asleep, but she knew the little one would be up soon. Emily lay back on her pillow and stared up at the ceiling. She had headed straight to bed when everyone started to wind down for the night. She had pulled the bassinet into the room to keep Hope close.

She could tell that Shawn had wanted to talk to her, but she managed to avoid it. She was not ready for that conversation yet. Her focus now needed to be on the new group and Hope. She had managed to grab the town ledgers before bed and had already picked out houses for the new group if they decided to stay. She also picked out a spot where a church could be built if the priest wanted to stay. He would still need to take on some other role to help out. Emily thought that having a church and a priest might help people cope with the world. She wouldn't force religion on anyone, but thought it reasonable to give them a choice.

Hope began to stir, and Emily knew she had to get up. Emily tossed back the blankets and sat up in bed. She looked down at Hope and smiled. Emily quickly went to the bathroom and got dressed for the day. She grabbed Hope and proceeded to get her ready for the day. As Emily finished, Marley jumped from the bed and walked towards the door. Emily opened the door and could not help but smile as she saw Shawn sitting against the wall, asleep.

Emily stood for a moment just looking at him. She remembered the day on the couch and holding his hand in the truck. Emily pushed the thoughts from her head as Shawn started to stir.

"Did you sleep here all night?" Emily asked as he looked up at her.

"Yeah," Shawn replied as he began to stand up.

"Next time, you should at least take the couch," Emily laughed.

"The priest took the couch. Didn't want to know the cosmic consequences of kicking a man of the cloth to the floor."

"Well, I'd better prepare breakfast before I know the consequences."

Emily laughed as she headed downstairs. She prepared a bottle for Hope and fed her. She then let Marley outside and set to making enough eggs and toast for everyone. A few minutes later, Shawn came into the kitchen, made coffee, and put the dishes in the dining room. Slowly, everyone emerged, and Emily had plenty of hands to help carry everything to the dining room.

Everyone sat down, and Emily could see that everyone was visibly more relaxed today. She enjoyed watching them all and could not help but believe everyone would stay. Once breakfast was finished, Emily stood to begin clearing the table.

"We got it," Cara said as they all stood and cleared the table.

"Shawn, could you please get my books from my room? I think it's about time."

Shawn nodded and headed upstairs. Emily felt lazy as she watched the group clearing away breakfast. Shawn returned just as they finished, and everyone gathered around the table. Emily could tell from their faces that they were ready to talk.

"I get the feeling you all have made a decision," Emily said with a smile.

"We all want to stay," Ben spoke. "We are just wondering what happens now."

"Well, I will just need to get an idea of what each of you did before the flash and see where you would be most helpful."

"That's what we are a little worried about," Ben grabbed Margaret's hand as he spoke.

"Margaret has a hard time standing, and I'm afraid that she wouldn't be able to be useful."

"I disagree," Emily smiled.

She had been thinking about this, knowing that Margaret would need a job where she would be sitting.

"I spoke with Sarah, head of our communications. She says she needs someone to help monitor the radios during the day. Do you think that is something you could do?"

Emily could see the smile spreading on Margaret's face.

"Yes, yes," Margaret replied. "I could do that."

Emily made her way around the table, listening to everyone and assigning them jobs as she went. When she finished, it was decided that Ben and Father Nathan would be helping on the farm, Jose with construction, and Isabella would be working with Doc, Cara, and Samara would be helping with retail, and Alec would be working under Sam for security.

Emily passed around the census ledger and watched as everyone signed their name. Once they finished, Emily was ready to show them each to their new homes.

"I have homes for each of you if you're ready?" Emily smiled at them.

Emily could see the joy on their faces as they all began to stand. Emily turned to pick up Hope, but saw that Shawn had beaten her to it. Shawn smiled at her as he held the baby, and Hope seemed happy with the arrangement. Emily led the group outside and decided to take Ben and Margaret to their home first, so Margaret didn't have to walk as far.

Emily turned left once they reached the street. She wanted to keep everyone close together, but also had to keep an eye on the house size. Marley and Shawn walked beside her as she slowly made her way to the first house.

"I think this one will work nicely for Ben and Margaret." Emily motioned to the house. "All of the basics should be inside, and Jessica will help you with anything you may be missing. She will also have your credit cards later this afternoon, and Shawn will let you know your shift schedule for the wall."

"This is more than we ever dreamed we could have again," Margaret said with tears in her eyes. "We will take a quick look and then report for work."

"You don't need to start work until tomorrow," Emily stated. "I want you all to take today and get settled."

Emily watched as Ben helped Margaret into the house. Emily then led the other families to their new homes and showed Father Nathan to his apartment. Emily left an empty apartment between Father Nathan and Derick.

"Derick can be a handful, but if you have trouble, just let me know."

"Is he the gentleman who attacked you?" Father Nathan asked.

"He tried," Emily smiled. Emily turned to follow Shawn downstairs and allow the Father to settle in.

"I did have a question," Father Nathan called after her.

"Of course." Emily turned back and walked back to Father Nathan.

"I accept my job on the farm, but I was wondering if it would be possible for me to run services here for those who wish to attend."

"I planned to talk to you about that, but wanted to give you a chance to settle. I have plans to talk to the construction crew about either converting a building to a church or the possibility of building a new structure."

"If it's okay with you, I could do a service on the street until something can be decided."

"I don't see any problem with that. If you let me know when, I will help spread the word for those who would like to attend."

"Thank you." Father Nathan smiled as he entered his apartment.

Emily turned and caught up with Shawn and Hope. Emily followed them downstairs, and soon they were back outside.

"I've got to head to a shift on the wall and work on the shift schedules." Shawn turned and handed Hope to Emily.

"I wanted to apologize for yesterday," Emily began.

"There's no need for that," Shawn smiled. "You have a lot to deal with, and I get it."

Shawn turned and headed to the security room for his rifle. Emily turned and headed back towards her house. She was glad that Shawn wasn't upset with her and felt a knot in her stomach from not addressing her feelings. Emily was nearing the house when Marley suddenly turned and started running back up the street. Emily turned to see June and Howard walking toward her.

"Do you have a moment?" June called to her.

"Of course, I do," Emily replied.

"We were all talking, and Bobby gave us an idea. You have been saying that we are all a family, and we would like to have a family dinner with our newcomers. It would allow us to get to know them and let everyone relax and let loose," June explained.

"That's a perfect idea. It's something we could do every time we have newcomers."

"Exactly." Howard was grinning as he spoke.

"With the work schedule, I think it would be easiest to do this on Friday nights."

"That with give us a few days to get ready," Howard grinned. "I was thinking a town barbecue style of get-together. We could even have music with the walls if we didn't try to play it loud enough to wake the uninfected dead."

"We have this large section of road in front of your house that we could set up and ask everyone to bring something to contribute."

"I'll let Jessica know that everything for the party does not require credits." Emily resituated Hope as she spoke. "There will be many things to get together to make it happen," Emily began.

"I will gladly handle all the plans if that's okay with you," June offered. "The kids go home by three. Even with the extra students, I have plenty of time to do it. I could even have them make some decorations." Emily could tell that June was excited about the idea of planning this.

"That would be a great help," Emily replied. "Let me know if you need help with anything."

"I will," June smiled.

"I'll make some cookies for my contribution," Emily continued.

"I'll tell everyone the cookies are taken care of," June grinned.

June and Howard turned to head to work. Emily could tell they were both excited by their new project.

"We are going to have a party," Emily said to Hope as she began to walk toward the store.

She wanted to let Jessica know her decision and gather the supplies for the cookies while she was there. Jessica was thrilled about the party and excitedly helped Emily gather the supplies for the cookies. Emily headed straight home, and after feeding Hope lunch, she set up the credit cards. She quickly took them to Jessica to distribute and walked around town to ensure everything went smoothly.

Emily returned home and, after having dinner, tucked Hope into bed. Emily returned downstairs and pulled out her journal. She sat at the desk for a long time, writing down everything that had happened over the past few days. When she finished, she returned the journal to the shelf and headed to the shower. After a quick check on Hope, Emily crawled into bed with Marley. It didn't take long for her to find sleep, and soon the day melted into the darkness.

The next day flew by, and Emily was pleased to see the newcomers fitting in well. Jacob was excited to have the extra help on the farm and felt confident that production would be much higher than expected. Shawn's new wall schedule put three people on the wall during each four-hour shift. Shawn understood that Emily needed space and kept their conversations light and friendly. Emily spent most of the afternoon baking cookies for the party the next day and went to bed early.

Friday morning, the entire town was buzzing with excitement. Emily couldn't believe the sight on the street. Tables were set up, and lights were strung above the area. Emily did her regular morning routine with Hope secured to her back. By the time she returned to the house, the scene had grown. Pictures were hung with the lights, tablecloths were added to the tables and centerpieces, and some kids set up chairs. Emily headed into the house and grabbed all the cookies she had made the night before. When she got back outside, Bobby came to help her carry them all to the table.

Soon, everyone was gathered, except for those on wall duty, and the music started. Emily sat back and watched the scene unfold in front of her. Everyone laughed and ate, and some were even dancing. At this moment, it felt like nothing had changed. It felt like a flash never happened, there weren't dead outside the walls, and they didn't have a worry in the world.

As the sun began to set, it came time for the wall shift to change. Emily saw Ben and June join the party minutes after Julia, Jacob, and Father Nathan. Emily couldn't help but scan the scene for Shawn, who should have been joining them. After a few moments, Julia returned. Emily made her way toward Julia.

"Where's Shawn?" she asked.

"He sent me back," Julia responded. "He said I should come back to be with my family, and he would take my shift since he didn't have one."

"Oh," Emily couldn't help but feel both hurt and guilty.

"I plan to go after Bobby goes to bed and force him down," Sam said. "I just hope there's some food left for him."

Emily looked at the food tables and saw that the children were going crazy.

"I'll make him a plate and take it up to him. Would you mind keeping Hope for a few minutes?"

"Of course not," Julia said as she took Hope from Emily.

Emily headed over to the food tables and made a plate for Shawn. Once she finished, she headed up the wall with Marley and found Jacob in the control room.

"Have you seen Shawn?" Emily asked.

"He told me to stay here while he patrolled the west side of the wall, and Father Thomas took the east."

"Thanks," Emily smiled. "Alright, boy, go find him."

Emily couldn't help but laugh as Marley took off running on the wall. She followed behind him and, after several minutes, could hear Marley barking and Shawn laughing.

"Did you send your dog to hunt me down?" Shawn laughed as Emily approached.

"Well, if you had come down when you were supposed to, I wouldn't have to."

"It seemed like the thing to do. Julia has a family down there, and I…," Shawn spoke to his boots instead of her.

"What am I?" Emily asked, "Chopped liver?"

"I figured," Shawn started. "Since we returned, you have seemed like you don't want me around. I thought it best to stay away so you could enjoy tonight."

Emily felt her chest tighten as he spoke. She wasn't ready for a relationship, but she didn't want to lose him either.

"I'm sorry," Emily said, barely louder than a whisper. "I know I've been weird, but I'm just working through my shit. It doesn't mean that I want you to stay away."

"Is that for me?" Shawn asked, motioning to the plate.

"Yeah," Emily said as she handed him the plate. She then wiped the tears she felt welling up in her eyes.

"Thanks for this," Shawn said.

"You're lucky you got any cookies. The kids are going nuts."

"I bet they are," Shawn laughed.

"Sam will come up to do the last half of Julia's shift." Shawn opened his mouth to speak. "No arguing," Emily interrupted. "I will come up here and drag you down if I have to."

Shawn laughed and nodded in agreement. Emily patted her leg to call for Marley to follow and headed back to the party. After about an hour, she ran inside and put Hope to bed. She carried the baby monitor back out with her. Sam and Julia headed home to put Bobby to bed a short time later, much to Bobby's objections to the plan.

Emily waited and couldn't help but smile when Shawn walked under the lights.

"You've been quiet tonight," Ben spoke behind her.

"Just enjoying the view," Emily smiled at him.

"As well you should," Ben smiled back at her. "It's because of you that this is possible."

"I don't know about all of that." Emily looked back to see Shawn dancing with Margaret. She could see that he wasn't thrilled, but couldn't tell the older woman no.

"We all know it," Ben said confidently. "It looks like a younger man has stolen my dancing partner."

"Looks like," Emily laughed.

"Well, two can play at that game. Would you do me the honor?"

Emily turned to see that Ben was holding out his hand to her. Emily didn't even realize she had taken it until he led her to the makeshift dance floor.

"You have given everyone so much. I can't help but notice that you keep yourself from getting what you want." Ben spoke as they began to dance.

"I don't know what you're talking about?" Emily was genuinely confused by his statement.

"Everyone knows, my dear," Ben smiled. "But from what I gathered, you haven't allowed it to go beyond friendship." Emily suddenly understood that he was talking about her and Shawn.

"It's complicated." Emily felt the hollowness of the words as she spoke them.

"My dear, a lot is complicated, but this is not one of those things."

"I was married before all of this. My husband was cruel, and the only good thing he ever did was give me Hope." Emily felt sick to her stomach as she spoke of Chad. "My husband doesn't even know she exists."

"You speak of him as if he's still alive?"

"To the best of my knowledge, he is."

"And yet you still call him your husband. Do you hold on to the chance that you may be able to find him and reunite?"

"God no," Emily laughed. "I pray for a way out of my vows," Emily explained. "My vows were until death do us part, and I can't know if we have parted or not."

"Oh, that makes sense," Ben nodded.

"I just don't know how to teach Hope that vows are important if I break them. My luck, Chad would show up one day, and I would lose Hope's trust."

"You think far ahead," Ben smiled.

"Hazard of the job," Emily smiled back. "I have a suggestion if you want to hear it."

"Gladly," Emily responded.

"Your vows were between you and God. Based on what you described, your former husband violated those long ago. In my opinion, God would gladly release you from those vows. All you need to do is ask and release yourself from them in your heart."

Emily nodded but knew that it would not be as easy to do as he said.

"I think he'll wait while you work on it."

"How can you know that?" Emily allowed her gaze to move to Shawn.

"He looks at you the same way I looked at Margaret initially, and I waited for her to realize she was marrying the wrong man." Emily looked at Ben, and the smile on his face comforted her.

Chapter 6

The days and weeks flew by over the next couple of months. Soon, August was upon them, and Sanctuary was filling slowly every week. Emily had welcomed six more groups inside the walls, and their skill sets proved invaluable, especially those of Cole. Cole reminded Emily of someone in a movie trying to represent country folk but just making fun of them. She found it difficult sometimes to understand what he was saying, but he had no problems repeating himself until she did.

Cole was a mechanic before the flash and had plans to fix up their vehicles to run on a new fuel source, moonshine. He claimed he had an old family recipe that would work great and knew how to convert the vehicles to run on it. It just involved emptying and cleaning the gas tanks and overhauling the carburetor system. Emily had decided to let him start with the truck she used when she first came to Sanctuary.

It wasn't the conversion of vehicles that made her nervous, but moonshine brewing. The process was dangerous if something went wrong, but it also provided the challenge of keeping Derick out of it. They had decided to give Cole a house for him and his family closer to the farm, but away from the wall, just in case. Cole and his sixteen-year-old daughter seemed to have no problems being asked to live away from everyone.

Altogether, Sanctuary had gained twenty new people. There were fourteen adults and six children. Emily had stuck to the most important jobs before trying to fill those that were not essential at the time. Jacob had more farmhands than he could have dreamed, and the crops were being harvested on time.

Shawn had kept his distance since Emily locked herself in the bathroom. While he was still friendly when he saw Emily, he seemed to understand that she needed space. While she missed having him around all the time, she didn't want to risk hurting him any more than she already had. Shawn had taken Sam with him on his trips to return the walkies every time someone new came in and had continued to sleep in the hall each night that a new group stayed in her house.

It had been over a week since the last group joined, and Emily was preparing for another day. She had dressed and managed to make the bed while Marley waited for her at the door. Emily opened the door and followed Marley to Hope's room.

"What are you doing?" Emily gasped as she opened the door.

Hope was standing in her crib and began to laugh at Emily's reaction. This was the first time Hope had stood on her own, and seeing it brought tears to Emily's eyes.

"You can stop growing up so fast, you know?" Emily smiled as she walked toward the crib.

Emily reached in and picked up Hope, hugging her softly. It didn't take her long to get Hope dressed, and soon they were all downstairs enjoying breakfast.

"Emily, can you come to the clinic?" Doc's voice rang out over the walkie. Emily reached down and unclipped it from her waist.

"Is everything all right?" she asked.

"Yes," Emily could hear the hesitation in his voice. "I have the test results and would like to review them with you."

"I'll be there in a few minutes."

Emily returned the walkie to her waist and quickly ate the rest of her meal. Doc had been working on the blood work to see if anyone, including Hope, was immune to the infection. Doc had been working on this for months, and Emily was finally anxious to know Hope's results. Emily quickly secured Hope in the carrier and headed out into Sanctuary with Marley. Doc's office wasn't far, and Emily had arrived in just a few minutes.

"Good morning, Ms. Emily," Isabelle smiled. "Doc's waiting for you in the exam room."

"Thanks, Isabelle," Emily replied as she headed back to the room.

As she entered, Doc sat in a chair, looking at some papers in a folder. Emily walked to the exam table and took Hope out of the backpack while Doc closed the door.

"I'm sorry that the results took so long," Doc began. "To be honest, I ran the tests several times just to be sure."

"It's fine, Doc," Emily replied anxiously.

"I just wanted to be sure," Doc spoke again as if he had not heard Emily.

"Well?" Emily asked, "What did you find out?"

"We are all immune to the airborne. The corpse you brought me was not, obviously." Doc began to stare at his papers once more.

"I'm sure you know something that is not obvious," Emily teased.

"Oh, I do," Doc defended himself.

As he looked up at the smile on her face, he noticed that she was trying to lighten the tension and visibly relaxed.

"We only have one resident with the marker that makes them immune to the blood infection."

"Who?" Emily could not hide the excitement in her voice.

"Unfortunately, just you." Doc looked ashamed as he spoke.

"Hope didn't inherit the marker?" Emily asked, praying that he had just forgotten to say it.

"I'm sorry," Doc spoke again.

"It's not your fault, Doc." Emily tried to sound firm. "At least we know now and can move forward. I do want you to keep testing anyone else who may join us."

"I will," Doc nodded. "I've been taking the blood samples during the initial exams."

"Sounds efficient," Emily nodded. However, she could tell there was more than Doc wanted to say. "Is there something else?"

"Yes, I wanted your permission to bring Isabelle in on my research. She is quite knowledgeable and might be able to help me find a cure if someone is bitten."

"I trust your judgment, Doc," Emily began.

"Just explain to her that we are not publicizing your research."

"Thank you." Doc breathed a sigh of relief.

"While you're here, we should probably give Hope a quick exam just to check on her progress."

"If you could find a way of slowing her down, it would be greatly appreciated. I found her standing in her crib this morning," Emily laughed.

"Was she standing alone, or was she holding the crib?"

"She was holding the crib. Is she old enough to be standing on her own?"

"Not quite yet. I only asked because she seems to be reaching her milestones early. Her muscular and mental development is more advanced than any baby I've seen before."

"Is there something wrong with her?" Emily couldn't help but sound concerned.

"No, not necessarily," Doc smiled for the first time since Emily arrived. "It could be because her body knows the world is more dangerous, so she is growing up faster."

"Faster?! I'm sorry, Doc, but I can't have that. Slow it down now." Doc laughed as he continued with the exam, making notes as he went along.

"She is right on track for an infant about eight months old," Doc smiled as he closed his folder.

"But she is only six months old!" Emily exclaimed.

"I know, but she is growing fast," Doc smiled. "She is perfectly healthy, though, so I don't see any reason for concern."

"I'll take your word for it, Doc," Emily grinned back. Doc helped Emily secure Hope in the backpack and opened the door.

"Have a good day, Isabelle," Emily said as she left.

"You too, Ms. Emily," Isabelle called back.

Emily walked out the door with Marley and found herself on the main street. Across the street, Jessica was busy as usual, directing her people to stock the shelves, and the smell of fresh bread filled the air. Emily turned to head back to her house, but instead went to the construction area. On the back side of the main street, she had permitted the first house to be converted into a church. Most of the town seemed to enjoy the church service. Derick had thrown a fit about the work, but his objections never went further than talk.

Emily smiled as she looked up at the cross secured above the door. Emily opened the door and realized how long it had been since she had been there. The entire first floor had been opened up, and pews now filled most of the floor space. Emily walked up the aisle towards a staging area where Father Nathan read a bible at the podium.

"Looks like everything is just about done," Emily smiled at him.

"It is," Father Nathan smiled back. "And not a moment too soon. The Lord tested my patience with Derick this past month."

"If that's the case, he tests me daily." Emily could not help but laugh as she spoke. "Do you have everything you need to get set up?"

"Almost." Father Thomas looked down at his bible as he spoke. "Robert was a man of science and did not bring a supply of the good book inside. I would like to have more to distribute here during service."

"I will try to find some on my next time out. I can't promise anything, but I will try."

"I'm sure the Lord will guide you just as he did when you found Sanctuary."

"No offense, Father, but if the Lord guided me here, it was a messed-up way of doing it."

Emily couldn't help the image of Jeff smiling at her that flashed into her mind.

"I know you have some faith," Father Nathan smiled at her. "But I can see that you are having a bit of a crisis."

"More than a bit these days," Emily smiled back.

"Would you care to talk about it?" Father Nathan had been trying to get her to open up since he had arrived.

"This is between the big man and me," Emily replied.

"I'm sure he is guiding you, but maybe you need help understanding what he is saying." Father Nathan was not going to give up quickly this time.

Hope began to squirm on Emily's back, showing that she was either hungry again or needed to be changed. Emily shifted her focus to taking Hope out of the backpack and grabbing a jar of carrots.

Emily took a seat on one of the pews and began the process of feeding Hope. Marley curled up next to her in the aisle and soon began to snore. Father Nathan smiled and spoke to Hope as she ate. Once the jar was empty, Hope began to rub her eyes.

"Why not let her take a nap here today?" Father Nathan beamed. "That will give us a chance to talk."

Emily searched for an excuse to say no, but couldn't find one. If Hope didn't lie down as soon as she wanted, the whole town would know she was upset.

"I'd appreciate it," Emily smiled.

She took Hope upstairs and laid her down in a playpen that Father Nathan had purchased for nursery school. Marley lay down next to the playpen and resumed his nap. Emily returned downstairs and found Father Nathan sitting in the same pew she had left him in. Emily sighed and walked over to sit next to him.

"So, what is troubling you?" Father Nathan asked in his most soothing voice.

"I have no idea where to start," Emily rolled her eyes as she spoke.

"Why don't you tell me about Hope's father?"

"He was a selfish bastard, and the only good thing he ever did was give me Hope."

"I see, so your marriage was not a happy one?"

"It was a life of servitude. I gave him everything while he took and still wanted more."

"That must have been lonely."

"It's part of why my therapist told me to get Marley. I needed emotional support Chad couldn't give, at least to me."

"Well, now, there's more behind that statement." Father Nathan looked at her, trying to read the information from her expression.

"I thought we were trying to save our marriage," Emily began. "I found out the night of the flash that he had already moved on. He had gotten his girlfriend pregnant and was only still pretending with me to get as much as possible out of the divorce."

"I'm sorry," Father Nathan said in no more than a whisper.

"You want to know what's worse?" Emily felt tears rolling down her face. "I stayed and tried to repair the relationship because of wedding vows, which meant nothing to him. Even after I knew the truth, I told my family to pick up his girlfriend to protect her and her baby."

"Did you know you were pregnant at the time?"

"No," Emily replied. "I was bitten before we got out away from my house. No one in my family knows that Hope exists."

"Do you want Chad to know?"

"No." Emily felt the tears stop as she found no sadness that Chad could not take advantage of Hope.

"Do you want Hope to know about Chad?"

"I will tell her the truth about him when she's old enough, but for now, I'm going to tell her as little as possible. I don't want to lie to her, but I don't want to burden her with it either."

"Does part of you want to find him one day? Perhaps try to repair the relationship for Hope's sake?"

"Never," Emily replied without hesitation.

"So, if you are so sure you would not take him back, why do you stop yourself from pursuing new relationships?"

Emily remained silent as this was not something she was ready to admit.

"A few months ago, we all thought we would see a fairy tale come to life between you and Shawn. That you two had managed to find each other through all of the craziness of this world. However, I get the impression that you are the one who stopped it. Why?"

"How could you know that?" Emily was confused. Father Nathan had only been Sanctuary a few hours before she had managed to push Shawn away.

"I see things," he smiled back at her. "Plus, no one in town is shy to talk about it."

"I can't even consider any new romantic relationships," Emily explained. "I made a vow to Chad on our wedding day. While it may have meant nothing to him, it does to me. I want nothing more than to be free of him, but don't know how since divorce is no longer a thing, and I can't be sure if he is alive or dead."

"I see," Father Nathan smiled as she spoke. "I believe this is why I have felt so drawn to help you."

"What do you mean?"

"Your vows were said in a church, yes?"

"Yes."

"Then, you can be free of them in a church."

"I don't understand." Emily looked at him with a puzzled face.

"A priest listened to your vows and helped you through them. In hearing your story, I believe I can help you free yourself of your vows and move on however you wish."

"So, what's the plan?" Emily could not hide the skepticism in her voice.

"I will have to do some praying and see what direction I am led to help you."

"I would like to see what you come up with," Emily responded. "I can't promise that it will make me feel free of my vows, but I'm willing to try."

"I'll get to work on it. I'm heading over to the farm to help, but you feel free to stay as long as you need."

"Thank you," Emily smiled back as Father Nathan stood to leave.

Emily sat for a long time, thinking back on everything. She had let go of the anger she felt towards Chad long ago, but didn't realize how much it still affected her. Emily didn't move until she heard Hope begin to call out from upstairs. After a quick diaper change, her small family headed out of the church and backed out into town. Emily couldn't help but pray that Father Nathan would find a solution to her problem.

Emily made her way around town, checking in with everyone. Everyone was cheerful and told her of the progress they were making. Everyone except for Derick, of course. He complained about the wasted time and materials in the church. Emily let her mind wander as he repeated the same things he had been saying during the project.

"Are you even listening to me?" Derick asked with frustration in his voice.

"Of course," Emily smiled back at him. "I felt it was important and would give the people something they need."

"I think it was a waste of time," Derick sneered.

"Well, you are welcome to your opinion."

"We have nothing else on the books for my crew and me." Derick was done talking about the church, and Emily was relieved. "I was thinking about sending my crew to the farm to work, and I could go help, Cole. I know a little about cars, after all."

"I have another project for you guys," Emily said much faster than she intended to.

She knew that sending Derick to help Cole would just end with him breaking the rules against him drinking. It was better to avoid the temptation as much as possible.

"And what would that be?" Derick seemed to understand what she was doing.
"I want to finish a few more of the houses."

"Why? We already have so many that are empty."

"I think ahead, and we have already gotten so many people. I want to ensure we have more than enough room to grow."

"Why don't you say what you mean?" Derick scowled at her.

"Fine, I don't want you working with Cole or around the alcohol." Emily secured the straps on Hope's backpack. She was trying to clarify that this was not the time for them to have another physical altercation.

"You can't single me out like that." Derick's frustration was building, and Emily knew she had to shut this down.

"I'm sorry, Derick, but my decision is final." Emily watched as Derick's face turned red, and Marley positioned himself in front of her.

"Emily, I need you to go to the COM room." Sarah's voice called out on the walkie. Emily grabbed the walkie from her waist.

"I'm on my way," Emily responded and headed towards the COM room.

"This conversation is not over!" Derick called after her.

"Yes, it is!" Emily called back.

She was so relieved by Sarah giving her a reason to walk away from Derick that she didn't ask what Sarah needed. Emily walked through the door of the COM building, where Sarah was waiting. Emily could hear Margaret talking to someone on a walkie.

"Do we have another new group coming?" Emily smiled.

"Margaret is still answering some questions they have, but it looks like a yes." Sarah smiled.

"Shouldn't we have everyone report?"

"Not yet. They may not make it until morning. They are at the furthest station."

"So, this is just a friendly heads up?" Emily smiled at Sarah.

" I saw you were getting ready to fight with Derick, and Hope was on your back."

"I appreciate it," Emily grinned.

"You don't want to stay in town after dark," Margaret said to the person on the walkie.

"You will want to drive straight through and go a couple of miles past before you pull over and rest."

"Do you have people out here to meet us?"

"No, we won't meet you until you reach our gate."

"Then who are these people?"

Margaret looked back at Emily.

Emily and Sarah had turned and were staring back at the radio, trying to process what the voice just said.

Chapter 7

Emily ran after Sarah to the radio. She watched as Sarah pressed the button to talk.

"Those are not our people," Sarah spoke in an urgent voice. "Please turn around for your safety. We can give you an alternate route."

"They are blocking the road behind us! Please help us!"

Emily grabbed the walkie from her waist.

"Shawn and Sam, report to the COM building immediately!" Emily tried to sound calm, but she knew that she had failed.

"Are you in danger?" Shawn's voice rang out.

"I'm safe, but we have an emergency." Emily returned the walkie to her waist. Within moments, Shawn and Sam burst into the building.

"Are you still there?" Sarah was saying to the radio. The silence was the only response that she received.

"What's going on?" Shawn asked.

"Margaret was guiding a new group, and they were ambushed in town," Emily answered.

"Ambushed by who?" Sam asked.

"We don't know." Emily was removing Hope from the back as she spoke. "They said they couldn't turn around because they were blocked in and then went silent."

"Please respond!" Sarah pleaded with the radio.

"No need to be pushy, Love," a voice responded.

Emily felt the rage want to explode out of her as he spoke.

"Your friends are safe. If you just tell us where to find you, we would be glad to bring you into our community. Based on your voice, you would be very welcome."

Emily motioned for Sarah to step back from the radio and handed Hope to her. Emily stepped to the radio and stared at the walkie button for a moment.

"Are you still there, Love?" the voice rang out again.

Emily steadied herself as she pressed the button.

"I told you I will never be yours," Emily replied before releasing the button.

She didn't turn around, but could feel the confusion on everyone's faces.

"Do the smart move here, Jeff. Let those people go, and we won't have to come and get them."

"I know that voice. Is that you, Love? Tell me, was it a boy or a girl?" Emily could see the twisted smile on Jeff's face in her mind as he spoke.

"We are not going to talk about that," Emily replied. "We promised those people safety, and you will let them go."

"I don't think so, Love. But I'll tell you what, I would be willing to trade all of them for you. What do you say, Love? Are you ready to come home?"

"I am home," Emily replied. "Let those people go, Jeff!" Emily sounded forceful as she spoke.

"Come and get them."

With that, the walkie went quiet. Emily slammed her hand on the table that the radio sat on. She knew Jeff was still out there, but she prayed they would never cross paths again. Emily finally calmed herself to turn and face her friends. "Was that the leader of the rape gang?" Sarah asked.

"Yeah, it turns out he's still an asshole." Emily could feel her anger radiating off of her. "I have to go get those people."

"No," Shawn finally spoke. "I'll gather some volunteers, and we will go get them. He's looking for you, which means you stay here."

"There's no time to fight about this," Emily replied. "I'm going, and I am leaving in ten minutes. Find volunteers if you want, but I'm going either way."

"Fuck!" Shawn yelled as he went out the door.

"Are you sure about this?" Sam asked.

"I'm positive," Emily stated. "Sarah, could you take Hope to Julia's and let her know what's going on?"

"I've got it," Sarah answered.

"Margaret, how many were in the group?"

"Ten," Margaret replied. "Three of them are children under ten." Emily nodded and turned back to Sarah.

"I'll see you later, baby girl. I love you." Emily kissed Hope on the head and headed for the door.

Marley followed her as she made her way to the armory. Emily opened her locker and grabbed her backpack. She took the walkie from her waist and tossed it into the bag next to a couple of bottles of water and protein bars. She slid the bag on her back as Shawn entered the armory, followed by Sam, Jacob, Cole, Alec, and Jose. No one spoke, but they headed straight to their lockers to start the same process as her. Emily slid the knife she stole from Jeff onto her waist and grabbed her crowbar.

"We may need to risk the noise; take this." Emily turned and took the shotgun that Shawn was handing her. "Put a few extra shells in your pocket and the rest in the side pocket of your backpack for easy access."

Emily nodded and did as he told her.

"I'll open the gate and get the truck ready to go," Emily stated as she turned to leave.

She ran up the stairs and entered the code to open the gate. She was returning downstairs as the group was exiting the armory. They quickly loaded into the truck, and Shawn slid behind the driver's wheel. Emily stood outside the wall and watched as the truck drove through. She entered the gate code, and the gate closed. Emily then climbed into the cab of the truck with Shawn. Once the door closed, Shawn quickly accelerated down the logging road. Emily looked back to check on those riding in the bed and was surprised to see Marley looking back at her. She had not seen him jump in, but he was just as stubborn as she was.

Emily turned back to the front and saw they were already nearing the main road. She was sure the truck would need some repair when they returned, as rough as the road was. She saw everyone in the bed tense up as the truck tires hit the pavement, and Shawn went even faster.

"It will take us a while to get there. Hopefully, the bastard will stay put," Shawn growled from behind the wheel.

"He will."

Emily felt confident that Jeff would stay there for days if it meant he could capture her.

"What's the plan here?" Shawn asked. "You just plan on fighting in, or do you have a strategy that won't get us all killed?"

Emily felt the sharpness of his words cut at her heart.

"I was hoping you might have a suggestion," Emily replied. She heard Shawn huff when she finished. "I know you're not happy I came, but you must get over it. I'm responsible for those people, and I'm doing this!"

"How can you be responsible for people you have never met?"

Shawn still refused to look at Emily as he drove.

"I didn't kill that son of bitch when I had a chance! If I had, then they wouldn't be trapped…."

Emily let herself trail off as she looked out the passenger window and watched the trees sail by.

"It's not your fault," Shawn finally said.

"Either way, I have to help them."

"Then you will, and we will help you get this done."

Emily turned and could see Shawn looking at her. Emily felt relaxed as she looked into his eyes.

"Thank you," she whispered.

Shawn turned back to the road. It was nearly an hour before Emily felt the truck begin to stop.

"We shouldn't drive any closer," Shawn explained. "I want to see them before they see us."

"I agree," Emily nodded.

They opened the truck doors and climbed out. Everyone emptied the truck's bed, and Marley came to stand beside Emily.

"We stick together when we go in. I want to look at them without them knowing and then figure out the best way to approach the situation." Everyone nodded that they understood. "If we find the dead, we kill them silently, no guns."

Shawn emphasized "NO" as he spoke. Emily knew that they would lose the element of surprise if they shot at the dead.

Everyone lined up, and Emily took her position behind Shawn. They silently made their way through the streets. The sun had set, and darkness blocked their vision. Shawn did not risk a flashlight; instead, they moved very slowly. They had only gone a few blocks into the city when Marley let out a low growl. Emily immediately turned and saw a zombie on top of her and Marley. Emily had slung her shotgun on her back and grasped the crowbar in both hands. She quickly thrust the crowbar into the zombie's eye and pulled it out as the corpse slid to the ground.

Shawn turned back towards Emily as she made a slight noise with her kill. Emily straightened herself and nodded to tell him that she was okay. Shawn turned back and continued to lead the way through the streets. Emily heard the sounds of another zombie being killed every few minutes. They continued to make their way as quietly as possible. It was about twenty minutes before they saw the lights. Shawn motioned for them to stop, and they all gathered in the dark.

"How many are in the group?" Shawn asked as he surveyed the area.

Emily knew where they were, the dealership where Jeff had found Emily last time.

"Ten," Emily replied. "Three of them are young children."

"They have the roads pretty well covered." Shawn was trying to find a strategy to get them all in as safely as possible.

"There's a forest behind the dealership. If you cut through the trees, it leads to the logging road."

"Why didn't you say something earlier? We could have driven the truck through there."

"There's not a road, and driving through the forest is how I wrecked the SUV," Emily explained.

"I can probably find a way to sneak into the woods from here. We will need some kind of distraction to get them out."

"I can handle that." Emily straightened herself as she spoke.
"We are not going to risk that," Sam spoke next to her.

"I don't think we have a choice. I've gotten away from him before." Emily looked to Shawn and could tell from his face that he knew she was right.

"You will be taking Marley with you," Shawn spoke. "That's non-negotiable."

"I don't think he would give me a choice even if I said no." Emily petted Marley as she spoke.

"Give us about ten minutes before you head in," Shawn began. "Don't try to hide. Just walk straight towards them. Just keep them talking, and once we are clear, get out of there."

"I will. I promise." Emily touched his shoulder as she spoke.

"I'll see you soon." Shawn's eyes told her that he would make sure she got out.

Shawn began to make his way down the dark streets with the rest of the group. Emily waited in the dark with Marley for what seemed like hours. Finally, ten minutes had passed, and Emily stood and walked to the center of the road. Marley followed at her side as if he understood the plan. Emily began to walk up the road towards the lights at the dealership. It wasn't long before one of Jeff's lackies spotted her.

"Stop there, Love," he called out.

"My name is Emily. I'm here to see Jeff," Emily called back to him as she stopped.

The man laughed at her name and called back to someone she couldn't see. After a few moments, he motioned for her to come forward. Emily reached him and could tell Marley was having difficulty not eating the man alive.

"Dog stays here," the man looked at Marley as he spoke.

"He's going to follow me no matter what I say," Emily replied.

"Jeff said the dog stays or the dog dies. It's your choice."

Emily quickly pulled the knife from her belt and had it to the man's throat before he could react.

"He's coming with me," she sneered at the man. "Got it?"

The man nodded with a childish whimper. Emily pulled the knife away from his throat and continued into the dealership. She could see Jeff sitting on the roof of a car. Behind him was a group of scared-looking people. Emily could not help but look at the children clinging to the adults. "I was beginning to wonder if you were going to show, Love," Jeff smiled at her.

"Stop calling me that," Emily replied. "I'm here to get the people you are holding captive."

"Straight to business, I see," Jeff smiled. "I missed you, Love."

"You said you would trade them for me," Emily replied. "Here I am. Now let them go."

"I've changed my mind on that." Emily felt no surprise as he spoke. "I think I will take all of you, even that dog, back to our place."

"That wasn't the deal." Emily made sure not to let her eyes move from Jeff.

She could see Shawn and the group starting to make their way around the dealership. Marley kept his gaze focused on Jeff as well.

"I make the rules, Love. I like your fight, but you will bend to my wants."

"I thought you would have figured out by now that I do not bend to anyone's wants. I'm a fighter, and after all the pain I caused you, I thought you would have given up by now."

"I don't know how to," Jeff laughed. "Your fight just makes me want to break you even more."

One of the men stepped close to Emily, and Marley met him with teeth. The man quickly stepped back, and Marley returned to Emily's side.

"I don't suggest any of you try that again," Emily glared. "The last man who lost his arm."

Emily knew she was exaggerating, but Jeff's eyes lit up at the mention.

"I've decided to let you keep the dog, but you will ensure he is loyal to me."

"I can't do that." Emily petted Marley as she spoke. "He doesn't like assholes."

Jeff stood and began to walk toward her. Emily had the attention of everyone here just as she planned. She could see Shawn and the others make their way to the group and start guiding them.

"You can and you will, Love." Jeff looked behind Emily and then back at her. "Where is the baby?"

Emily felt her stomach churn as he mentioned Hope.

"Safe." Emily pulled her shotgun off her shoulder as Jeff got closer.

"That's a lot of gun for such a little girl."

"If you don't back off, there will be a large hole in your chest," Emily replied as she placed her finger on the trigger.

"You have a choice," Jeff smiled. "You can either hand over your weapons, or my boys will kill one of the people you came here to save."

Emily could see that Shawn and the others had gotten the group out. Emily knew it was time for her to find her exit strategy.

"What people?" Emily asked, looking behind him.

Jeff and the others turned quickly to look at the spot where their prisoners once sat.

"Where the hell are they?!" Jeff yelled.

"Looks like you found more people that you can't control."

Emily began to back up as she spoke. Marley followed her step by step. The men rushed around to try to look for their prisoners. Emily had finally cleared the men and turned to run. Before she could start, a hand grabbed her arm.

"Where do you think you're going, Love? You leaving was not part of the deal."

Emily didn't have to look to know it was Jeff. She heard Marley lunge and bite at him. The sound of the gun firing made Emily jump. Marley let out a cry as he fell to the ground.

"Marley!" Emily couldn't stop herself from yelling out.

"I told you he would have to be loyal to me. I wonder if we should do a headshot or not. Can dogs turn like humans?"

Emily turned her shotgun on Jeff, and he managed to push the barrel up just as she fired.

"None of that now, Love." Jeff's soothing voice made her sick. "You should say goodbye before he's gone."

Emily let her gaze drift back to Marley and could see he was still breathing. He was moving his legs to try to get up, but wasn't able to.

"I will fucking kill you!" Emily sneered at Jeff.

"You've tried that, Love, but now you are truly alone." Another shot rang out, and Jeff grabbed his shoulder, which was already covered in blood.

"No, she's not!" Shawn yelled out as he rushed towards her. Emily fell to the ground next to Marley as shots began to ring around her.

"We have to go!" Shawn yelled as he reached her.

"I'm not leaving him!" Emily yelled back.

Shawn looked down and realized that Marley was on the ground. Without hesitation, he picked up the large dog and began to run back up the road. Emily stood and ran behind him. Shawn had pulled the truck closer, and Emily could see the group all sitting in the bed. Emily ran to the driver's side door and threw it open. She slid across the seat, and Shawn slid Marley in beside her. Emily pulled Marley's upper half as far as she could to allow Shawn to get in.

"Keep pressure on the bullet wound," he instructed her as he began to speed down the road.

Emily knew she should check to ensure everyone got in, but couldn't take her mind off Marley. Shawn drove like he was trying to break the sound barrier as he went down the roads. They drove for nearly an hour before either of them spoke again.

"Is he still with us?" Shawn asked beside her.

"Yes," Emily cried back.

"Hold on, Marley, we are almost home."

Emily looked up to see them turning onto the logging road. She tightened her hold on Marley to keep him from bouncing around. Shawn slowed as they neared the gate.

"I'll take him. You need to enter the code."

"No, you do it. The code is…."

"Stop!" Shawn yelled. "You still have to lead. I got him. You enter the code."

Emily waited as Shawn lifted Marley from her lap, and she ran to the gate and entered the code. Shawn drove the truck past her. Emily entered the code to close the outer gate and ran through before the gate closed. Emily could see Doc running towards the truck as Shawn stepped out. Someone must have radioed what happened.

"Get him to the clinic," Doc demanded.

"Can you help him?" Emily asked.

"I can try, but if he loses too much blood, it's over before I can."

Doc turned and ran behind Shawn towards the clinic. Emily could hear Hope crying somewhere beyond the inner gate. Emily looked down at her clothes and hands and saw that she was covered in blood. She knew that Hope should not see her like this. She tried to wipe her hands on her jeans, but the blood would not clean away.

"Thank you," a voice spoke from the truck's bed.

Emily turned to see a little blonde girl looking back at her. Emily tried to find the words but couldn't.

"Will the doggy be okay?" the little girl asked.

"I don't know," Emily finally spoke. "I hope so."

Emily heard the sound of engines and horns outside the gate. She looked back to ensure that they were sealed and breathed a sigh of relief that they were. Gunshots began to ring out as the trucks stopped just outside.

"I normally have a whole speech and a tour for you, but I can't now. I'll explain later, but for now, there are cabins just through that door," Emily pointed to the door that Derick had built. "Make yourselves comfortable, and I will be back as soon as I can."

Emily watched as everyone climbed out of the truck and headed for the cabins.

"I remember this place, Love," Jeff's voice shouted at the gate. "It was you who shot at us that day. I'm ready to come home now, to Sanctuary."

Chapter 8

Emily allowed the rage to fill her as she took off running for the wall steps. Sam ran towards the group that stood inside, and Emily could see them all head to the armory. Emily began her run up the stairs and was winded by the time she reached the top. She carefully looked down the wall and saw Jeff and his gang below her.

"Are you still saying goodbye to the mut?" Jeff yelled up at her.

Emily felt someone nudge her and saw Sam handing her a rifle. She glanced down either side of the wall and could see everyone except for Margaret and the children. They were armed and had their weapons pointed down at the men below. Emily locked eyes with Shawn for a moment and could see he was covered in blood just as she was. His eyes told her that Doc was trying, and Marley wasn't gone yet.

"I gave you a choice, you son of a bitch!" Emily yelled down at Jeff.

"You did?!" Jeff yelled back.

"Yeah, I did. You chose the wrong ass hole!"

Emily looked at her friends on the wall once more.

"Fire!" Emily yelled as loud as she could.

Gunshots rang out all over the wall. Emily couldn't get a shot at Jeff as he ducked as soon as the gunfire started. She watched as several men dropped to the ground. The remaining men scrambled to get into the vehicles and began to drive away. Everyone continued to fire until the trucks were out of sight.

"Open the gate, and I'll make sure they stay dead," Shawn said as he headed for the steps.

Emily made her way to the control room and entered the code for the outer gate. She listened as the gate opened and saw Shawn go outside through the cameras. Emily forced herself to stand and wait until Shawn walked back in. She closed the outer gate and made her way back down. Emily met Shawn as he walked back through the inner gate.

"We didn't get him," Shawn said, not looking at her.

"Are you sure?" Emily asked him before she could stop herself.

"I'm positive," Shawn answered. "I'll burn the corpses tomorrow. You should get cleaned up. I'll go check on Marley." Shawn turned and headed toward the clinic.

Emily made her way home and stood for a moment holding the door before she realized that Marley would not be following. Emily closed the door and made her way up to the shower. She turned on the hot water and began to peel off her blood-soaked clothes. Emily then stepped under the hot water and watched as the water ran red off her skin. Emily allowed herself to cry freely as she washed. Once she finished, she quickly dried and dressed in a fresh set of clothes. Emily looked back at the bed and felt her heartbreak as Marley was not lying on the covers.

Emily quickly made her way out of the house and to the clinic. Isabelle was not at the counter, but Emily could hear voices coming out of the surgery room. Emily made her way down the short hallway and into the room. Marley lay on the table with a white bandage wrapped around his shoulders. Emily stood still and finally saw that his chest was rising and falling.

"How is he?" Emily asked.

Doc, Isabelle, and Shawn all turned toward her. Shawn had changed his shirt, and the bloody one was lying on the floor.

"As far as I can tell, it missed all his vital organs," Doc began. "I stitched him up as best I could, but we just have to wait."

"What does that mean?" Emily began to cry as she spoke.

"Doc's not a vet," Shawn explained as he stepped forward. "He gave Marley a fighting chance. It's up to him what happens now." Shawn stood in front of her as he finished talking.

"I can't do this without him," Emily cried.

Shawn stepped forward and pulled Emily close. Shawn held Emily and allowed her to break down. After a few moments had passed, he loosened his grip on her.

"You should go sit with him," Shawn whispered to her. Emily pulled back and dried her face. "He needs to know that you want him to fight."

Emily nodded and made her way over to Marley. Doc moved a chair closer to the operating table. Emily made her way towards it and sat down next to Marley. His eyes were closed, and she couldn't help but miss them looking back at her. Emily reached up and began to run her hand through his fur.

"You got this, baby boy," Emily whispered
to him. "You are strong, and that's no more than a
bug bite."

Emily lay her head down on the table next
to him. "I need you to fight for me. I need you."

Emily continued to run her hand over his
fur and listen to him breathe. Emily lay this way
for a long time and eventually drifted to sleep.

Emily woke suddenly next to Marley, her
arm still draped over him. His breathing seemed
stronger. Emily began to run her hand through his
fur once more.

Thump, thump, thump…

Emily turned her head and saw Marley's tail
rising and falling against the table. Emily turned
and couldn't help but smile to see those big brown
eyes staring back at her.

"There you are, sleepyhead." Emily smiled
at him as she petted his head.

"How is our patient this morning?" Doc
asked as he entered the room.

"He's awake," Emily smiled at him.

"He is a strong one," Doc remarked as he
walked towards Marley. "We need to change his
bandage. I'll lift him if you want to unwrap the one
he has on."

"Whatever he needs," Emily replied.

Doc slowly lifted Marley's top half, and
Marley's tail started to wag again. Emily undid the
fastener on the bandage and unwrapped it. Once
she finished, Doc laid Marley gently back down
on the table. Doc pulled off the final square
bandage to reveal the stitches under it. Emily
watched as Doc cleaned the stitches and placed a
new square bandage.

"Ready to wrap him back up?" Doc asked.

Emily nodded, and Doc lifted Marley once more. Emily rewrapped the bandage to hold it and secured it again. Once Marley was lying on the table, Emily returned to sit next to him.

"Does this mean he's going to be okay?" Emily asked.

"It's a good sign. I only worry about whether he will regain his mobility. He won't have much of a life if he can't walk."

"So, we need to know if he can move his legs?" Emily questioned.

"Yes, but not too much, or he could pull his stitches."

"If he can move, he will try to get up when I leave." Emily looked down at Marley as she spoke.

"I am afraid of that. I've been researching all night on dog reflexes. I think I can test them, but I need your help to keep him calm while I do it. Once we're done, I can give him something to help him sleep."

Emily stood and traded spots with Doc and began to pet Marley. She watched as Doc started to test each of Marley's legs for a reflex much like he tested Hope's reflexes. Emily tried to contain her excitement as each of her legs responded.

"I may not be a veterinarian, but I expect this guy to recover fully," Doc smiled. "He will need to be on bed rest for the next couple of weeks until the stitches come out."

"I will make sure he does," Emily smiled.

She watched as Doc injected a medication into the IV, and Marley slowly fell asleep.

"Did you say morning?" Emily asked,
realizing how Doc had greeted her. "Yes,
you stayed here all night."

"Hope..." Emily began.

"Shawn picked her up from Julia's and took
her home. I saw him walking down the road this
morning with her in her carrier. It was quite a sight
to see, if I say so myself." Doc laughed as he
spoke.

"I bet it was," Emily smiled. "How long
will he be asleep for?"

"Hours," Doc replied. "I can radio you
when he starts to wake up if you want."

"That would be great, Doc."
"I'll ask Isabelle to keep an eye on him, and
I'll come to do the exams on the new people."

"I'll see you there." Emily ran her hand
through Marley's fur and then headed outside.

The sunlight hurt her eyes as she stepped
out, but she quickly adjusted. Emily reached for
the walkie on her waist to discover it was gone.
She remembered that it was still her backpack
back at her house. Emily turned and quickly made
her way home. She found the bag on the floor in
the bathroom and pulled out the walkie.

"Shawn, I have an urgent need to see the
monkey on your back," Emily said.

"And she has one to see you," Shawn
laughed. "I'll meet you at the base of the stairs."

"Roger that," Emily replied.

She clipped the walkie on her waist and
quickly made her way outside and up the main
street. She felt herself break out into a run as she
spotted Shawn with Hope in his arms.

"There's your mommy." Shawn comforted Hope as Emily ran up and took Hope into her arms.

"Thank you for taking care of her," Emily said to Shawn.

"It was my honor," Shawn smiled back at her.

Shawn continued to smile as Emily held Hope, and Hope laughed.

"We have some scared people on the other side of this wall," Shawn said. "We have been ensuring they get food and the supplies they need, but they are waiting to talk to you."

"Well, I guess I'd better get to work."

Emily held Hope on her hip and walked through the opening in the inner gate. The group from the night before all stood staring at her.

"I'm sorry for the delay," Emily began. "Normally, I would have given my big speech, shown you all the town, and welcomed you to stay in my home for the night. However, circumstances threw things a little off schedule."

"Is the puppy going to be okay?" the little blonde girl asked again.

"He is," Emily smiled back at her. "He will need to rest for a few weeks but will return to chasing chickens soon."

"Chickens?" a tall, slender man asked.

"Yes, chickens." Emily smiled.

She listened to herself as she explained about Robert and Sanctuary. She continued with all their resources and how the town worked. She then explained that they would need to let Doc examine them, though she expected they would know by now if any of them were sick. After about half an hour, Doc began to take them into the exam room and gave each new person a clean bill of health.

Emily then invited them all in and began her tour through town. She watched as each of them gasped at the sights and the resources. She skipped explaining that Jessica would help them with fresh clothes, as she could see they had already received them. Instead, she led them all to her home and invited them inside.

"Please take a moment to relax and think about everything," Emily told them. "I know it's a lot to take in. The children are welcome to watch television if the adults need time to talk. I'll be here if you have any questions."

"Why do you let people in?" a blonde woman asked. "Especially after those guys last night. Why would you risk it?"

Emily looked down at Hope as she spoke.

"If I hadn't opened the gates to strangers, neither of us would be here."

With that, Emily turned and headed to the kitchen.

"I'm proud that you handled that so well with everything that's happened," Shawn said as she sat down.

"Someone reminded me that no matter what, I have to lead," Emily looked him in the eye as she spoke.

"Well, whoever that was sounds smart to me. He probably deserves a raise or something," Shawn grinned back at her.

"I'll take it under advisement," Emily grinned back.

"So, Marley is going to be okay?" Shawn asked.

"Doc says all signs point to yes. He woke up this morning and was wagging his tail. Doc tested his reflex and got a response on each leg. He says Marley will need to be on bed rest for a few weeks but should make a full recovery."

"That dog will rest if I have to strap him to my back to make him be still."

"Now that I would like to see," Emily laughed.

"Hey, I make the baby carrier look good," Shawn joked back.

"You were rocking it," Emily laughed.

"Have you eaten anything today?" Shawn asked with a look of knowing on his face.

"No, I've been a little busy," Emily replied.

"Well, prepare to watch me rock making a sandwich."

"Should we offer some to the new group?" Emily couldn't help but feel lousy eating while they were still in the living room, talking.

"I'll make you one and put everything in the dining room for them," Shawn replied as he walked towards the cabinets.

A few minutes later, Shawn slid a plate in front of Emily with a sandwich and some apple sauce.

"Thanks," Emily said as she picked up the sandwich.

Shawn grinned and started to carry things into the dining room. After a couple of trips, she heard Shawn tell the living room group that the food was in the dining room. Shawn then returned as Emily was starting on the apple sauce.

"I'm going to feed the monkey and try to lay her down. She threw a fit last night that Marley wasn't in the room."

"Thank you for helping with her. I feel awful that I completely spaced and fell asleep at the clinic."

"This is what family does," Shawn smiled. "Besides, who will she be safer with than the head of security?"

Shawn set to work feeding Hope. Emily couldn't help but smile as she watched the big man holding the tiny baby and feeding her. Once Hope was done eating, Shawn headed out of the kitchen to take Hope upstairs.

"If you are ready, she will meet you all in the dining room in just a few minutes," Emily heard Shawn say from the living room.

The group must have decided whether they wanted to stay or not. Emily finished eating and put her plate in the sink. She then headed to the study and grabbed the ledgers to take with her. As Emily walked back out, Shawn was just reaching the bottom of the stairs.

"That was fast," Emily remarked.

"She didn't sleep much last night, so she passed right out. You ready for this?"

"It feels strange not to have them stay with me for a day before reaching this point."

"They seem like good folks," Shawn smiled. "If it helps, I like them."

"It does," Emily grinned.

With that, she turned and headed into the dining room. The new group was sitting around the table. Some of them had sandwiches.

"We've decided we are not going back out there," the blonde woman said.

"I understand," Emily smiled.

"Your friends explained a lot last night, and you confirmed everything today," a brown-haired man said.

"I think we are all forgetting to say the most important thing," a gray-haired man chimed in. "Thank you for last night. You didn't know us yet. You risked everything to save us."

Emily looked around at the group and saw that they all agreed with the man.

"When you all took the walkie and agreed to come, I agreed to keep you safe," Emily said.

"Still, not many people like you, especially in this world." The gray-haired man smiled at her. "So, what's the next step for us to join your family here?"

"First, you all sign the census. After that, I will need to know each of your skills to assign you a job, and then I will give you each a place to live based on your family size."

"I'm ready to sign!" the blonde girl smiled.

Emily grabbed the census ledger and handed it to the little girl to pass around the table. She watched as each of them signed, and the ledger made its way back to her. Emily then explained that children were required to attend school and how the credit system worked. She then went around the table and asked them what they did before the flash and what skills they felt were strong.

After about twenty minutes, everyone was assigned a job, and Emily was excited to have filled a new position. One of the women, named

Kathy, was a scientist who worked for the CDC. Emily was sure that Doc would appreciate the help with his project. Emily assigned them a house and prepared to set out just as Hope made it clear that she was awake.

"You get started," Shawn said as Emily turned to head for the stairs. "We will catch up with you."

"Alright, let me show you guys where you will be living." Emily opened the front door and headed outside.

"We will give you guys a couple of days to settle into your homes and basic jobs. Then Shawn will let you know when your shift on the wall will be. If you cannot take your shift, you need to talk to him or me."

Emily made her way down the street and showed each family to their home. Only two single women were in the group, and they seemed pleased with the apartments they were assigned. Emily had just left the apartments when she spotted Shawn walking toward her with Hope. Hope was changed into a fresh outfit, so Emily could only assume a slight complication with the diaper change.
"Everything go okay?" Emily smiled at him.

"She just wanted to prove to me that she was in charge, just like her mother," Shawn laughed as he held Hope in his arms.

"Emily, Marley is beginning to wake up." Doc's voice came over the walkie.

"On my way," Emily responded. "Do you want to see Marley?" Emily asked Hope.

Shawn said Hope was confused by not having Marley around, and Emily prayed that seeing him might help.

"Yes, she does!" Shawn replied for Hope. "I would like to see him too if that's okay?"

"Of course," Emily grinned.

The three of them turned and headed toward the clinic. When they entered, Isabelle was in the exam room, and Emily knew she was with Derick. Emily walked quickly past the door and into the surgery room, where Marley was still resting. Hope began to coo and clap as they entered, and Marley's tail began to thump against the table. They walked closer and stood in front of Marley.

"Did you miss Hope?" Emily asked as she petted Marley on the head.

Marley's tail continued to hit his tail against the table. Shawn held Hope closer, and Hope began to touch Marley's nose. Marley began to move his legs, and Emily could tell he would try to stand up.

"You have to lie down." Marley looked up at Emily with confusion and hurt in his eyes.

"You have to rest." Emily felt like she was pleading with him to stay on the table.

"Is the patient ignoring the doctor's order?" Doc grinned as he walked in.

"I think the table might be getting to him," Emily replied as she petted Marley.

"I thought it might," Doc grinned. "Shawn, would you mind helping me move him to the recovery room?"

"Sure thing, Doc," Shawn said as he handed Hope to Emily. Emily watched as Shawn picked up Marley and carried him to the room that Emily woke up in after her surgery.

"We will have to let him go for a couple of short walks starting tomorrow," Doc explained as Shawn set Marley down on the bed. "We will just have to be extra careful to make sure he moves slowly and no jumping."

"Can we take him home tomorrow?" Emily asked.

"I want to keep him here a few more days to be safe, but after that, yes."

Emily sat on the edge of the bed next to Marley. She and Hope were petting him as Doc gave Marley his next dose of medication. They stayed with Marley until he was fast asleep.

Chapter 9

The next few days went by in a blur for Emily. She spent as much time at the clinic as she could with Marley, leaned on Shawn for help taking care of Hope, and worked with all the residents of Sanctuary to keep things running smoothly. Marley kept getting stronger, but Doc continued to make him sleep when Emily was not there.

Emily was going to Doc's this morning to bring Marley home. He had been doing well on his walks over the past couple of days and seemed to understand that he had to move slowly, finally. Doc had told her that as long as he kept resting, she could take him home. Emily opened the door to the clinic and thought about closing it and returning later. Derick stood in the clinic's lobby, and the look on his face told her he was ready to argue.

"Good morning, Derick," Emily greeted him as she walked through the door.

"We need to talk," Derick glared at her.

"I can meet up with you later. Right now, I need to…."

"I know what you are here for," Derick interrupted her. "That's what we need to talk about."

"I don't understand." Emily stopped and looked at Derick.

"Our medical supplies are not unlimited, yet you have chosen to let them be wasted on that damn dog!" Derick screamed at her.

"He is part of this place and was shot protecting...."

"He got shot protecting you!"

Derick's temper was in full swing. Emily stood quietly and looked at Derick, trying to figure out how best to handle this.

"It's because of shit like this that a woman should not be allowed to lead."

Emily sighed as she stood in the lobby. Derick said that Emily was unfit to lead since he first arrived at Sanctuary.

"Derick, we are not going to do this again."

Emily tried not to roll her eyes as she spoke. Emily saw Doc walk into view and motioned for him to go back. While Doc was a genius, he was only brave when faced with no other choice.

"Just give me the gate code and get out of my house. Then we will not have to do this again."

"Derick, I'm not going to...."

Emily took a step closer as she spoke, and she smelled it. She felt like she could get drunk just standing this close to him.

"Have you been drinking?" Emily asked him.

"That's none of your damn business," Derick spat back.

"It is." Emily grabbed her walkie from her hip and pressed the button. "Sam, can you please come to the clinic?"

"What the hell do you need him for?!" Emily ignored Derick as she waited for Sam to respond.

"I'm on my way. Is it an emergency?"

"We have a case of drunk and disorderly," Emily responded and returned the walkie to her hip.

Sam burst through the door a few minutes later, breathing hard. It was clear that he had run all the way here, from wherever he was.

"Did the crew finish the project we had talked about?" Emily asked as he came in. "They finished last week. I always knew he would be the first occupant." Sam turned towards Derick. "You know the law says you are not allowed to drink. Where did you get it?"

"I am a grown man! I don't have to explain myself to you!" Derick began to sway a little where he was standing.

"You're right. You don't. But I do need you to take a walk with me."

"You think because this bitch says so, you're the law around here!? I don't have to do shit!"

"Derick, you are going with Sam." Emily began to walk closer to Derick, and Sam did the same. "The only question is, are you going to do this the easy way or the hard way?"

"If you think you will force me to do anything, you have lost your damn mind!"

Emily had managed to get Derick to turn towards her with Sam standing behind him. Sam suddenly lunged at Derick and took him to the ground. Sam quickly had Derick's hands bound in rope before Derick could react. Emily watched as Sam pulled Derick to his feet and began to walk him towards the door.

"I'll let you know once he sobers up in the cell."

"Since when do we have a fucking cell?" Derick was confused by the statement.

"I had your crew working on them when you were too sick to work." Emily felt a smile spread across her face. "After our last conversation, you made me realize that sometimes we need to hold someone who poses a threat to Sanctuary."

"And I'm a threat?" Derick laughed at her.

"Yes," Emily replied as she watched Sam push Derick out the door.

Emily turned and headed for the recovery room. Doc already had Marley on a leash, and Marley looked ready.

"Is the excitement over?" Doc asked as she entered.

"For now," Emily smiled. "Is he ready to go?"

"He is," Doc replied as he handed her the leash. "He needs his morning walk, and then he'll need to rest. Don't let him do any stairs until the stitches come out."

"Got it," Emily smiled and turned to leave.

"Don't forget these." Emily turned and took a small pill bottle from Doc. "It's his pain medication. He can have one pill twice a day." "Thanks, Doc," Emily said, looking at the small bottle, and remembered Derick screaming that they were wasting medical supplies on Marley.

"You know he was wrong, right?" Doc spoke as if he knew what she was thinking.

"What do you mean?"

"Sam radioed as soon as you guys were on the road and said Marley was shot. He told us that Marley was alive but bleeding badly. Everyone was waiting for you to return and heard the radio as Sam spoke."

"I was wondering how you knew what was going on."

"There was no hesitation by anyone. We gathered the veterinary medicine books, and I quickly studied how best to treat him while everyone helped me prepare for your arrival. We decided before you even opened the gate that we had to try to save Marley."

Emily felt a tear roll down her cheek as he spoke.

"Why would you all do that?" Emily asked.

"He is part of our family, and we protect our family."

Emily readjusted the leash in her hand and nodded. She strolled with Marley out of the clinic and onto the street. Emily turned and walked home to allow Marley to do his business. Once he finished, Emily led him up the ramp that the construction guys had put in for him. Marley seemed excited to be home, finally. Emily led him over to a pile of blankets she had set up for him to lie on. Marley made himself comfortable and settled onto his new bed.

"I'll be back in a while," Emily said to Marley after making sure that the baby gate was blocking the stairs leading to the upper level. "You stay here, and I'll be back for lunch."

Marley let out a soft whimper that Emily took as his way of asking her to stay.

"I have work to get done to keep this place safe. I don't have the luxury of lying around all day," Emily teased.

Marley lay his head down in defeat and let out a huff. Emily smiled and headed back outside. The morning was well underway, and everyone was busy doing their work. Hope would be somewhere on the wall with Shawn. He had agreed to bring her home by lunchtime. Emily felt herself turn right and head to the church. She wasn't sure if Father Nathan would still be there or if he would have left for the farm by now. Emily made it to the doors just as Father Nathan walked out.

"Good morning, Emily!" he called out as he saw her.

"Good morning, Father," Emily smiled back. "Heading off to the farm?"

"I was coming to find you," Father Nathan smiled. "I was wondering if you had a moment to talk about the issue we discussed."

"Have you found something you think will do the trick?" Emily laughed as she spoke.

She didn't mean to, but it escaped her before she could stop it.

"Why don't we talk inside?" Father Nathan smiled back at her.

Emily followed him inside and sat in one of the front pews.

"I've been doing a lot of studying on how to handle your situation."

"I'm sure there's not much information on how to get divorced in an apocalypse."

"Not exactly, but I still believe I have a solution," Father Nathan laughed. "The process I have in mind will take time, but I think it will clear your soul of the burden of your vows."

"But will it release me from the vows with God?"

"I believe He released you a long time ago. I believe what is holding you back is not being able to release yourself."

Emily wanted to believe that he was right, but couldn't help but be skeptical.

"The first step I propose is that you pray on it," Father Nathan seemed confident in his answer.

"That's your solution? I just have to pray on it, and I'll be free?"

Emily felt the hope that she had in Father Nathan being able to help her begin to slip away.

"Not exactly," Father Nathan smiled at her in his all-knowing way. "This is just the first step in the process. Well, it's the second step."

"What happened to step one?" Emily asked.

"You did it on your own. You found your inner strength and proved you're a good person to yourself."

"I did this recently?" Emily thought she had done this long ago, before the flash.

"When you selflessly went out to help those people and faced Jeff alone."

"I wasn't alone. I had Marley with me." Emily looked down as she spoke. "And I almost got him killed."

"But, according to Shawn, even though it looked hopeless, you stayed by his side and refused to leave him. Trust me, we all see it, and as you move through the process, you will also."

"So, what is the next step after praying?" Emily couldn't hide her skepticism as she spoke.

"I'll let you know when you get there. That's how this is going to work. I'll tell you when you're ready for the next step and what it is."

"I'll try, Father, but I'm not sure about this." Emily stood as she spoke.

"That's okay," Father Michael smiled. "If you didn't have a faith issue, you wouldn't need my help."

"As I said, Father, I'll try."

With that, Emily stood up and left the church. She felt the frustration building in her as she walked. Emily couldn't see how his plan would get her any closer to being free of her vows or Chad. Emily walked without paying attention to where she was going.

"Didn't expect to see you out here today," Jacob's voice interrupted her thoughts. Emily looked around to see that she had walked to the farm.

"Didn't expect to be here," Emily replied as she looked around. "I was lost in thought, I guess." "Is everything alright?" Emily could hear the concern in Jacob's voice as he spoke.

"Yeah, I'm fine," Emily replied, finally shaking the cobwebs out of her mind. "How are things going here today?"

"Ahead of schedule, which is nice for a change," Jacob smiled. "When you get time, Buttercup is still waiting to give you a riding lesson."

"We will set that up real soon." Emily smiled as she thought back to the first time she met Buttercup.

"Are you doing anything right now?"

Jacob knew she wasn't busy if she was just wandering around town without knowing where she was going.

"I just saddled her up for a ride, but I think she would rather go with you."

"Let's do this," Emily smiled.

Emily followed Jacob to the barn and spotted Buttercup standing near the door.

"Look who has finally come to keep her promise," Jacob said to Buttercup. "Do you know how to get on?" he said, looking back at Emily. "I've seen it done in movies. Let's give it a shot."

It took Emily a few tries, but eventually, she climbed into the saddle. Jacob led Buttercup out of the barn and instructed Emily on the basics. Emily paid as much attention as she could.

"Alright, you should be good to go," Jacob said, looking up at her.

"That's it?" Emily felt like there should have been more instruction.

"That's it," Jacob stepped back and leaned against the barn.

"Alright, be nice, Buttercup." Emily did as Jacob told her to, and Buttercup began to move forward.

They moved at a slow pace for quite a long time. Emily enjoyed the freedom she felt riding the horse.

"Okay, let's see what you can do."

Emily signaled Buttercup to run, and the horse did not hesitate. They ran through the fields, and Emily felt like she was flying. They did several laps through the fields before Emily slowed Buttercup to a trot as she returned to the barn. Emily brought Buttercup to a stop and could feel the smile glued to her face.

"Looks like the two of you had fun." Jacob walked towards Emily and took the reins.

"We did," Emily laughed. "I will try to get out here more often for a ride."

Emily climbed down from Buttercup and felt the soreness in her legs. She knew that she probably looked hilarious the way she was standing.

"It's normal," Jacob laughed. "You will get used to it after a few rides."

"I hope so," Emily said as she rubbed her legs. "I'd better get home to meet Shawn and Hope for lunch."

"I will see you later then." With that, Jacob turned and began to walk Buttercup back into the barn.

Emily began the struggle of walking home on her sore legs. The walk seemed to take forever, and Emily feared she wouldn't make it home before dinner. Emily finally reached the front door and headed inside. She could hear that Shawn was already in the kitchen, but her legs were not going to make it that far. Emily wobbled her way over to the couch and collapsed.

"Are you okay?" Shawn asked from behind her.

"I took Buttercup for a ride, and now my legs hate me." Emily continued to rub her upper legs as she sat on the couch.

"Have you ever ridden a horse before?"

"I rode the ponies several times when I was a kid."

"So, no?" Shawn laughed as he walked into her view.

"I don't need your criticism. Unless you have a new pair of legs for me, I don't want to talk about it." Emily looked away from him and pretended to pout.

"Fine, I'll wait until you feel better to give you criticism."

"Thank you," Emily laughed.

"Hope has finished eating, so I was just on my way to lay her down. I'll be back in just a few minutes." With that, Shawn began the walk upstairs. Emily heard him come back down, but his footsteps stopped.

"Would you be okay with it if I carried Marley upstairs during Hope's nap?" he asked. "I'm sure he and Hope will sleep better, and I would bring him back down."

"Yeah, that's fine. Please just move the gate to the top so he can't try to come down on his own."

"On it, boss lady."

Emily turned to see Shawn carrying Marley up the stairs. Once Marley was settled and the gate moved, Shawn finally joined her on the couch.

"Are you hungry?"

"I'm too sore to eat right now." Emily leaned back on the couch and closed her eyes.

"Well, we do have some business to talk about."

"My work is never done," Emily teased as she opened her eyes.

"I was thinking back to when we had everyone shooting from the wall when Jeff's gang was here." Shawn had a severe look on his face, and Emily knew the time for jokes was over. "I watched as almost no one knew how to aim properly, and more ammo was wasted than I can even count."

"What do you think we need to do?" Emily knew that if he was bringing it up now, he already had a plan.

"I want everyone to go through a weapons course until they are proficient enough. Having them guarding the wall is not good if they can't hit the broadside of a barn."

"I think that would be amazing. Would you be running the course?"
"Sam said he would be willing to help me."

"Then I give it my seal of approval," Emily smiled.

"There's more," Shawn continued. "I also want to run a separate class for kids fifteen or older to start making them comfortable with the weapons. In case of a major attack, they could help us defend Sanctuary."

"I like the idea, but I'm worried that parents will have a problem with it. I'm unsure how I would feel about Hope in the class."

"I could work with Howard and June to see if we could build it into the curriculum and make it more than weapons training. We could also teach them about the town's structure and have them pitch in when needed."

Emily could tell that Shawn had put a lot of thought into this plan.

"We could also make a requirement that they meet a certain grade requirement to participate in range practice."

"If you want to speak with Howard and

June to confirm they are on board, I think I can approve that. I would just need all of the final details."

"I'll get them as soon as I can." Shawn looked pleased with her decision.

"Is there anything else?" Emily asked, ready to lean against the couch and take a little nap.

"Yes, I want permission to take a group outside the wall to hunt down Jeff and the others."

Emily felt her entire body tense as Shawn spoke.

"Why would we risk that?" Emily asked him, not trying to hide the confusion in her voice.

"They know where you are now and have proven they are willing to kill to get you. They have seen the stations and will keep intercepting travelers looking to find Sanctuary. It would be safer to take them out on our terms rather than having to keep facing them on theirs."

"I understand what you are saying, but didn't you just say that most of our people are not capable of defending the wall?"

"Well, yes." Shawn looked confused at her statement.

"So, you would take our few good fighters with you, and we would be left defenseless."
"Well, perhaps going out right now would not be the best plan."

"We can discuss this again once everyone is properly trained and we are capable of defending this place with our fighters gone."

"I think that is the best decision," Shawn agreed.

"Are we good?" Emily forced herself to lean forward to try to catch Shawn's gaze.

"Yeah, I just hate that he is still out there. Letting him get away is my biggest regret."

"You saved Marley and me. We will get him; we just have to be patient." Emily smiled as he finally looked at her.

"I'm pretty good at being patient," he smiled at her.

"I hope so," Emily thought to herself as she leaned back and closed her eyes.

Chapter 10

Emily continued her work in town and took care of her small family. Shawn carried Marley upstairs to sleep with Emily and brought him downstairs each morning. Emily kept Hope with her daily; Shawn was busy setting up the defense classes. The first class was set up for today, and Shawn planned to gather the whole town at once for the first class. Emily was excited as today was also the day Marley's stitches were ready to come out, and he could go back to regular activity.

Emily had Hope secured in the baby carrier as she hooked Marley's leash onto his collar. Emily knew that Marley was more than ready for this day. She walked her small family out of the door and to the clinic. Everyone would do their daily jobs quickly this morning to enjoy their Saturday. Emily walked into the clinic and straight to the exam room where Doc was waiting.

"Is my favorite patient ready?" Doc grinned as she entered.

"More than ready," Emily smiled back.

"We'd better get started then."

Doc set to work and had all the stitches out in just a few minutes.

"That will do it," Doc said as he finished.

"So, he's good to go back to normal life?" Emily asked.

"He should be fine, but he may tire more easily until he builds his strength back up."

"I will make sure to make him take plenty of naps."

"I'd better get everything in order here so I can attend the afternoon lesson."

"Are you nervous?" Emily could hear the apprehension in Doc's voice.

"A little," Doc admitted. "I chose a life where I would save lives, and I'm not sure I feel comfortable taking them."

"I understand that, Doc," Emily empathized with him. "But you knowing how to defend Sanctuary will lead to us being able to save the lives of our family."

"I know that," Doc sighed. "I will be there and do what I have to. I just don't want to be okay with killing."

"That's what makes you an amazing person," Emily smiled back at him.

Doc seemed to find comfort in her words as he smiled back and left the room. Emily removed the leash from Marley's collar and saw his hesitation to move as she left the room. Emily turned as she reached the lobby to see him still standing where she had left him.

"Are you coming?"

Marley turned and cautiously walked towards her. Emily led him to the door and opened it. Marley continued to stroll out of habit. Emily checked the straps on Hope's carrier and looked down at Marley.

"Catch us if you can, slowpoke!"

Emily teased as she began to run towards the wall. Marley only hesitated a moment and then ran to catch up with her. Emily continued the runup to the top of the wall, where she and Marley needed to stop to catch their breath.

"Go find him," Emily said while pointing at the wall.

Marley took off at a run to begin his search for Shawn. Emily waited a few more moments and then began to follow. Emily didn't have to walk long before she heard Shawn's voice.

"Are you finally free?!" Shawn said as he wrestled with Marley.

"He sure is, though Doc said he may still need more naps."

"Hey, I could do with a nap prescription," Shawn laughed.

"Me too," Emily smiled.

"Is everything set for the class today?" Emily asked as they started to walk back to the control room.

"Yeah, I'm going to have everyone meet in the armory and bring them up for target practice."

"When do you want to set up the targets?"

"I'd like to do it now if you have time to work the gate for me."

"No problem," Emily smiled. "Do you need a hand carrying anything?"

"I've got it," Shawn said as he walked towards the steps.

"I'll get it open then." Emily entered the control room and entered the code to open the gates.

She watched on the screen as Shawn carried out the various targets he had made for everyone. It took him about half an hour to get everything set up, and he gave Emily the thumbs up as he entered the gate for the last time. Emily entered the gate code and heard it close below her.
Emily turned to see that Marley was taking

a nap on the floor next to the couch. She stood and walked to the door, and he jumped up to follow her. Emily led the way back down to the road where Shawn was waiting.

"Are you sure you will be okay alone on the wall while I do the armory part of the class?" Shawn asked her.

He had already asked her this several times over the past few days.

"I am sure," Emily rolled her eyes as she spoke.

"Just remember if something happens…." Shawn started.

"I radioed for backup, and you all can be there in a matter of minutes," Emily interrupted Shawn. "It's going to be fine."

"Alright then," Shawn laughed. "I'll stop repeating myself and asking the same question."

"Is that too much to ask?" Emily teased.

"I also feel better knowing Marley will be up there with you. I know he can't do anything up there, but it still helps."

"I feel better with him there, too." Emily reached down and petted Marley on top of the head.

"You'd better make your rounds then, and I'll see you at noon."

"Yes, sir," Emily saluted him as she spoke.

Shawn laughed and shook his head as he walked away. Emily quickly made her way through town, checking that everyone would make it to the class. Shawn had arranged with the parents that all of the children would be present for at least the safety part of the class. Emily headed home and prepared lunch for Hope and herself before heading for the armory. She opened her locker and grabbed her rifle and ammo.

"You have everything you need?" Shawn asked as they walked in.

"Yup, I have lunch, and I'm armed," Emily teased.

"I won't stand in your way then," Shawn said as he held his hands up.

Emily laughed as she walked past him and led Marley up the stairs. She set the lunches in the control room and watched as Cole, June, and Howard headed to the armory. Emily headed out and did a walk around the wall with Marley. She spotted a few dead in the distance, but not close enough to worry about taking them down. Emily removed Hope from her carrier and grabbed the lunches from the control room. She sat on the wall, fed Hope, and then returned her to the carrier. Emily ate the sandwich she had made herself as she did another round on the wall. She returned to the control room as everyone came up the stairs.

"Everyone, take a position on the wall and find the targets," Shawn instructed as he walked toward Emily. "We will have this side covered if you don't mind watching the other until we're done."

"I got it, boss," Emily grinned as she and Marley began to walk to her new post.

Emily reached her latest post, and Marley curled up on the wall. Emily watched and noticed she could barely hear the sounds of gunfire on the other side of the wall.

After an hour, Emily began to think that things were worse than they believed with everyone's shooting abilities.

"We are all clear!" Shawn's voice made her jump as it rang out over the walkie. Emily grabbed the walkie from her waist.

"I'm on my way back."

Emily nudged Marley to wake him, and they walked back to the control room. Shawn was waiting for her by the stairs.

"How did it go?" Emily asked as she walked toward him.

"Some surprises," Shawn replied.

"Good or bad?" Emily asked.

"Both, some of them need a lot more practice," Shawn began. "But Margaret had to have been a sniper in a previous life."

Emily felt shocked as he finished.

"Margaret?" Emily asked to make sure she heard him correctly.

"Yeah, I would have never guessed it. Remind me never to make her angry."

"You should never make a woman who is armed angry," Emily laughed.

"That's a good point," Shawn laughed. "I will be setting up a regular schedule for everyone to get some practice."

Emily noticed that Shawn did not look happy about the results of his first class. "Is something bothering you?" Emily asked.

"I hoped they would prove that I was worried about nothing, and we could set out to hunt down that bastard."

"He will get what he deserves, but we can't let it consume us," Emily replied. "Our priority has to be that Sanctuary is safe."

"I know, and I agree, but when I think of him, I just…." Shawn clenched his fists as he spoke.

"I know," Emily remembered Shawn running towards her as Jeff told her she was alone. "We will be safe, and we will get him."

"I'm sorry." Shawn tried to relax but wasn't successful in the attempt. "I need to walk this off." Shawn walked past Emily and began to walk around the wall.

"Emily, just a reminder that Derick's sentence is up today," Sam's voice rang out over the walkie.

"Do we have to?" Emily whined back to him.

"Well, it's your call," Sam answered.

"Fine, I'll be right there."

Emily began the walk down the stairs, but was in no hurry to get to the cells. She had tried to talk to Derick when he sobered up, but gave up when he spat on her. She had sentenced him to remain there until today to think about whether he wanted to stay or not.

Emily reached the security room door and found Sam sitting at a desk. He stood as she entered and led the way down the hall. The four small back offices had been converted into cells. Sam stopped in front of the first one, and there sat Derick.

"Good afternoon, Derick," Emily smiled. "I trust that this conversation will go better than our last."

"Yeah," Derick replied without looking at her.

"Have you made your decision?"

"I'm staying," Derick said as he spoke. "But I still believe you are the wrong choice to be in charge, and I have a right to say it."

"You do," Emily tried her best to be patient. "But by staying, I need you to understand that as long as I am in charge, you will follow the laws I put into place."

"Yeah, I get it." Derick looked to be trying to hold back his temper. "Follow your rules or be locked up like an animal."

"Well, you were acting like one," Sam shot back.

Derick rolled his eyes and did not reply.

"You are to report to your wall duty starting today and back to work on Monday," Emily began. "I have made Jose the head of the construction crew."

"But that wet...." Derick started.

"Don't, Derick," Emily interrupted. "Many people wanted you gone, and I couldn't let you stay in a position of power after what you did. You can accept this decision or get out."

"Yes, ma'am," Derick said with his jaw clenched.

Emily nodded to Sam, who opened the cell door. Derick walked out and headed out the door without hesitation.

"You know this won't be the end of it?" Sam asked.

"I know," Emily sighed. "But Cole will be locking all of the moonshines up now, and

hopefully, he will at least be sober for the next
fight."

"I think I'm going to head over to Cole's
and check to make sure that building is secure,"
Sam said as they walked back to the front. "I know
Derick will search for a way to get to it."

"I can't argue with that," Emily agreed. "If
you need anything to secure it better, just talk to
Jose. I'm sure he would be glad to help."

"Oh, I'm sure he will, too," Sam smiled.

Emily walked with Sam outside and
watched as he began the walk to Cole's garage.
Emily had plans to build Cole a better structure,
perhaps closer to the main street. However, she
wanted to ensure that his process would work and
not explode them all.

Cole had been set back thanks to Derick's
thirst. Derick had drunk or spilled almost the
entire small batch of moonshine that Cole had. He
said the engine was ready but would have to wait
until the next run to test it. Emily had insisted that
he make sure she was present when he did. She
was either going to celebrate with him or be blown
up. Either way, she was going to be there to
support him.

Emily made her way down to the store
called "Baby." Hope was growing fast, and her
new clothes were already too small. She waved to
Jessica across the street and entered the store. She
made her way through the racks and picked up
clothing in the next size. Emily heard the bell ring
behind her as Jessica walked in.

"Has she outgrown her clothes again?"
Jessica asked.

"Just about," Emily laughed. "Maybe I should stop feeding her to get her to slow down."

"Oh, I don't think even that would stop her," Jessica smiled.

Emily finished gathering the new clothing and walked to meet Jessica at the counter. Emily watched as Jessica added up the credit for each item, and then Emily handed Jessica her card.

"I feel like most of my credits go to baby clothes these days," Emily laughed.

"I had an idea about that," Jessica smiled.

"Kids grow so fast that most of the time, their clothes still look new, but they can't wear them anymore. We could allow parents to return the clothes to receive their credits back."

"As long as they are still in usable condition, I don't see a problem with that. It's not like we have an endless supply, and it would keep the store stocked."

"That was my thought, too," Jessica grinned. "With your permission, I would like to get it going immediately. I know Bobby has already outgrown his clothes, and Julia could use the credits."

"You have my seal of approval," Emily smiled. "I will gather all of Hope's clothes and bring them back by tomorrow." Emily gathered all the items on the counter and headed for the door. Emily stepped outside as Jessica followed her out.

"You know," Jessica spoke. "One of Derick's arguments was that you lied when you said you would listen to us and take our advice." Emily turned to look at Jessica. "But you always listen, and while there is some stuff you tell us no on, you always have a legitimate reason."

"I try," Emily replied.

"I just wanted to say that you are the best person for the job, and anyone who wants you gone will have to go through me."

"Well," Emily grinned at her. "My reign is forever safe."

The two women parted ways, with Jessica heading back to the grocery store. Emily called for Marley, who was resting near the baby store and had been since she went inside. Marley stood and stretched before walking toward her.

"It has been a full day, boy," Emily smiled as she patted him on the head.

Marley yawned back at her in response. Emily took it as a sign that he was done and ready for bed.

"We got a bit longer before bedtime, but you can nap once we get home."

Marley looked pouting but stayed beside her as she walked through town. Emily checked on Jose to ensure that Derick did not try to start anything. Jose worked with Cole and Sam to make up some loose boards in the garage. Emily knew Sam would find something to fix and was glad to know that Derick would have a harder time stealing the moonshine. Emily then made a surprise visit to Derick to ensure he was sober. Derick was not thrilled by her visit but kept his answers short and civil for the most part.

The afternoon would soon be turning to evening. Emily headed down the stairs from the apartments and headed home. Marley strolled behind her, obviously worn out from his day of full activity. Emily opened the door to the house and led them all inside. It wasn't quite time for dinner yet, so she grabbed a book, sat on the couch, and read to Hope. Hope stared at the pages as Emily read, and it looked almost like she was reading along.

Once they finished, Emily headed to the kitchen and made supper for everyone. Marley ate his food with his usual gusto and slept on the floor before Emily had finished feeding Hope. Emily set Hope on the floor to snuggle Marley while she ate dinner. Hope had not been allowed to play with Marley until his stitches were out, and she missed her puppy time. Emily allowed Hope to continue playing while she did the dishes and cleaned up the kitchen.

"Time for bed, you two," Emily said as she finished and carried Hope upstairs, and put her to bed.

Marley hesitated at the base of the stairs but followed after a bit of encouragement. Emily tucked in Hope while Marley curled up under the crib. Emily looked up at the bandana on the wall and then returned to the door.

"I'll come back for you later," Emily said to Marley as she left the room and closed the door.

Emily walked to her room and sat on the bed. She grabbed the photo album from her nightstand and flipped through the pages. She looked at her family's faces as she slowly turned the pages. She paused and looked for a long time at a picture of her, Joe, and Rachael. The photo must have been taken from Joe's senior year of high school, and the three of them looked like they were all sharing an inside joke. Emily focused on Joe and the bandana he was wearing. It was the same one he wore in his motorcycle accident. The doctors couldn't explain how he survived, but Joe was convinced it was because of his lucky bandana.

Emily whispered goodnight to her family and returned the photo album to the nightstand. Emily went to the bathroom, took a quick shower, and brushed her teeth. Emily then returned to the bedroom and sat on the bed. Emily folded her hands together and closed her eyes. She prayed for God to give her the strength and wisdom to keep Sanctuary safe. She prayed for Hope and everyone in her family. Lastly, she prayed to be free of her vows to Chad. Emily opened her eyes as she finished. She had not prayed this much since she was a child, and her mother made sure she said her prayers each night.

Emily stood and went to Hope's door. Marley stood as she opened it and began to walk towards her. Emily looked at Hope asleep in the crib and then at the bandana on the wall.

"I hope you left a little bit of luck in it," Emily smiled as she closed the door and led Marley to bed.

Marley carefully jumped onto the bed and snuggled down. Emily flipped off the light and crawled in beside him. Marley slept on the floor while he recovered, and Emily missed him lying next to her. She threw her arm over the massive dog and closed her eyes. Tonight, Emily felt at peace and allowed herself to relax. Emily lay in the dark, listening to Marley's rhythmic breathing for only a few minutes before she drifted off to sleep.

Chapter 11

Emily found herself running down the main street of Sanctuary. She could feel the heat of the fire from the nearby buildings, and the sound of screams and gunfire filled her ears. Emily looked down and could see Marley running beside her. There was bright red blood wet on his fur, and Emily could not be sure if it belonged to him or someone else. Emily didn't have time to stop, though, and continued running. She was near the gate when she saw him.

Jeff was standing there holding Hope in his arms. Hope was screaming, and the blanket she was wrapped in was covered with blood spatter.

"You let her go!" Emily yelled at Jeff.

"Now, Love, we had a deal."

"I would never give you Hope!" Emily reached for her knife, but found it was not at her waist. "You let my daughter go, you son of a bitch!"

"Not you, Love." Jeff smiled in his creepy way.

Jeff then turned towards someone, and Emily's eyes followed. She watched in horror as Jeff handed Hope to Chad.

"A deal is a deal," Chad grinned as he took Hope into his arms. "You can have the bitch."

Jeff began to walk toward Emily with his hand out to her.

"You are free of your vows; now you belong to me."

Emily stood frozen and watched as Chad walked out the gate holding Hope. She looked down at Marley, but he was no longer by her side.

"Come on now, Love. It's time for us to go home."

Emily woke covered in sweat and discovered Marley was lying on top of her. He was awake and looked like he was trying to hold her down. Emily patted the bed to call him off of her and sat up. It had been a long time since she had a nightmare, let alone one that vivid. Emily ran her hand through her hair and tried to calm her heartbeat. Nothing in the dream made sense. How would Jeff find Chad? How did Jeff get into Sanctuary?

Though Emily knew the dream did not make sense, it shook her. She glanced at the clock to see that it was three in the morning. Emily tossed back the blankets and quickly got dressed. The range on the baby monitor was pretty far, though she had not tested it. Emily threw on a jacket and put the monitor in her pocket. She opened the door as Marley jumped from the bed to follow her. Emily turned and opened the door to Hope's room and ushered Marley inside.

"You lay in here for a bit, and I'll get you when I come back," Emily said as he walked in.

Marley seemed confused, but curled up under Hope's crib. Emily shut the door and headed outside the house. She checked the monitor as she walked to ensure she could still hear the sounds of Hope and Marley sleeping. Emily made her way to the armory, grabbed her rifle from the locker, and headed up to the wall. Isabelle was on watch at the control building and looked confused as Emily walked up.

"Is everything all right?" she asked as Emily walked towards her.

"Yeah, just couldn't sleep and figured an extra set of eyes couldn't hurt." Emily was not up to going into the details and prayed that Isabelle would not ask.

"You've been through a lot lately. I'd be concerned if you weren't having some trouble sleeping," Isabelle smiled. "If you want, I'm sure Doc could give you something to help."

"No, I just needed to get some air," Emily replied. "How much longer until the next shift change?"

"It's at four," Isabelle replied.

"Okay, I'll be watching the road for a while."

Emily turned and walked to the edge of the wall. Emily looked down over the edge and scanned the road. Emily set the baby monitor and the ledge and listened to Hope and Marley sleep.

Emily had no idea how long she had been standing at her post when she spotted movement on the road. Emily raised her rifle and looked down at the scope. She would have thought it was a living man if it weren't for how it walked. Emily couldn't get a clear enough view of his eyes to see for sure. Emily waited as the man shuffled closer down the road. As it neared, she saw the clothing torn in several spots. Emily was sure that this man no longer had a heartbeat. Emily carefully lined up the shot and squeezed the trigger. She watched as the bullet penetrated the skull and the body fell limp to the ground.

"Nice shot," Shawn said behind her.

Emily pulled down the rifle and turned toward him.

"How long have you been there?" Emily asked.

"A little over an hour." Shawn looked at her.

"You looked focused, and you warned me about armed women."

"What time is it?" Emily asked, noticing for the first time that the sun was starting to peek over the horizon.

"Nearly six-thirty," Shawn replied. "Are you going to tell me what's going on?"

"I have to get home. Hope will be waking up soon."

Emily picked up the baby monitor and headed for the stairs.

"Are you not going to tell me what's going on?!" Shawn called after her.

"I just couldn't sleep!" Emily called back as she ran down the stairs.

Emily walked in her door as Hope began to make noise. Emily made her way upstairs and got Hope from her crib. She set to work changing Hope and dressing her for the day. She then led Marley down the steps to the kitchen and set to feeding everyone. Emily worked quickly and soon had them all out the door. Emily was surprised to find Father Nathan standing in front of her house.

"Good morning, Father," Emily greeted him as she walked out.

"Good morning," he replied. "Though I hear you were awake before the sun this morning." Emily rolled her eyes and breathed heavily.

"Who told you?" she asked.

"Shawn. He's worried about you."

"It was one night, and I couldn't sleep. Why does everyone think something is wrong?"

"It's just not normal for you, and we all know you have been through a lot."

"So, are you here to be my therapist?" Emily knew she sounded annoyed, but couldn't help herself.

"You have confided in me before, and I thought it would be easy for you to talk to me if something was wrong."

"But why would Shawn think that? Have you told him what we talked about?"

"Oh, my no." Father Nathan shook his head.

"That man sees everything and noticed you coming to the church and staying. He assumed we were talking and asked me to speak with you."

Emily looked at Father Nathan with both annoyance and a bit of anger. However, if she had raised enough red flags with Shawn for him to seek out the father for help, perhaps she should talk with him to quiet the worries.

"We could talk after service if you like," Father Nathan spoke.

"I will ask Julia if she can watch Hope," Emily responded shortly.

"I will look for you afterward." Father Nathan smiled as he began to head towards the church.

Emily walked onto the road and slowly made her way towards the church. She was in no hurry to make it to service this morning but felt compelled to ensure Hope still attended. Emily finally arrived to see Shawn waiting in front of the church.

"Since when do you attend service?" Emily glared at him as she spoke.

"Do you hate me now?" Shawn asked, looking at his boots.

"No," Emily felt part of her anger slip away. "Are you coming in?"

"Would you like me to?" Shawn asked.

"I think it's only fair." Emily tried to sound angry but knew that she didn't.

She walked up the steps into the church. Shawn reached past her and opened the door. Emily entered and sat down in the pew towards the center. Shawn took a seat next to her and sat in silence. Marley lay next to the pew on the floor.

Shawn had never attended the services before, and Emily felt he was only here to try to smooth things over with her. Emily turned back to the front just as Father Nathan began to speak. Emily found it hard to concentrate on the service. While she heard the words, she didn't fully register what they were.

Emily kept looking out of the corner of her eye at Shawn. She knew that he was worried about her behavior this morning. He didn't want to force her to talk to him and tried to find someone she would speak to. Suddenly, everyone started to stand, and Emily realized the service was over. Emily stood with Shawn and followed him to the door.

"Shawn," Emily asked, and he turned to face her. "Would you mind watching Hope for a while?"

"Sure," he replied. "Is everything okay?"

"Yeah, I'm going to hang back and talk to
Father Nathan for a while." Shawn nodded and
took Hope. "You go too, Marley," Emily looked
down at Marley.

Marley followed Shawn out the door and
looked back at Emily several times. Emily smiled
at him and then closed the entrance to the church.

"I half expected you to try to slip out with
the crowd." Emily turned to see Father Nathan
sitting in the front pew.

"I considered it, but I am a woman of my
word," Emily grinned.

Emily walked towards him and sat down in
the pew.

"So, what brought you to the wall late last
night?" Father Nathan wasn't wasting any time.

"I had a dream, and it scared the hell out of
me." Emily thought he might let her get away
without telling her the details.

"What was the dream about?" Emily should
have known he would ask.

Emily took a deep breath and searched for
the words.

"Take your time," Father Nathan
encouraged her.

"I dreamed that somehow Jeff had gotten
into the walls," Emily began. "He was burning
everything, and I heard gunfire and screams."

"That does sound terrifying." Father Nathan
tried to comfort her.

"He had Hope and traded her to Chad for
me." Emily felt the tears roll down her face.
"Where was everyone else?" Father Nathan
asked. "Your family, the townspeople?"

"There was no one else." Emily continued to cry. "Marley was with me initially, but when I saw Jeff, he disappeared."

"Well, that should tell you it was nothing more than a dream." Father Nathan's voice was soft. "We would never leave you, and Marley has proven that not even a bullet can make him leave you."

"Chad said he was setting me free of my vows and giving me to Jeff." As she said the words, Emily felt like her mouth was full of ash.

"Have you been saying your prayer each night?"

The question caught Emily off guard.

"Of course," Emily replied, wiping the tears from her face. "I have every night since you told me to."

"I think your dream may have partially been my fault." Father Nathan confessed. "The prayers combined with your recent trauma may have been too much."

Emily looked at him and couldn't believe what he was saying. How could her screwed-up dream possibly be his fault? Emily looked down at her hands and realized she was twisting her wedding ring. She hadn't realized that she was wearing it.

"No, Father, you were right." Emily smiled as the tears started to fall once more.

Emily slid the ring off her finger and felt like she had just removed a weight. She held out the ring to Father Nathan.

"I don't need this anymore," Emily said with a surprising amount of confidence.

"Are you sure?" Father Nathan asked as he took it.

"I'm sure," Emily replied. "I can't promise my late nights on the wall are done, but that has more to do with Jeff still being out there. I can say I'm done believing that Chad is still in control of my life."

"Well, I think that completes step two," Father Nathan smiled.

"I get the feeling that step three involves more prayer?" Emily smiled at him.

"Yes, but perhaps the prayer should change. Maybe now, instead of praying for freedom, you should pray for the strength to follow your heart."

Emily nodded and allowed the last few tears to fall.

"I appreciate your help, Father."

"I'm always here if you need to talk," Father Nathan said, stood, and held out his hand to help Emily to her feet.

Emily took his hand and stood, feeling different than she had when she had sat down. She followed Father Nathan to the door and smiled at him as she walked out. The summer breeze greeted her and guided her down the stairs. Emily stood for a moment and allowed the wind to dry the tears away from her cheeks.

"You look happy." Cole's voice brought her back to earth.

"Hello, Cole," Emily smiled.

"I didn't mean to interrupt. I was hoping to talk to you after the service. When you went back in, I decided to wait."

"That's perfectly fine, Cole." Emily smiled at him. "What's going on?"

"I got a batch of our new fuel source ready, and the truck retrofitted. I thought you would like to be there when I fired it over."

Emily couldn't help but notice that he spoke slowly so she could understand him with his accent.

"Let's do it!" Emily was excited to see Cole's plan in action.

Cole smiled and led Emily to his home/ garage. Emily looked at the old flatbed truck and couldn't see anything different. Cole removed the gas cap and placed a funnel. He then started to pour in jars of a clear liquid that Emily knew was moonshine. Once he finished, he removed the funnel and replaced the gas cap.

"That should do it," he said as he walked towards the cab.

Emily watched as he climbed inside and turned the key. The truck cranked but didn't fire over.

"It can take a couple of tries to work it through the fuel lines," Cole explained.

He turned the key again, and Emily nearly jumped when the truck roared to life. Cole couldn't contain his excitement as he clapped his hands and celebrated.

"Time for the final test," he said to Emily.

"Would you like to go for a ride?"

"Oh, I'm not being left behind," Emily smiled as she walked over and climbed into the passenger side.

Cole put the truck in gear, pulled it out of the makeshift garage, and began driving through the streets of Sanctuary. The truck went smoothly, and Emily could not help but be surprised. Cole slowed the truck to a stop when they reached Emily's house.

"You did an amazing job, Cole," Emily beamed.

"Thank you, ma'am." Cole was grinning like a kid who managed to steal a warm cookie. "With the remaining fuel turning to sludge, would you like me to set to work on the other vehicles?"

"Definitely." Emily couldn't help but be excited. "Let's get the pickup done next if you can."

"I'll get started on it in the morning."

Cole jumped out of the truck, walked over to the passenger door, and opened it for Emily. Emily blushed as she allowed Cole to help her out of the truck. Cole walked her around the truck and then, with a tip of his hat, was back in the truck and driving back to his house. Emily waved goodbye and turned back to her house. Shawn sat on the porch steps while Hope and Marley played in the grass.

"Was that a date?" Shawn asked in a mocking voice.

"A test drive," Emily laughed. "The moonshine fuel works like a charm."
"That's a good thing. Our remaining gas is almost gone."

"He's going to start on the pickup tomorrow morning."

"That is our primary one," Shawn replied. "You sure that it's a good idea?"

"I do." Emily placed her hands on her hips as she spoke. "Are you questioning my judgment?"

"Nope," Shawn smiled. "I know better than that."

"Good man." Emily smiled as she joined him on the porch steps.

"I'm sure you're mad at me for going to Father Nathan," Shawn said, not looking at her.

"Not mad," Emily spoke. "Frustrated but not mad."

"I understand that," Shawn said. "I was just worried."

"I know," Emily nudged him as he spoke.

"I'm not going to say there won't be any more late nights on the wall, but I'll be okay."

Shawn nodded as he watched Hope and Marley play in the grass. Emily leaned against him and rested her head on his shoulder as she watched Marley and Hope play. They sat together until the sun started setting, and Hope began rubbing her eyes.

"I'd better get her fed and in bed before this turns ugly," Emily said as she began to stand up.

"I need to work on the schedules anyway," Shawn said as he stood behind her. "Remember, if you need anything, just radio."

"I will." Emily waved goodbye to him after she picked up Hope.

Emily led her family inside and once again set out to make dinner. She noticed her food supply was finally running low and resolved to make herself a shopping list after Hope was in bed. They all ate dinner quickly, and Hope remained pleasant through a bath. Emily laid Hope down in her crib while Marley took his position under the crib.

Emily quickly gathered the clothes Hope had outgrown and replaced them with the ones she had just picked up. She then returned downstairs and grabbed the bags of clothes she had stored there over the past couple of months. Emily loaded them all into the washer together and started it. She wanted to ensure they were all as clean as possible before taking them to Jessica in the morning.

Emily headed upstairs, set to do some basic house cleaning, and wrote her list while the washer ran. Once it was finished, she loaded everything into the dryer and headed upstairs for her shower. Emily finished and headed back to the bedroom to get dressed. She knew she should be exhausted because of the very little sleep she had gotten the night before, but she was wide awake. Emily opened the closet, but instead of her pajamas, she wore jeans and a t-shirt.

Emily grabbed the baby monitor and listened to ensure Hope and Marley had fallen asleep. She then put on her jacket and tucked the baby monitor into the pocket. Perhaps a walk around the wall would help her unwind and sleep. Emily quickly headed out the door and made her way towards the wall. The sun was down, and the street was empty.

Emily retrieved her rifle from the armory and then headed up the wall. Emily was relieved that no one was in the control room and knew they must be doing patrols. Emily took up her post by the road once more and placed the baby monitor on the ledge. She then took her rifle from her shoulder and began the process of scanning the road just as she did the night before. Now and then, she would hear someone walk behind her, but none of them said anything. The street was quiet tonight, and Emily felt her mind begin to relax. After a few hours, Emily pulled the monitor from the ledge, placed it in her pocket, and headed back down to the armory. She returned her rifle to her locker and made her way home.

Emily quickly changed into her pajamas and retrieved Marley from Hope's room. Soon they were both snuggled into the bed, and Emily allowed herself to glance at the clock. It was threethirty by the time she got into bed. Emily allowed herself to yawn and fell into a dreamless sleep in minutes.

Chapter 12

The rest of the summer flew by, and Emily kept her same routine. After putting Hope to bed each night, she returned to the wall and would not go to bed herself until about three-thirty. Hope was beginning to resist being in the carrier since she had mastered the art of crawling and preferred to move. Emily was forced to take more frequent breaks to give Hope a chance to get out and move around. Marley was back to his old self; if it weren't for the scar, no one would ever know he had been injured.

Shawn had continued with his classes and even had Margaret helping him teach. Derick was not allowed in the classes. Shawn said he was only a spotter during his wall shift and was not allowed a weapon for security reasons. It was not safe to allow Derick a gun at any time. Emily had followed his suggestion, and Derick had made his feelings clear. However, while he vocalized them, he always knew when to stop and return to work.

It was the end of October, and Emily had planned an event for everyone. She had been working with some of the townspeople, and they were going to celebrate Halloween. The only rule is no zombie costumes. They had been working with the parents and helping them make the children's costumes. They would have a little party and allow the kids to trick-or-treat around different tables.

Everyone had been on edge since the encounter with Jeff, and they had not seen any new groups. Emily told them that people were probably trying to find a place to hunker down for winter. However, she knew what they all were thinking was perhaps true. Jeff was probably intercepting the groups or had at least done something to the stations. Shawn knew that Emily would disapprove of a group going out to take out Jeff. While everyone's accuracy improved, Emily felt the risk was too high for them.

Cole had converted all of the vehicles to run on moonshine. It was just in time as the last of the gas had turned to no more than sludge. He had been back stocking their new fuel source and had even managed to brew an extra for "grown-up time." Since the attack, Emily had not felt comfortable sending a group out on the run. She had searched the empty houses, come up with about a dozen Bibles, and gave them to Father Nathan. She knew that he wished for more, but seemed grateful for what she was able to give him.

Emily made her way through the streets doing her daily check-ins. Everyone was in high spirits, and many expressed to Emily that they were excited about the night's event. Emily had baked her cookies the night before. Once Emily had finished, she headed back to her home to find some of the guys already setting up. Hope began to squirm and fuss on Emily's back. Emily stopped, removed Hope from the carrier, and placed her in the front yard. Hope began to crawl, and Marley followed her through the grass. Emily sat on the front step and watched them play for a while.

She could see that the tables were all nearly ready, and the lights were all up. Hope crawled towards Emily and showed that she was prepared for her lunch. Emily scooped up Hope and took her and Marley inside. She fed Hope lunch, laid her down for a nap, and read her a short story. Emily had found herself reading to Hope every chance she got.

Once Hope and Marley were both asleep, Emily took the baby monitor from her room, grabbed the cookies, and headed outside to help set up. Emily was helping Bobby set up chairs as Hope began to make noise.

"I'll be back in a bit," Emily said to Bobby.

"I'm almost done," Bobby smiled back at her. "You guys should start to get ready."

"Well, you'd better run home to get ready too," Emily grinned at him.

"I will as soon as I'm done." Bobby could barely contain his excitement as he spoke.

"Is it true that the grownups are dressing up too?"

"It's true," Emily grinned.

"Even Shawn?"

"I'm not sure, to be honest. I guess we will have to wait and see."

Hope began to grow louder over the monitor. She was upset that Emily had not arrived yet.

"I'd better get going," Emily smiled at Bobby as she headed towards the house.

"I can't wait to show you my costume!" Bobbie yelled back at her.

"I can't wait to see it!" Emily called back to him as she walked into the house.

Emily made her way upstairs just as Hope began to make her frustration known. As Emily opened the door, Hope went quiet. Emily saw Hope standing in her crib, smiling, and Marley sitting beside it.

"It's a good thing I didn't name you Patience," Emily teased as she picked up Hope and gave her a diaper change.

"Mommy will get dressed first, and then we will get you and Marley ready."

Emily walked Hope to her room, and Marley followed. Emily closed the door and allowed Hope to crawl around with Marley watching over her while she got dressed. Emily had worked hard on their costumes over the past month. Hope would be a princess; Marley would be her noble steed, and Emily would be a queen. She had protested at first, but Julia and June insisted. Emily slipped into her dress and then set to work on her hair. Once Emily was done, she put her crown on the bed and picked up Hope.

Hope cooperated in putting on her costume and was soon dressed as an adorable princess. Emily had made herself a pink dress with tulle and had glued gems over the bottom of the dress. Emily had also made herself a cone princess hat and draped pink cloth on the top. Emily was pleased with how it turned out. Hope seemed happy with her new outfit as well. She didn't try to pull the hat off but was fascinated with the gems. The gems helped to keep Hope distracted while Emily put Marley into his costume. Marley stood still while Emily secured his saddle and attached ropes as reins to his collar. Once everyone was dressed, Emily grabbed her crown and walked everyone back downstairs and outside. Emily realized she had taken a while to get ready, as everyone was already gathered and the music was playing. Shawn had changed the wall shifts so everyone would only have to be gone an hour at a time during the event. Emily walked out to the street and began greeting everyone.

"A queen should never be seen without her crown," Shawn spoke from behind her.

Emily quickly placed the crown on her head and turned to face him. Emily couldn't help but laugh as she looked at him. Shawn was dressed as a grizzly bear.

"Where did you…?" Emily couldn't finish her sentence because she was laughing too hard.

"Margaret helped me," Shawn laughed. "Do you like it?"

"I love it," Emily grinned.

Shawn offered her his fuzzy arm, and Emily took it. Shawn then led them through the party. Everyone was laughing and having a good time.

"So, I may have told one person that the costumes were required," Shawn grinned while looking over Emily's head.

"You what?" Emily laughed.

"Yeah, I had Margaret help me with his required costume."

Emily turned to see Derick walking towards them dressed as a court jester. Emily quickly had to look away as she burst out laughing.

"I'd better tell him it was all me before he sees you guys and thinks you did it. It was worth it, though." Shawn bowed and then took off, walking towards Derick.

"You're an asshole!" Derick's voice rang out over the music and talking.

"I know," Shawn said as he continued laughing.

Emily smiled and made her way to a table to sit down. Hope continued to look around and smile at everyone.

"What do you think of my costume?" Bobby ran over to her. Emily looked at his cop costume and knew he had chosen to look like his dad.

"It's perfect!" Emily remarked.

"Ready for a family picture?" Jessica said as she walked toward Emily.

Emily couldn't help but smile at Jessica's costume. Jessica was wearing a cheerleader outfit. Jessica had talked about being a cheerleader in high school and carried her uniform with her even after the flash. Emily assumed that this was her actual high school uniform.

"Family picture?" Emily asked, realizing what Jessica had asked her.

"Yeah, I found a camera and a printer. I thought everyone would like to have a picture to remember tonight."

"That's a great idea," Emily replied. "Do you think you can take one of everyone dressed up? It would be nice to have a town picture."

"I figured out the timer function, so yes," Jessica smiled.

"If you can, maybe we should take a yearly picture of everyone."

"I can." Jessica was grinning big. I can get the original group together for a picture in the next couple of days, and then we can take one every year on Hope's birthday."

"Why is Hope's birthday?" Emily asked.

"Technically, that's the mark of the first day you opened the gates. It seemed like a day that should be remembered. Not that celebrating Hope is not enough, of course," Jessica tickled Hope as she spoke.

"I like it," Emily smiled.

"I hoped you would," Jessica said proudly.

"Well, let's do this," Emily replied. Emily turned to Marley, who was already standing next to her.

She carefully positioned Hope on the saddle. Hope immediately grabbed the ropes and was excited. Marley stood still while Emily turned back to look at Jessica. Jessica snapped a few pictures of the three of them.

"Got it," Jessica smiled. "I will try to get everyone together here in the next few minutes to get it done before the kids get on a sugar rush."

"Where do you want us all to stand?" Emily asked.

"If it's okay with you, I was thinking in front of your house. It's the focal point of the whole town."

"It's fine with me," Emily smiled as she picked up Hope and turned to make her way back to the yard.

A few minutes later, everyone was gathered in front of the house, and Jessica positioned them all. Jessica had Marley lying in the grass in front of everyone. Hope refused to sit still on Marley's saddle and insisted that Shawn hold her. Jessica even managed to get Derick to stand in the shot, though Emily was sure he would not be smiling. Jessica set the timer on the camera and ran back to join all of them. The camera flash went off, and Jessica ran back to it.

"First try!" Jessica yelled as she looked at the photo. "I will get these printed up and have them at the store if you guys want to pick them up tomorrow."

Everyone smiled and thanked Jessica as they began to spread out into the street. Emily stood and watched as everyone went. While she had been there to welcome them each in and invite them to stay at her home, she had not truly realized how many people were now in Sanctuary.

"I think they are ready to do the trick-ortreating," Shawn said while handing Hope back to Emily.

"Well, I'd better get the princess out there to see her subjects," Emily laughed.

Emily walked with Hope between the different tables. At each, Hope received a treat or a toy of some kind. Once they had finished, Hope began to rub her eyes. The excitement of the day was wearing her out quickly. Emily managed to get Hope to eat and then headed inside to put her to bed. Once Hope was out of her costume and Marley's saddle was removed, the two of them fell asleep before Emily could close the door.

Emily headed back outside to see that the sun was down enough that the lights were on. Most of the children were still up, but Emily knew they would be sent to bed soon. She made her way through the crowd and sat down at a table.

"Did you manage to find time to eat?" Howard asked behind her.

"I knew I forgot something," Emily laughed.

"June thought that maybe the case. She had me put a plate together for you." Howard set a plate on the table beside Emily.

"Thank you," Emily said, and Howard turned to head back over to June.

She began to take small bites of the food and realized her hunger. Emily began to eat so quickly that she was sure she was disgracing all queens. She finished and let herself relax in her chair.

"Is it safe?" Shawn asked as he walked toward her.

"What do you mean?" asked Emily.

"Well, the way you attacked that plate, I was afraid you might turn cannibal on whoever was closest to you."

"Very funny," Emily rolled her eyes at him.

"I wanted to let you know that the kids are going to bed. Cole has some moonshine under lock and key in the truck to keep a certain individual out of it. Would you like a little bit?"

"Yeah," Emily smiled at him. "But just a little bit."

"Right, I'll get you a big glass," Shawn teased as he walked away.

Emily watched as the parents all took the children home and slowly returned. Once everyone was back, Cole opened the door to the truck and poured a small glass of moonshine who wanted it. Shawn came back and offered one to Emily.

"Have you ever had this before?" he asked as she took it.

"Nope," Emily said as she sniffed the contents. "But it smells like rubbing alcohol."

"That just means it's good," Shawn laughed.

"Take it slow, though. It's very strong."

Emily followed his advice and took a small sip. Shawn burst out in laughter at the face she made. Emily tried to compose herself, but it took her a few minutes.

"Yeah, going to go very slow with that." Emily set her glass down on the table.

"Just don't walk away from it," Shawn warned. "I guarantee Derick will ensure the glass is empty when you return."

"Understood," Emily smiled.

Shawn sat next to her, and they continued to sip on their drinks. Emily could only drink half of what Shawn brought her and poured the rest into Shawn's glass.

"You know I'm not going to let you work on the wall tonight, right?"

"You think you can stop me?" Emily grinned back at him.

She had already planned on heading up to the wall once the party was over.

"First, you have had alcohol, and second, you need sleep." Shawn took another drink from his glass.

"Sleep is not an option these days." Emily felt herself saying the words, but couldn't stop them from coming out. "Every time I sleep for more than a few hours, I have that damn dream. I just can't take it."

"What dream?" Shawn casually asked.

"The one where Jeff is inside the walls, the town is burning, everyone is gone, and he has Hope."

Emily felt relieved to tell Shawn what had been bothering her, finally. Yet, simultaneously, she could not help but be embarrassed.

"Where was I?" Shawn asked while drinking casually from his glass.

"You were just gone, like everyone else."

"Well, then you know it will never happen," Shawn spoke. "For him to get in and get to Hope, I would have to be dead in the street. I think even my zombie self would try to kill him."

"It just feels so real when it happens." Emily looked down as she spoke.

"Then, when it happens, radio me, and I will come to sit guard all night if I have to." Emily looked up to see Shawn looking at her. "You can't keep going at this pace, or you will kill yourself."

"I'm not trying to," Emily sounded like a little kid as she spoke.

"I know, it was scary as shit out there, and I'm not too big of a man to admit I have had my share of nightmares about it. Let me help you get through this, and then, one day soon, we will hunt down that bastard. We will become his nightmare."

"That would be fun." Emily grinned at the thought.

"By the way, you are a talkative drunk," Shawn laughed as he spoke.

"I'm not drunk," Emily replied. "I think you're drunk."

"Oh, we will have to test it to see who's drunk." Shawn quickly finished his drink and stood up. "You game?" Shawn asked Emily as he held out his hand.

"What are we doing?" Emily asked as she took his hand.

"Well, drunks are notoriously good dancers." Shawn grinned as he led Emily out into the open area.

Emily knew as she was walking that perhaps she had drunk too much, but wasn't going to admit it now. It quickly became apparent that Shawn had no rhythm as he danced. Emily simply smiled and joined him. Emily lost count of how many songs she played, but she and Shawn continued dancing. By the time the last song of the night played, they were holding each other more for stability than anything. However, both of them were laughing and genuinely having a good time.

After the last song, everyone still on the street clapped. Emily suddenly realized that she and Shawn were the only ones still dancing. Emily knew that she would typically be embarrassed, but instead, she simply bowed and walked with Shawn back to the tables.

"So, I can't drink, but you can make fools of yourselves!" Derick glared at her from his chair.

Emily straightened herself as best she could and turned towards Derick. Emily had plans to tell him that while they enjoyed the recreational drink, they didn't do it daily. Emily also planned to call Derick an ass somewhere in her rant. However, when she turned and saw that Derick was still in his gesture costume, she lost all of her thoughts. Emily couldn't contain the laugh that escaped her mouth.

"Derick, if you can stay sober and not break any laws before Hope's birthday, I will allow you to have a small amount of alcohol at events."

"Why would you do that?" Derick asked, and Emily could see that even Shawn was confused.

"You stayed in that costume and were a part of our community. If you are willing to try, I am also willing to."

Emily turned, still laughing, and headed for the first chair she saw.

"Don't sit," Shawn warned her as they approached the chairs.

"But I need to rest," Emily reached for the chair anyway.

"Then let's get you inside and in bed," Shawn held her by the arm and guided her towards the house.

"Are you telling me it's my bedtime?" Emily asked as she walked.

"Yes," Shawn laughed. "It's your bedtime."

Emily allowed Shawn to walk her inside and up to her room.

"Are you up to changing your clothes?"

"Nope," Emily replied as she crawled into the bed. "Marley!" Emily yelled as she tried to get up.

"You stay," Shawn said as he pushed her back into the bed. "I'll get him."

Emily watched as Shawn left the room, and a few moments later, Marley jumped into the bed.

"Good boy," Emily said as Marley lay down beside her.

"You need anything else?" Shawn asked from the doorway.

"Did you mean what you said about I could call you if the nightmare came back?" Emily could feel the fear of sleeping creeping over her.

"Of course," Shawn replied, taking a step into the room. "But if it's okay, I was thinking about sleeping on the couch downstairs tonight."

"Are you trying to make sure I don't sneak out?" Emily asked as she pulled the blankets up around herself.

"Maybe," Shawn smiled as he turned off the light and shut the door.

Emily cuddled into the bed next to Marley and felt herself relax. Emily closed her eyes and allowed sleep to overtake her.

Chapter 13

Emily woke the following day and was surprised that she didn't have a headache. Emily tossed the blankets back and sat up as she would any other morning. She instantly regretted her decision. Emily considered lying back down as her stomach began to churn. Emily sat for a few minutes until it calmed down. She slowly stood and made her way to the bathroom.

After removing her costume, Emily managed to drag herself into the shower and was surprised at how much the water helped her. While she wasn't normal, she felt much better when she returned to the bedroom to get dressed. Once dressed, Emily turned to the bed and realized that Marley was not sleeping there. Emily scanned the room and noticed a note on her nightstand. Emily walked over and picked up the note.

Hope woke early, and I wanted you to rest. I have her and Marley downstairs when you are ready to come down.

Shawn

Emily smiled as she placed the note back down on the nightstand. Emily took her time making the bed before heading downstairs. She stopped at the bottom of the stairs and watched the scene unfolding in her living room. Shawn was sitting on the floor with the "Ugly Duckling" open. He was reading to Hope, who sat in his lap, looking at the pictures. Marley was lying on the floor and looked to be listening to himself. Emily thought back to his costume and smiled at the thought of how accurate it was.

Emily waited until after Shawn finished the story before she walked toward them.
"Are you three having fun?" Emily smiled.

"I think so," Shawn replied. "How did you sleep?" Shawn stood with Hope in his arms as he spoke.

"Good, I didn't realize how tired I was. Thank you for helping out."

"It's no trouble," Shawn smiled. "Maybe now you won't do any more late-night trips to the wall."

"I might still do it, but I will let you know before I do. It's channel one, right?" Emily teased.

"Well, I guess I'll have to take it. But at least now I know how to force you to get some rest."

"Now that's cheating. Hand me my baby, before you corrupt her too." Emily took Hope as she laughed.
"She will be ready for lunch soon," Shawn smiled.

"Lunch!" Emily glanced at the clock on the wall. She couldn't believe that it was a little after twelve. "How could you let me sleep so long!"

"I told myself that one was the cut-off time," Shawn smiled.

"Well, as long as you had set a limit," Emily laughed.

"My wall shift is at one today. Otherwise, I probably would have let you sleep until tomorrow."

"I didn't do my rounds today," Emily began. "Everyone is probably wondering if I have become a drunk who has started ignoring my responsibilities."

"No, they all were proud that you took the day to rest."

"You told them I slept away the day?"

"No, I told them you took a vacation day. You remember those, don't you?"

"Vaguely."

"You earned it," Shawn smiled. "Even if you had to be forced into it."

"Didn't you have a wall shift coming up?" Emily desperately wanted to end this conversation.

"Yes, ma'am. I'm heading out now, but I mean what I said."

"I know, and thank you again for taking care of Hope and Marley."

"Any time. Remember, channel one."

"I will."

Emily walked Shawn to the door and closed it behind him.

"You ready for lunch?" Emily asked Hope as she walked toward the kitchen.

Marley followed her and watched as she made Hope lunch. Once Hope finished her meal, Emily took her upstairs for her nap. Emily hated to have spent so little time with her today, but knew that she had to let Hope rest. Once Hope and Marley were tucked in, Emily headed back downstairs to the study.

She pulled out the ledgers and sat at the desk. Emily spent the next hour updating the housing ledgers and inventory lists, a task she failed to make time for. Once she finished, she also pulled out her journal and updated it. When she finished, she headed upstairs to see Hope awake and ready for round two.

Emily did a quick diaper change and headed downstairs. Emily looked around the house and realized how little time she had spent there. Everything was still organized and decorated just as Robert had left it. Other than setting up the nursery, Emily had changed nothing. It was almost as if she were staying here until Robert got home.

Emily made her way to the front door and headed to the store. Jessica was standing behind the counter, flipping through the pictures. Emily opened the door and walked inside.

"I thought you were taking the day off?" Jessica raised an eyebrow as she spoke.

"This is personal, not official," Emily smiled. "I wanted to pick up some things for the house and see if the pictures are ready."

"They are," Jessica grinned. "I assumed you wanted the town picture as well." Jessica handed Emily the pictures.

Emily looked at them, trying to keep Hope from grabbing them. The first was Emily, Hope, and Marley. Emily smiled as she flipped to the entire town next, followed by an original group picture. The last photo was of Emily, Hope, Marley, and Shawn. Emily knew when it was taken and when they were waiting for the town to gather. They played with Hope, trying to keep her happy until everyone was ready.

"I didn't know you took this one." Emily looked up at Jessica.

"I hope you don't mind. It seemed like the perfect moment, and I thought you would like to have it."

"I love it," Emily said, looking down at the picture again. "Do we have frames that these could go in?" Emily looked around the store as she asked.

"No, but I could talk to Jose to see if he can make some."

"If he can, I would appreciate it." Emily looked around the store once more. "I'm going to look around the stores for a bit."

Jessica looked at Emily and seemed both shocked and confused. Emily grabbed a cart and started to make her way through the store. She grabbed some groceries she knew she was running low on and headed back to the front.

"Do we have any decorative type of stuff?" Emily asked Jessica.

"Not much," Jessica admitted. "I have some stuff in the back that I found. Are you planning on redecorating?"
"More like personalizing," Emily explained.

"It's time to make it look more like my place than Robert's."

"I get that," Jessica said. "I did the same thing with my apartment. The pictures will help, but maybe putting a playpen downstairs for Hope and a dog bed for Marley. What helped me was rearranging things."

"Thanks for the advice. I'll look at what's back there, and then I'll be back."

Emily walked back and found one section of the shelf with decorative items. However, none of them spoke to her. She returned to the front and allowed Jessica to add up the credits for her things.

"Go ahead and add a dog bed and a playpen. I'll pick them up later."

"You got it," Jessica smiled. "Isabelle came in while you were looking and said that Jose was already making her a frame, so she would ask him to make more for everyone."

"Great." Emily smiled as she handed Jessica her credit card.

"I'll make sure to put four back for you," Jessica replied as she handed Emily her card.

"I appreciate it. Do you mind if I take the cart home and bring it back? I didn't quite think this out." Emily laughed, looking at everything and then at Hope.

"Of course," Jessica smiled.

Emily pushed the cart out the door and up the street to her house. It took her a few trips to get everything inside, but soon it was done. Emily put away the groceries and thought about what Jessica had said. Emily walked into the living room and looked around. She couldn't move the television as the stand was built into the wall, but everything else in here was movable. Emily glanced into the study. It had always seemed odd to her to have the desk in the center of the room.

"Alright, I got the little stuff, you got the big stuff?" Emily asked Hope.

Hope stared around the room without making a sound.

"Fine, I'll do it all," Emily laughed.

Emily started with the couch and chairs. She pushed them further from the television and switched the lamps with the ones in the study. She then removed some art sculptures from the shelves and carefully stacked them on the couch. Emily headed into the office and began to carry the children's books to the shelves. On the top shelf, Emily placed the census books and the journals. It would be easier for her if they were in this room instead of the study.

Emily then pushed the desk so that the hidden control panel was behind it, and she could access everything without having to move around. Once she was done, she carefully looked at each art statue she had taken down. While she was sure Robert loved them, she didn't like them. Hope was still playing with Marley on the floor while Emily worked. Next, Emily removed some pictures from the walls and added them to the couch. Looking at the empty wall, she could see family pictures hanging on it.

"What do you guys think?" Emily asked as she looked around. She looked down to see that both Hope and Marley were ignoring her. "Thanks for the help." Emily bent over and picked up Hope. "Let's go get...."

"Delivery!" Shawn called as he walked through the door.

"I didn't schedule a delivery," Emily smiled as he walked in carrying the playpen and dog pillow.

"I take it that means that I'm not getting a tip. Well, where do you want these?" Shawn tried his best to look defeated.

"Over there is fine," Emily pointed behind the couch. Shawn walked over and set everything down.

"There are a few frames in the playpen, a box of nails, and a hammer." Shawn was looking at the couch. "What are you doing with this stuff?"

"It wasn't me, so I was going to send it to the store for someone else to have if they want it." "I was going to take the cart back. I can load it in there and take it for you."

"You sure?" Emily asked.

"Yeah, I probably should get some food anyway."

"I'd appreciate it. You want some help loading it up?"

"No, I think I got it," Shawn smiled.

Shawn grabbed some of the statues and made his way to the door. Emily set up the playpen and found the stuff inside. She grabbed the pictures from the table and secured each of them in the frames. Emily then put a nail on the wall for each of them. Shawn continued to carry the stuff from the couch out as she worked. Emily had the pictures on the wall by the time he finished.

"They look good," Shawn remarked.

"It's the start of something, I think," Emily smiled.

"I think so. I'd better get this stuff to Jessica before she heads home for the day."

"I'll see you in the morning," Emily smiled at him.

"Remember to call if you decide to do a late-night walk."

"I will." Emily could not help but roll her eyes at him.

Shawn just laughed and headed out. Emily finished setting up the playpen and put the dog pillow in place. Emily picked up Hope once more and placed her in the playpen.

"This will keep you from getting into trouble while I cook," Emily smiled at her. "I'll go grab some toys from your room before I start."

Emily quickly made her way upstairs and grabbed a few tiny toys she had for Hope. Once back downstairs, she gave Hope the toys and started to work on dinner. Emily had done everything to make the house feel more like hers, but having the playpen helped more than she could imagine. Preparing dinner without worrying about what Hope could get into while Emily was cooking was easier and faster.

Emily could see Hope from the kitchen, and she was not quite as thrilled with the new arrangement. It was probably because she had always been able to do things differently from other babies because of her mom's job. Hope was used to always being on the move and having freedom when she wasn't in the carrier. Part of Emily worried if this life was going to have a negative effect on her. Emily forced herself to push the thought from her mind. Hope would grow up seeing that her mom was strong and figured out how to make an impossible situation work.

Emily headed to the living room, picked up Hope from the playpen, and carried her to the kitchen. Hope was eating regular foods more often. Emily carefully ensured that everything was soft and small enough for Hope to eat. Emily still held Hope while she fed her, though she knew it was more than time for Hope to be in a highchair and perhaps trying to feed herself. Emily wasn't ready to let go of this time together.

Hope didn't fuss and ate her dinner without complaint, allowing Emily to take bites of hers as they went. Soon everyone was finished, and Hope was back in the playpen while Emily cleaned up dinner. Once she finished, Emily went to the books she had moved earlier that day and took a look. After a few minutes, she grabbed "The Wonderful Wizard of Oz" from the shelf. It may be a bit too much for a child of Hope's age, but Emily was sure they would re-read the series many times.

Emily then picked up Hope from the playpen and sat on the couch. Marley jumped up and joined them as Emily got comfortable and opened the book. Hope sat quietly, staring at the pages as Emily began to read the story. Emily read the first few chapters to Hope, waiting for Hope to become restless or show that she was done with this particular activity. However, by the time eight o'clock came, Hope had done neither.

"We will read some more tomorrow," Emily smiled as she closed the book.

Hope began to rub her eyes, and Emily knew she had to be exhausted. Emily stood with Hope and returned the book to the shelf. As she did, Marley jumped down from the couch and waited for them to head upstairs. It didn't take Emily long to get Hope ready for bed. Emily closed the door as Marley and Hope were heading off to sleep.

Emily grabbed the baby monitor and headed back downstairs. While this was a reasonable bedtime for Hope, she was nowhere near ready. Emily walked around the house searching for something to do, but found herself sitting on the couch. Emily reached and pulled her walkie from her waist, surprised that no one had radioed all day. She smiled to see that it was set to channel one.

"I'm bored," Emily said into the walkie after pressing the button.

"I don't think I've ever heard you say that before," Shawn replied.

"Well, I am," Emily laughed. "Is there anything I can help with?"

"You are welcome to come to keep me company on the wall if you want."

"So, just to be clear, I have permission to come to the wall?"

"Permission granted," Shawn replied.

Emily quickly returned the walkie to her waist. She grabbed the monitor from the table and headed out the door. She never thought she would miss having things to do outside of her home. Emily made her way down the street to the armory. Once she had her rifle, Emily began to walk up the stairs. She found Shawn waiting for her at the top.

"I'm on the far side tonight if you want to join me," Shawn smiled.

"Let's get going then," Emily said as she began to walk.

Shawn shook his head and followed Emily as she began the walk around the wall. They walked in silence until they reached Shawn's post for his shift. Emily leaned her rifle against the wall and looked out into the distance.

"We should probably clear back the tree line to give us more of a line of sight," Shawn remarked as he walked up beside her.

"I've been thinking the same thing," Emily replied. "Hopefully, we will have more people next spring and can get that done."

"I agree." Shawn placed his hands on the ledge and looked at Emily.

"What?" Emily asked while laughing.

"You said you were a glorified receptionist before the flash."

"I was," Emily smiled.

"I just find it hard to believe," Shawn said without looking away.

"Why?"

"You seem to have a deep understanding of not only how to run this place but of security and strategy."

"I just do what I think is right." Emily realized that her knowledge of the situation was strange.

"I think it proves that you were meant to lead this place." Shawn looked back out into the distance.

The sun eventually disappeared, and the temperature began to drop. Emily suddenly regretted not bringing her jacket with her. Emily wrapped her arms around herself and tried to hide the fact that she was freezing.

"Come here before you freeze to death," Shawn said as he put his arm around her and pulled her close. Emily welcomed the warmth and felt the shivers begin to slow.

"I thought you would tell me to go home," Emily laughed.

"Would you have gone if I did?" Shawn asked.

"Probably not," Emily smiled. "Do you want it, or can I take it?"

Shawn turned his gaze back to the tree line as a zombie walked out towards the wall. This person was turned by the bites that covered their body.

"You take this one," Shawn said as he released her.

Emily grabbed her rifle from where it leaned and took her time lining up the shot. A few moments later, the sound of the shot rang out, and the corpse fell lifeless to the ground.

"We are starting to see more and more of them. There was a time when we could go weeks without seeing one."

"Well, there's less and less living every day," Emily replied.

"True, but I still don't like it."

As soon as Shawn finished talking, they heard a shot ring out from the west side of the wall.

"I don't like it," Shawn said, looking in the direction of the shot.

"We can handle it," Emily smiled. "I will check and make sure everything is okay on my way home."

"You had enough of the wall tonight?" Shawn smiled.

"Just a little cold, and if I don't get rest, someone will force me to." Emily skeptically looked at Shawn as she spoke.

"Damn straight," Shawn laughed.

"Goodnight," Emily said as she started to walk towards the west.

"Goodnight," Shawn replied. Emily made her way to the west and found Cole staring into the distance.

"Just a dead one," Cole said as she approached. "Now it's dead."

"Glad to hear it," Emily replied as she walked by.

Emily made her way home and gladly snuggled into her warm bed next to Marley for the night.

Chapter 14

The cold November air whipped through Sanctuary the following day. Emily had made sure to bundle up Hope before heading out into town for the day. Things at the farm were quiet as most crops were done for the season. Everyone seemed to be doing well and in high spirits as she visited. Several people were even talking about celebrating Thanksgiving.

Emily was surprised to find Sarah standing by the gate as she reached the end of the main street.

"What's going on?" Emily asked as she approached.

"I was reviewing some of the wall blueprints and found that there should be another panel here to enter the codes. I thought if I could find it or maybe hook one up, it would help save you from running up the steps all the time."

"My legs would greatly appreciate that," Emily smiled.

Emily helped Sarah look at the wall, and, almost at the same time, they both noticed four screws that formed a square and seemed out of place on the metal sheet. Emily watched as Sarah removed the screws and revealed a bunch of wires behind the plate.

"The keypad must be here. I will see if I can get this hooked up."

"I'll ask everyone to keep an eye out in case they come across it."

"Could you ask them to bring any electronics like that to the COM building? It would be better to know what I had to work with to help enhance our situation."

"Sure," Emily smiled.

"I have almost nothing to do these days since the calls stopped coming in." Emily could tell that Sarah was still unhappy about the decision not to check on the stations.

"Sarah, we talked about this," Emily started.

"I know," Sarah interrupted. "I just wish I knew they were okay. I hate the idea of people freezing out there over the winter." Emily knew Sarah would be worried all winter if the stations were not checked at least once.

"I'll see if I can arrange a party to go out and check," Emily finally said.

"Really?!" Sarah jumped around and looked at her.

"Really," Emily breathed. "We probably should do one more run before winter sets in to ensure we have everything we need."

Emily knew they had more than enough of the essentials to get through winter, but knew this would help her justify the run to herself.

"If you need me to go, just let me know." Sarah quickly screwed the plate and ran back to the COM room. Emily shook her head as she grabbed her walkie.

"Shawn, are you available for a meeting?"

"I'm currently at security," Shawn's voice replied.

"I'm on my way." Emily returned the walkie to her waist and made the short walk to the security building. Once inside, she saw Shawn and Sam sitting at a table. Emily took Hope out of her carrier and went to join them.

"We have an emergency, boss?" Shawn asked as she approached.

"No emergency," Emily replied as she sat down. "I have decided it would be okay to do one more run before winter sets in. We should sure up our supplies and check on the stations."

"Really?" Shawn smiled at her.

"It's not the hunting mission I know you were hoping for, but I think we need to go out."

"I'll take it." Shawn looked at Sam. "You never know what or who you may find."

"Shawn, you must promise we will stay focused on what we are going out for."

"Wait, are you planning on going?" Shawn asked with concern on his face.

"Of course," Emily replied. "I have gone on all the runs outside the wall, and I don't plan to stop now."

"I hoped you would until Jeff was no longer out there," Shawn admitted.

"I'm not going to let him scare me into hiding. We need to go out, and you're not leaving me behind."

"I think it will be fine," Sam said. Shawn turned and looked at Sam with anger on his face. "As long as she agrees to stay too close to you or me the entire time."

Emily knew there had to be a catch to Sam agreeing that she would be fine. While she didn't believe she needed a babysitter, Emily knew that this was the only way she could end the debate.

"I agree," Emily interjected. "Can we move on to planning the run now?"

Emily could tell that Shawn was not happy, but knew that he had to let it go. The three sat for the next few hours and planned their route, areas they would be looking to scavenge, which they would be taking, and what the wall team put in place while they were gone. They decided to head out the following day if the weather cooperated.

Once they finished, Emily left Shawn and Sam to complete the planning and let everyone know what would happen. Emily headed towards her house. Marley walked beside her as if understanding what they were planning. Emily had considered leaving him at Sanctuary, but knew he would never stay.

Once inside the house, Emily fed Hope a quick lunch and tucked her into bed. Emily returned downstairs and updated her journal with their plans. She wanted to keep some kind of record just in case something happened to her. Once she finished, she went through the house quickly and did some chores.

Once she finished, she got Hope and Marley up from their nap and spent the rest of the day at home. Everything was quiet the rest of the day. After dinner, Emily grabbed "The Wonderful Wizard of Oz" and read Hope a few more chapters. Emily then got Hope ready for bed and tucked her in. However, Marley refused to take his usual position under the crib and insisted on staying with Emily.

Emily closed Hope's door and walked with Marley back downstairs. Marley seemed to be glued to Emily's side and followed her everywhere. Emily grabbed a jacket and the baby monitor. She then headed outside with Marley. She hoped that the fresh air might help to calm down a bit. Emily made her way to the wall and started her walk around. She hadn't grabbed her rifle, but didn't have any intentions of working tonight.

Emily worked her way around the wall with Marley at her side. After a while, she spotted Shawn looking over the fence. Emily expected Marley to take off at a run to greet Shawn, but Marley remained close to her side.

"Anything tonight?" Emily asked as she grew closer to Shawn.

"We've killed seven tonight," Shawn replied as he turned to face her.

"So, they are coming more often," Emily replied.

"Yes, but nothing we can't handle," Shawn smiled. "I expected him to be with Hope," Shawn said, looking at Marley.

"He refused," Emily replied. "It's like he knows what we are doing in the morning. I hoped a walk would help him relax."

"I can't blame him for being on edge. He did get shot last time."

"I'm trying not to think about that." Emily petted Marley as she spoke.

"You know he won't stay here, right?"

"I know," Emily breathed. "I don't know how he learned to be so headstrong."

"I have no idea," Shawn laughed. Emily laughed with him, knowing that he was referring to her.

"I guess we'd better finish our walk and head home," Emily said.

"You need some rest. I'll be going straight home once my shift is over."

"I'll see you in the morning," Emily said as she continued walking.

Marley didn't relax during the walk, and Emily eventually had to give up and head home. After a quick check on Hope, Emily and Marley headed to bed. Once Emily lay down, Marley insisted on lying on top of her. Emily understood that he was scared and decided to let him if it made him feel better. It took her a while to fall asleep, but eventually, she did.

Emily woke early the following day and set to getting ready for the day. When Julia walked through the front door, Emily had just finished getting Hope ready. Emily stood with Hope to greet her friend.

"Good morning," Emily greeted her.

"Good morning," Julia smiled back. "I'm here to pick up my assistant for the day."

Emily tried to hand Hope to Julia, but Hope grabbed onto Emily's shirt and began to fuss.

"I think she knows that you're leaving," Julia remarked.

"I'll be back." Emily tried to comfort Hope.

Hope continued to fuss and cry as Emily pulled Hope from her shirt and handed Hope to Julia. Emily's heart broke watching Hope be so upset by her leaving. Emily turned and grabbed a book from the shelf.

"This may help," Emily said as she handed Julia the book. I have read her a few chapters every day before bed, and she seems to enjoy it."

Julia took the book and looked at it.

"I don't think I've read this since I was a kid," Julia smiled. "We will be fine. You just make sure to come home."

"I will." Emily smiled and took a step forward. "I've got to be going," Emily said to Hope. "You be good, and I will see you tonight." Hope began to scream after Emily kissed her head and went out the door. Emily had a hard time not turning around and grabbing Hope. However, she knew this was something that she had to do. Emily made her way to the armory just as the sun began waking up the world. Emily saw that everyone had arrived as she walked in.

Today, it would be Emily, Shawn, Cole, Sam, and Jose. Emily found her backpack in her locker and grabbed her weapons. The men all headed towards the gate as Emily headed upstairs to enter the code. Emily couldn't help but think about how much easier this would be if Sarah could hook up the panel. Emily joined the code and headed down as the doors opened. Everyone was divided between two cars. Shawn took the pickup, as usual, and Sam was driving the box truck. This would be the first time they were doing a run with the vehicles using moonshine.

Emily walked out the gate and waited as the vehicles drove out. Emily entered the code and watched as Marley jumped into the truck's bed with Cole. Emily then climbed inside the cab with Shawn. Shawn didn't say anything but started driving down the logging road. Emily watched out the windshield as they drove. Shawn didn't speak, and neither did Emily. Shawn began to slow the truck before they reached the end of the road.

"What's wrong?" Emily asked, trying to see where he was looking.

"There is something by the station," Shawn said.

As they drove a little closer, Emily saw what he was talking about. There was a zombie chained to the station. Shawn brought the truck to a stop, and they both jumped out. Marley and Cole climbed out of bed and walked toward the station.

Emily walked towards the man and could tell he wasn't killed in a flash. He had lived for some time in this world. Emily saw that his throat was cut, and blood covered the front of his plaid shirt.

"He was killed and chained before he turned," Shawn explained. Shawn walked past Emily and stabbed the man in the brain.

"Jeff left him for us to find and to keep people away from the stations."

Emily walked closer and saw that while the small bag of supplies was gone, the walkie remained at the station. However, a note was nailed by the walkie.

I told him all he had to do was grab it, and help would come. I grew tired of waiting and made sure he wouldn't get lost.

Husband

Emily pulled the note from the station and crumpled it. Emily threw the crumpled paper on the ground.

"How long do you think he's been here?" Emily asked without turning around.

"Hard to say since they don't decay," Shawn replied. "It's not fresh. The blood is dry on his clothing and almost completely washed away on the ground. Our last rainstorm was a month ago, so I would say at least a month."

"Let's get him off the station and move on to the next."

"Jeff could be watching us," Cole spoke.

"I don't think so," Emily said. "Otherwise, he would have kept adding fresh bodies for me to find."

"I agree," Shawn said. "I'll get the cutters from the truck."

Emily stood with Marley and watched as Shawn cut the chain and dragged the corpse into the tree line. Cole followed him with a shovel, and they buried the corpse in a shallow grave. Once they finished, they all loaded back into the truck and continued down the road.

Emily looked toward Shawn, but it was clear he was still not up for talking. Emily silently watched as the tree line blurred outside the window. Emily couldn't help but notice the number of dead they passed. They had only seen one when she and Shawn set up the stations, and now there were dozens.

Shawn slowed the truck as they approached the next station. Emily held her breath and didn't exhale until she saw that the station was untouched. Shawn drove closer, and Emily looked at the station as they went by. The bag of supplies was missing, but the walkie was still in position. Shawn pressed down the gas once more, and they continued on their way. Emily was glad to see that the same sight waited for them at the third station.

However, she couldn't help but become anxious as they drove towards the last. The last station was in town, the same place where Jeff had been, and Marley was shot.

Shawn remained quiet as they drove. Emily tightened her grip on her crowbar as the town came into view. Shawn moved in slowly and stopped the truck in front of some stores. Emily reached for the door handle to jump out.

"Remember," Shawn spoke. "You don't go anywhere alone."

"I know," Emily replied as she cracked the door open.

"And that doesn't mean with just Marley," Shawn looked at her, knowing what her way out of the arrangement would be.

"I understand."

Emily then climbed out of the truck and shut the door without looking back. Marley jumped out of the truck and stood beside her. Everyone gathered around the front of the pickup and waited for Shawn's instructions.

"We will check the last station on the way out," Shawn began. "We will break up into two groups to see what we can find. Emily, Marley, and Sam will take the left side. Jose, Cole, and I will take a right. Stack anything you find on the sidewalk, and we load it together when we are done."

Emily was surprised that Shawn didn't pair himself with her, but didn't say anything. Instead, she turned and followed Sam to the first store. Emily stood with Marley as Sam walked towards the door and knocked on it several times. She did this process herself when she was on her own and knew what he was doing. After a few moments of silence, Sam opened the door. Emily and Marley followed Sam inside, shutting the door behind them.

"Let's split up to see what we can find," Sam said. "Call out if you get into any trouble."

Emily nodded and began to make her way through the small store. The shelves were mostly picked clean, but she found a few canned goods. Emily was finished going through her part of the store and met back up with Sam.

"The storeroom is back here, but I thought it best if we do it together," Sam said barely above a whisper.

"Let's do it," Emily replied.

Sam led the way to a door at the back of the store. Once again, Sam knocked on the door and waited. Emily felt herself jump as a thump came from the other side of the door.

"There's at least one in there," Emily said as she gripped her crowbar.

"You ready?" Sam asked as he grabbed the handle.

Emily nodded as she raised the crowbar, and Sam opened the door. As the door opened, two men with milky white eyes burst through. Emily backed away slightly, trying to get them to separate enough to give her a window of opportunity. One of the men caught sight of Sam and turned towards him. Emily stepped forward quickly and hit the first zombie, and it fell to the floor. The second had gotten on top of Sam before he had time to act. Sam was struggling to keep the zombie from biting him. Emily ran towards him and stabbed the zombie, which fell limp in Sam's grip. Sam threw the corpse to the ground and steadied himself.

"I guess there were two," he said, slightly out of breath.

"Looks like," Emily replied. "Are you alright?"

"Yeah, the son of a bitch just caught me off guard."

Emily turned and looked down at the corpses.

"I don't see any wounds," Emily remarked.

"Looks like they have been in here from the start."

"This could be good for us." Sam looked into the open door. "Shall we?"

Emily nodded, and Sam led the way into the room. Closed boxes lined the walls, and Emily began to look with Sam through them.

"I think we should just take it all," Emily remarked after looking in several.

"We should probably just take the essentials," Sam said as he kept looking. "Finds like this will get rarer, and it will take us hours to go through it all."

"You're right," Emily said, looking around. "We'd better get to work then."

Emily returned to the front of the store, grabbed a couple of carts, and returned to Sam. The two quickly filled the carts and pushed them to the sidewalk. Marley stuck with Emily as they did these trips several times.

After the last boxes were on the sidewalk, Emily looked for the first time across the street. Several shopping baskets were on the opposite side, but she did not see the other group.

"They probably moved on to the next building. We should do the same."

"You're right," Emily said as she turned towards the hardware store next door. Emily knocked on the door and waited. "Looks to be empty."

"Just keep your eyes open," Sam said.
Emily opened the door and started to step inside.

"SHIT!" Cole's voice rang out through the street. Emily turned quickly but couldn't see him. Sam had grabbed his walkie and was trying to reach Shawn.

"REPORT!" Sam yelled again into the walkie.

"We have to go!" Emily yelled at him. "We don't know what we are running into. Shawn specifically said not to."

Emily knew Sam was just trying to follow the procedure, but she was not good at being told what she could or could not do.
"We are not losing anyone," Emily replied. "Marley, where is he?"

Marley ran across the street, and Emily followed. Emily could hear Sam's footsteps behind her.

Chapter 15

Emily reached the door of the building across the street and followed Marley more slowly inside. Marley led the way through the building and to the back door. Emily watched as Marley headed out the back door. The rule had been not to leave the stores, no exploring. Sam pushed the door the rest of the way and followed Marley out. Emily looked back at Sam, who looked just as surprised as she was. Emily suddenly understood that this was why Shawn did not want to be in her group. He wasn't here for supplies or to check the stations. He had gone rogue and was hunting for Jeff.

Emily followed Marley but knew he would be leading her to the dealership. It didn't take long to arrive, and Emily could see Jeff wasn't there. He had, however, left them a present. The dealership was surrounded by the dead, and the second group was trapped inside based on the cursing being yelled at.

"What the fuck?!" Sam exclaimed behind her.

"Jeff knew that if we were to hunt him down, we would start here. He left a trap, and those dumbasses walked right into it."

"We can't kill that many," Sam kept staring at the dealership.

"No, we can't, but we must get them clear enough for the others to get out." Emily began to look at the surrounding area for something that could help.

"There," Emily said as she pointed at a police car.

"There's no way it will start," Sam said, looking at the car.

"We don't need it to," Emily said. "We just need the battery to have enough juice to turn on the siren for at least a few minutes. It should draw enough of the dead from the dealership for them to get out."

"It will also draw all of the dead for miles!" Sam said.

"It's the only choice we have. We will get them out and have to hunker down until the siren stops and the dead lose interest. If you have a better idea, let's hear it."

"Let's do it," Sam said after a couple of minutes.

The three of them began to make their way toward the police car. Sam and Marley stood guard while Emily climbed into the car. Emily was happy to find the keys in the ignition. Emily held her breath as she turned the key to the auxiliary. Emily exhaled as the lights on the dashboard came to life. She began to look and found the switches for the lights and sirens. "Ready?" Emily asked Sam.

"As ready as I can be," Sam replied, looking around.

Emily quickly flipped the switches and climbed out of the car, joining Marley and Sam. Emily could see that the dead in the dealership were beginning to turn and head straight for them.

"Get back to the stores!" Emily called Sam.

"What about them?!" Sam asked.

"We have to hope that's where they will run to."

With that, Emily turned and began to run with Marley and Sam back to the stores. They ran up the street and climbed into the back of the box truck, only a few minutes before Shawn, Jose, and Cole climbed inside, shutting the door behind them. Emily stood towards the back of the truck, shaking with anger as she looked at Shawn.

"Something set off a police car," Shawn breathed heavily. "We will be stuck until it stops."

"What took you so long?" Emily asked. "We were in a store a few doors down, and the dead started to fill the street from the sound," Shawn said, still trying to catch his breath.

"So, you will lie to me twice in one day?" Emily replied, trying hard not to yell.

"What are you talking about?" Shawn asked as he leaned against the wall and looked angrily at her.

"So, you didn't plan to go to the dealership to hunt Jeff and get caught in a trap?"

Emily watched as Shawn's face told her he finally understood that she knew the truth.

"I broke the rules and came looking for you all when Cole yelled," Emily explained.

"The police car didn't go off by accident, did it?" Shawn asked.

"No," Sam answered. "We set it off to save you, idiots."

"Look," Shawn began and took a step toward Emily.

"Don't," Emily said as she stepped farther back from him.

"I was just trying to help. You know he needs to die." Shawn tried to look stern as he spoke.

"I know we came out here for two reasons. We needed to check the stations and look for supplies."

"Those were my reasons, but I had one more objective that Cole and Jose agreed to help me with. I thought you would be grateful!" Shawn yelled.

"Grateful?!" Emily yelled back. Emily clenched her fists and looked down for a few moments, trying to find the words. "You're right, Shawn, thank you. Thank you for risking not only your life but all of your lives! Thank you for getting us trapped in this box and ensuring none of us would make it home to our families tonight! Thank you for doing the one thing you said you never would!"

"What was that?" Shawn asked, still angry.

"Hurting Hope and me. I always come home the same day until today. She won't understand, and I can't keep her from that pain. The pain that you caused by going out here."

Emily couldn't find the energy to yell anymore and allowed herself to slide down the wall of the truck to the floor. She pulled her knees up to her chest and dropped her head.

"I wasn't trying to…." Shawn started.

"Leave her alone," Sam interrupted. "She can't take any more right now."

Shawn walked back towards the truck's door and leaned against the wall. They all sat silently for hours, listening to the police siren go off and the dead occasionally running into the truck. The battery had more life than Emily had hoped for and showed no signs of dying anytime soon.

"You need to eat." Emily looked up at Sam, who was handing her a sandwich. "Julia gave them to me before we left."

"I'm not hungry," Emily replied.

"I know, but you still need to eat."

Sam held out the sandwich, and Emily could tell he wouldn't stop. Emily took it and forced herself to eat a bite as Sam watched. Sam then sat down next to her and began eating as well. Emily looked around and saw that he had given everyone something to eat, even Marley. Emily forced herself to finish the sandwich and drink some water. As she finished, they all noticed the siren's sound had disappeared.

"It will still take hours for them to settle down," Cole said. "But we still might be able to make it home tonight."

Shawn reached beside him and cracked the door on the truck, maybe an inch or two. Emily could see that the sun was long since gone, and night had already settled in. Shawn shut the door and leaned back against the wall. None of them needed to say it. They all knew they weren't making it home tonight. Emily pulled the walkie from her backpack and tried to radio home.

"Sanctuary," Emily spoke into it. She noticed she didn't hear her voice in Shawn's or Sam's walkies.

"I couldn't get it to work earlier," Shawn said, not looking at her.

"So, we have no way to call home?" Emily asked out of frustration as she stuffed the walkie back into her backpack.

"I didn't mean for this to happen," Shawn said, looking down at her.

"I'm going to get some rest," Emily said. "I suggest you all do the same. We will still have to fight tomorrow to get out of here."

Emily turned, lay her head on Marley's stomach, and closed her eyes. Emily knew that she wouldn't be able to sleep, but wanted a reason not to have to talk anymore. Emily felt herself allow a few tears to run into Marley's soft fur.

"You had to try to be a hero, didn't you?" Sam asked after several minutes had passed.

"You wanted to hunt him down just as much as I did," Shawn said with almost no emotion in his voice.

"I did, but when the time was right. I didn't plan to sneak away and put everyone's life in danger to do it." Emily had never heard Sam sound this angry before.

"You wouldn't understand," Shawn replied shortly.

"I wouldn't understand?!" Sam raised his voice. "I was there, remember?! I helped kill those bastards to get her out! I care about her too, you know?!"

"I wasn't saying you didn't, but it's different."

"Are you telling me that if I went rogue with a half-baked plan, didn't tell you, and put everyone in danger, you would be okay with it?!"

Shawn sat quietly and didn't answer.

"That's what I thought," Sam said sternly.

The truck fell silent once more, and Emily heard a few of them lie down, though she couldn't be sure who. Emily lay still but didn't cry anymore. Emily lay for a long time but eventually fell asleep despite trying not to.

"Emily," Sam's voice pulled her awake as he shook her shoulder.

Emily forced herself to sit up and look around. Everyone was standing, and Shawn was looking towards the door. Emily stood and grabbed her crowbar as Marley stood to join her.

"We haven't heard the dead in a while now," Jose explained. "It's time to deal with stragglers and get the hell out of here."

"Then let's do this," Emily said as she walked towards the door.

Shawn opened the door quickly, and the sunlight burst in. Emily held up her hands to shield her eyes until they adjusted. On the street behind the truck, there was only one zombie. Shawn jumped down without speaking and proceeded towards it. Emily jumped down and moved towards the front of the truck. Everyone worked in silence to kill the few dead that remained in the street. Once they were finished, everyone began to gather around the back of the truck.

"We should get going," Cole said, looking around.

"Not without what we came for," Emily replied. "You three load the stuff on the sidewalk while we check the hardware store."

Emily didn't wait for anyone to reply and turned to go to the hardware store. Marley and Sam followed her to the door. Emily knocked and waited to ensure no dead had gotten in during the night. When no sound followed, she looked at Sam, who nodded in silent agreement. Emily opened the door and headed inside. She and Sam loaded a couple of carts with boxes of nails, hammers, and various other supplies. Once they had everything they thought they could use, they pushed the carts back onto the street.

When they returned, Emily saw that all the boxes on the sidewalk were loaded. Emily and Sam pushed their carts over to the back of the truck to be loaded. Emily then turned and went to get into the back of the pickup with Marley, and Sam climbed into the driver's seat of the box truck. After a few minutes, Jose joined Sam in the box truck. Shawn looked at Emily as he walked by to climb into the pickup's cab. Emily could see in his eyes that he was sorry, but she wasn't ready to forgive. Cole walked to the cab and climbed inside, where Emily typically sat. Emily was grateful that he did not join her in the truck's bed.

Emily sat by Marley as the truck roared to life and began down the road. She heard muffled voices in the cab for a few minutes, but couldn't understand what they were saying. Emily didn't turn to look through the window but watched the side of the road as the scenery whizzed by. Emily didn't look around until the truck began to slow. Emily turned to look at the station, but couldn't get a good look at it. Emily stood in the truck's bed and jumped out before Shawn could bring it to a complete stop.

"What the hell are you doing!?" Shawn yelled at her as he climbed out of the truck. "My job!" Emily yelled back as she reached the station.

"Sanctuary, do you copy?" Emily spoke into the walkie. "Sanctuary?" Emily repeated after a few minutes. "None of the walkies are working," Emily said to the others.

"This is Sanctuary." Margaret's voice came through the walkie. "Emily, is that you?"

"Yes," Emily replied. "We ran into a complication, but are on our way home."
"How far out are you?" Margaret asked.

"About an hour," Emily replied.

"We will see you then." Margaret sounded relieved.

Emily returned the walkie to the station and jumped back into the truck's bed with Marley. Shawn walked past her without speaking and climbed back into the cab. Emily heard the muffled voices, and then the truck began to move. Emily watched the trees go by and felt the truck turn onto the logging road after about an hour. Emily watched as they passed the old SUV, showing they would soon be home. Emily could tell it was nearly noon and was sure everyone was concerned they wouldn't be coming home.

Emily felt the truck come to a stop and knew that they had reached the wall. She climbed out of the truck with Marley and entered the code on the keypad. The gate roared to life, and Emily walked through the gate before the trucks could. She ran the stairs to the control room and entered the code to close the gate just as the last truck passed. Emily ran back downstairs and immediately spotted Julia holding Hope. Emily dropped her backpack and weapons at the base of the stairs and ran towards them.

"Hope." Emily took Hope from Julia and wrapped her in a hug.

Emily breathed in Hope for several minutes and had no plan to let her go again.

"What happened out there?" Julia asked.

"I can't talk about it right now," Emily forced herself to look at Julia. "The important thing is we all made it back."

"Was it Jeff again?" Ben asked.

"No, this was…this was…." Emily couldn't find the words.

"You're all safe," Ben smiled. "That's all that matters."

Emily nodded and shifted Hope to her hip. Emily looked towards the inner gate just as Shawn and the others entered.

"We brought back quite a bit that will need to be brought in, sorted, and inventoried," Emily said, looking away from Shawn.

"Sounds like I'm up," Jessica spoke as she walked towards the gate.

Julia and Isabelle followed Emily towards the gate. Emily knew they were eager to see their husbands. Emily focused her attention on Ben.

"Was everything alright here while we were gone?"

"Derick tried to get an election this morning to put him in charge," Ben smiled. "We may have accidentally locked him in the construction trailer."

Emily felt a smile spread across her face.

"Someone should let him out and give him the good news," Emily replied. "I take it that everything else is okay."

"Oh yeah, we all knew what we were supposed to do, and it got done," Ben smiled.

"I'm glad to hear it," Emily smiled. "If you'll excuse me, I think it's time for a diaper change."

"Of course, she's probably beyond ready for a nap. I know she kept half of us up all night screaming for you to come home."

Emily nodded and walked with Hope and Marley to their house. Emily opened the door and took her family inside. Emily closed the door behind Marley and walked upstairs to change Hope. Emily took her time with the diaper change and laid Hope in the crib. However, Hope refuses to let go of Emily's hand. Emily picked Hope up once more. Emily carried Hope over to the rocking chair and sat down. Emily held Hope in her arms and began rocking back and forth. Marley lay in front of the chair a little way, most likely to protect his tail from the rockers. Hope tried to fight sleep, but she was fast asleep in Emily's arms after fifteen minutes. Emily knew she should lay Hope back in the crib, but she wasn't ready to let go yet. Instead, she continued to rock.

"Can we talk?"

Emily glanced up to see Shawn standing in the doorway.

"Not now," Emily replied, looking back down at Hope.

"Please?"

Emily could hear the sound of pleading in Shawn's voice.

"Shawn, I just can't," Emily replied, still not looking at him.

"I'll be downstairs if you change your mind." Emily heard Shawn walk away.

Emily continued to sit with Hope for a while longer. Then she stood and placed Hope in the crib. After washing up, Emily headed to her room and changed into a fresh pair of clothes. Emily then headed downstairs to find something to eat. Emily stopped at the bottom of the stairs as Shawn stood up from the couch.

"I just want to say I'm sorry," Shawn said, not moving from where he stood.

"I know you are, but that doesn't make it all go away," Emily felt her anger boiling back up to the surface.

"I thought if I killed him, it would protect you and Hope. I never wanted to hurt you."

"But you did," Emily spat back at him. "You were so set on your belief that I need a hero to save me that I ended up having to save you."

Emily worked hard to steady herself before she went on. She refused to allow tears to fall at this moment.

"I need time to sort through everything," Emily said, looking at him again. "Until then, none of you are allowed outside the walls."

"I understand," Shawn nodded. "I just want us to be okay."

"We are not," Emily interrupted. "But that was your choice, not mine. Please, I need you to go."

Shawn stood still and showed no intention of leaving.

"JUST GO!" Emily yelled at him.

Shawn turned and headed out the door without looking back. Emily looked around the now-empty living room and felt darkness trying to swallow her from all around. Emily fell to her knees and allowed the fear she had felt the night before to explode. She felt the fear of losing the guys in the dealership, of never seeing Hope again. She let it all out until there was nothing left. Emily sat back as she felt the last of her fear drain from her body and looked around the room.

Emily forced herself to stand and walk over to the pictures she had hung on the wall just a few days ago. Emily looked at them slowly but forced herself to look at the picture with Shawn. She smiled, looking at him in his bear costume. Emily wanted to go back to that night when everything was perfect. Emily jumped as a knock came at the door. Emily dried her face and opened it.

"I just wanted to ensure that you were okay," Father Nathan said.

"I'm alive, and so is everyone else," Emily replied.

"I saw Shawn leave, and he looked to be upset." Father Nathan pointed in the direction that Shawn must have gone.

"I don't care if he is." Emily didn't look in the direction Father Nathan pointed.

"What happened out there?" Father Nathan asked.

"My best friend lied to me and put us all in danger."

"I'm not sure I understand," Father Nathan asked.

"Neither do I." Emily felt herself wanting to fall apart again. "I just want to be alone right now, Father."

"I understand," Father Nathan smiled. "I wanted to thank you for the box of Bibles you brought back."

"To be honest, I didn't know what was in most of those boxes," Emily admitted. "It was just luck that they were in there."

"Still, thank you," Father Nathan smiled. "I will be around if you need to talk."

"Thank you, Father." Emily didn't wait for a reply as she stepped back and closed the door.

Chapter 16

Emily spent the next few weeks avoiding Shawn, Cole, and Jose. Shawn seemed to know she was not ready to talk and gave her space. Their conversations were short and only about Sanctuary. Hope didn't understand but was upset by Shawn's absence. Emily couldn't help but feel her pain every day in not understanding why Shawn didn't stop and talk to her. Emily tried her best to comfort Hope and distract her from what was happening in town.

To help make things like they used to be, they were all planning to celebrate Thanksgiving. While they did not have turkeys, they did have plenty of chicken for each household. Emily was finishing her walk with Hope and Marley around the wall to check on everyone before heading home to start their dinner.

Emily was nearing the final checkpoint and slowed her pace as she saw Shawn standing ahead. Emily steadied herself and began walking in his direction. Marley seemed to understand that things were not okay with Shawn and didn't run ahead. Marley stayed by her side and paid Shawn no attention.

"I just wanted to let you know that no one has objected to the shifts. The wall will be fully guarded through the night, and I don't have another shift until tomorrow."

"I'm glad to hear it," Emily said as she continued on her way.

As she continued, Hope began to cry in the carrier. Hope continued to cry for the rest of the walk to the store. Emily wanted desperately to calm her, but she knew she could not give Hope what she wanted. Emily tried to look calm as she entered. Jessica was waiting for her by the counter.

"Hey, Jessica," Emily smiled. "I just wanted to ensure everyone got their chickens this morning."

"They did," Jessica smiled. "I only had to put three into the freezer."

"Who didn't take theirs?" Emily asked.

"Father Nathan invited Derick over for dinner. I think he is still trying to save Derick's soul," Jessica laughed.

"Well, I wish him luck with that. And the other two?" Emily asked, laughing.

"Shawn said he was just going to have a sandwich tonight and refused to take his." Jessica was looking at Emily with knowing in her eyes.

Emily knew everyone saw the rift between her and Shawn, but she still had not discussed it with anyone.

"Well, I'm sure that's a single guy's idea of Thanksgiving." Emily tried to hide the concern in her voice.

"Maybe," Jessica replied. "Here's the stuff you asked for," Jessica said as she handed Emily a bag. "If there's nothing else, I'll head home and get to work. Sarah and I are planning to have dinner together."

"That sounds like fun," Emily grinned. "I'd better get home and start myself."

"I hope you guys have fun," Jessica smiled.

"You too," Emily replied.

Emily left the store and walked back out into the cool air. The temperature was dropping faster these days, and Emily felt like she was bundling Hope up like an Eskimo every time they left the house.

"Ma'am, do you have a moment?" Emily turned to see both Cole and Jose walking toward her.

"Unless it's essential, I really should be heading home.

"Allow me to carry that for you," Cole said as he took the groceries from her.

Emily considered insisting that she could do it herself, but was too cold to fight about it.

"We just wanted to apologize," Jose spoke as they began to walk.

"I'm not up to talking about this," Emily replied.

"And we don't mean to push, ma'am, but you should clean out a wound so it can heal," Cole looked ashamed as he spoke. "We know an apology won't mean much now, but we just want to try at least to get things out in the open."

Emily stopped on the front porch, removed Hope from the carrier, and held her in her arms.

"I just don't understand," Emily felt herself blurt out. "I had explained why, and you guys did it anyway."

"We didn't plan it," Jose began. "We cleared the stores and couldn't stop talking about what happened that night."

"I kept thinking that bastard could get his hands on my little girl," Cole said more to his shoes than Emily.

"We know how strong you are, and he almost got you. We wanted to make sure that he was not around to hurt our girls," Jose spoke next.

"Shawn told us that you had said no," Cole started. "But we kept talking and asked if he would be able to live with Jeff getting his hands on Hope."

"That's when he changed," Jose said. "And we headed out the back door."

"Did you think he would be waiting for you at the dealership?" Emily asked.

"We thought he might have set up his camp there," Cole explained.

"His camp is at a farm. I've been there, remember?" Emily asked.

"But you have never told us where, so we thought...." Jose began.

"I've never told you because I was afraid something like this would happen!" Emily felt herself yelling now.

"We understand that now," Cole spoke. "We do."

Emily stood for a long time, allowing their words to sink in fully.

"I understand you wanted to protect your daughters," Emily said calmly. "I'd be lying if I said I didn't have nightmares about Jeff getting Hope. But we must be smart or risk leaving them without us to protect them."

"We agree," Jose spoke.

"We are going to get him, and I would like to trust you both enough to have you by my side when that day comes." Emily smiled at Jose and Cole. She could see they were both shocked by her words.

"If you have concerns or fears, talk to me," Emily continued. "I trust you both and would like it if you could trust me enough to talk to me."

"Yes, ma'am," Cole and Jose both spoke.

They sounded like children who had been scolded.

"You both better get home," Emily smiled. "I will see you tomorrow."

Jose and Cole both nodded, and after Cole had set the groceries down, they headed home. Emily carried the groceries inside and felt grateful for the warm air around her.

Emily placed Hope in her new highchair while she set to work cooking. This would be the first Thanksgiving dinner Emily ever had where her family was absent. She worked through preparing the various dishes, talking with Hope and Marley as she went. Hope had plenty to say, but her words were not quite understandable. Emily didn't mind, though, as she enjoyed their little conversations.

Once there was nothing left to do but wait, Emily picked up Hope from the highchair and went to the living room. Emily had every intention of reading more of Hope's book, but Hope's screams stopped her in her tracks as she walked to the couch. Emily looked down at Hope to see what had upset her and saw Hope pointing at the wall and screaming. Emily looked and saw that Hope was pointing at the pictures on the wall.

While Hope couldn't say it, Emily knew she was pointing at Shawn. Emily looked at the pictures and focused on her, Shawn, Hope, and Marley. They all seemed so happy that it was hard to believe it had been taken less than a month ago.

Looking at the picture, they looked like a family. Emily knew that Hope missed Shawn. Emily did too. She missed having him around to talk to. She missed knowing that he was always there for her. But he had made his choice, and Emily didn't know if they could get past it.

"I'm sorry, little one," Emily said in a soothing voice. "Let's go over here and read more about Dorothy."

Hope continued to cry and refused to settle while Emily tried to read. Usually, Hope was quiet and still when Emily read. But Hope was not letting go of how upset she was and making it known. Emily had barely managed to make it through one page before the timers started going off in the kitchen. Emily stood and placed Hope in the playpen before heading to the kitchen. While it may not be great parenting, Emily needed a break from the screams for a minute. Hope was still upset and continued to scream to make it known. Emily finished setting the table and returned to get Hope from the playpen. Emily carried Hope to the dining room and finally stopped crying.

Emily placed Hope in the highchair she had brought in, and Marley sat by the bowl that Emily had carried in. Everything was almost perfect. Emily took a deep breath and reached for the food to start making their plates. Emily picked up the fork and knife to get the chicken, but stopped. Emily glanced at the chair on her left, where Shawn had always sat when he was here. Emily tried to shake off the feelings that overtook her, but she missed him. While she wasn't ready for a relationship, she wasn't prepared to lose her best friend.

Emily slammed the fork and knife back onto the table.

"Well, shit!" Emily said under her breath. "You win, kid. Let's go."

Emily picked up Hope and bundled her up in a coat before heading out into the town. The wall shift change must have occurred as several people made their way toward the wall. Emily spotted Margaret nearing the COM building. Margaret had just finished her shift on the wall and looked to be on her way home. Emily took off at a run with Marley by her side.
"Margaret!" Emily called as they got closer. "Margaret!"

Margaret stopped and waved at Emily as she neared.

"Happy Thanksgiving, Emily," Margaret smiled at her.

"Happy Thanksgiving, Margaret," Emily said, breathing heavily. "Can you do me a favor and watch Hope for just a minute?"

"I'm supposed to be heading home. That husband of mine might burn everything if I'm late," Margaret smiled as she spoke.

"I know, and I'm sorry," Emily breathed. "I just really need to talk to Shawn and..."

"Well, I've fixed his cooking screwups before," Margaret interrupted. "Who am I to stand in the way of young love?"

"No," Emily replied. "We are just friends, and I'm going to get my best friend back."

"Oh, I know, dear," Margaret smiled. "And trust me, the first fight is always the worst. I'm sure you two will figure it out."

Emily couldn't bring herself to waste any more time explaining that she and Shawn were just friends. Instead, she simply nodded and watched Margaret walk into the COM building with Hope.

"You too, boy," Emily said to Marley. Marley looked at the door and back at Emily. "I'll be fine," Emily insisted. Marley turned and followed Margaret into the COM building.

Emily turned and ran over to the apartments. Emily ran up the stairs two at a time and down the long hall to Shawn's door. Emily knocked loudly and quickly on the door while she tried to catch her breath. After doing the stairs on the wall, Emily thought she would be in better shape by now. Emily listened and could hear Shawn move through the apartment and towards the door. Emily felt her breath leave her once more as the door opened. She stood looking at Shawn, who was holding his dinner sandwich.

"Emily," Shawn finally spoke. "Is something wrong?"

"Yes," Emily replied firmly. "Who eats a sandwich on Thanksgiving?!"

"You ran over here to yell at me for my choice of dinner?" Shawn seemed even more confused.

"Yes," Emily felt herself losing her nerve now that she was here. "I mean no, not really."

"So, why are you here?" Shawn asked. "Because you were supposed to be having dinner with us," Emily blurted out.

"I had planned on it, but after the dealership, I thought you wouldn't want me there."

"What happened at that dealership ruined everything." Emily felt her anger turning to pain. "I lost my best friend because of what happened at that dealership!"

"I know. I'm sorry," Shawn spoke. "I don't regret wanting to go after that prick, but I do regret going behind your back and hurting you."

"You did," Emily felt tears in her eyes, and hated it.

"Emily, I'm sorry." Shawn stepped forward as he spoke and pulled Emily into his arms.

Emily allowed the tears to escape as she felt Shawn's arms wrap around her. They stood for a long time, neither of them saying a word. Emily finally felt the tears stop, but allowed Shawn to continue to hold her.

"So, should we go eat before dinner gets cold?" Emily finally asked.

Emily felt Shawn pull away and looked up at him.

"Unless you would rather just keep eating your sandwich?" Emily smiled.

"I think I can save it and eat it tomorrow," Shawn smiled.

Shawn walked back into the apartment and set the sandwich on the counter. He then joined Emily in the hall and shut the door to the apartment.

"Where are Hope and Marley?" Shawn asked as if just realizing they were not with Emily.

"Margaret is watching them in the COM building," Emily replied as she turned to leave.

Shawn followed her down the hall and back outside. The sun was setting, and the temperature was dropping even more. Emily wrapped her arms around herself and suddenly realized that she had forgotten to get herself a coat when she left. The wind cut right through her, and Emily wrapped her arms around herself to keep warm.

"Where's your coat?" Shawn asked.
"On the coat rack at home," Emily replied. She looked and could see Shawn shaking his head. "So, maybe I didn't think this plan all the way through," Emily laughed.

"Well, I know what that's like," Shawn smiled as he took off his coat. "Put this on before you freeze to death. We last need to wait for spring for you to defrost."

"Very funny," Emily said as she took the coat and wrapped herself in it.

Emily and Shawn walked together to the COM building to pick up Hope. Margaret was sitting in the chair by the radio, singing to Hope, and Marley was waiting for them as soon as they entered the door. Marley seemed surprised to see Shawn with Emily, but soon bounced around, excited to have his friend back.

"Thank you, Ms. Margaret," Emily said as she took Hope. "You are a lifesaver."

"It was my pleasure," Margaret smiled. "Everything okay?"

"Yeah, we're friends again," Emily replied.

"Well, I'd better get home to make sure there's something edible for dinner," Margaret smiled as she made her way out the door.

"I heard that dinner would be getting cold if we don't hurry," Shawn said from the doorway.

"You're right," Emily smiled as she walked toward him with Hope.

"Hey there, Hope," Shawn spoke to Hope for the first time in weeks. Hope began to try her best to get out of Emily's arms and to Shawn.

"Fine, you like him better. I get it." Emily laughed as she allowed Hope to crawl into Shawn's arms.

"Well, mom says no, where I say yes," Shawn laughed. "Of course, that makes me the favorite."

"Let's get going," Emily laughed as she led them back into the street.

Soon, they were all gathered in the dining room and enjoying the chicken dinner Emily had prepared. Emily felt at peace for the first time in months. She felt herself laugh freely as they all enjoyed the meal. Once they were all stuffed, Shawn helped Emily tuck Hope into bed.

"This was nice," Shawn said once they were back downstairs.

"It was, but don't get used to it," Emily smiled. "I'm not cooking like that again until Christmas."

"Are you inviting me to Christmas dinner?" Shawn asked.

"No, it's a requirement." Emily gave him her best serious face.

"Yes, ma'am," Shawn laughed. Emily walked over to the couch, and Shawn sat down beside her.

"I hate what he did to you," Shawn said.

"Not just that day, but even before I knew you. But I hate that I hurt you even more."

"I know," Emily smiled. "Jeff will get what he deserves, but for now, we need to take care of our family here, in Sanctuary."

"You're right," Shawn agreed. "I won't do anything else until you give the okay."

Emily nodded and leaned back against the couch.

"Let's put it behind us and move on," Emily sighed.

"I can do that," Shawn said.

Emily and Shawn talked for hours. Shawn didn't attempt to leave until Emily accidentally let a yawn escape.

"You should get some rest," Shawn said as he stood.

"Probably," Emily said. "I really should finish cleaning up before I do."

"Why don't you rest, and I'll take care of it?" Shawn offered.

"You were a guest," Emily replied. "Guests don't do dishes."

"I thought I was family, and family helps with the dishes."

"You're right," Emily smiled. "Plus, I am too tired to argue."

"Then I win," Shawn laughed. "Now, you go to bed, young lady."

"Yes, sir," Emily yawned as she walked toward the stairs.

Emily dressed for bed once she reached her room and then proceeded to Hope's room to get Marley. Emily slowly opened the door and saw Hope and Marley fast asleep. Marley looked up as Emily made her way over to the crib. Hope looked peaceful as she slept, and Emily knew that it was because the tension was gone. Emily kissed Hope on the head and walked back towards the door. Marley followed and headed to Emily's room while Emily shut Hope's door. Emily could hear Shawn downstairs doing dishes as she headed into her room. Emily crawled into bed beside Marley but didn't fall asleep right away. Emily lay awake until she heard Shawn leave and the front door close.

Emily remembered the day's events, and her heart felt warm. The three men she thought had betrayed her had simply been trying to protect the children. Emily felt sure that none of them had anything in common before the flash, and they probably would have never known each other existed. However, inside these walls, they were all family. They all cared about each other and wanted to keep everyone safe. Emily reached over and ran her hand through Marley's soft fur. Marley was still awake, and Emily felt him begin to sniff at her hair.

"It's hard to believe, boy," Emily whispered to him. "A year ago, it was just you and me against the world."

Emily could feel Marley's tail hitting against the bed as he wagged it.

"It's still you and me," Emily laughed. "We just got more people to protect."

Marley moved closer to Emily as if knowing she needed to go to sleep. Emily wrapped her arm over the big dog and snuggled her face against his fur. It didn't take long for Emily to fall asleep.

Chapter 17

Emily felt like the next month went by in a blur. They had not had any new groups come in, but they had not ventured out due to the cold. Things stayed busy inside Sanctuary. Everyone worked together and decorated the main street to look like a movie set with all the decorations. Father Nathan planned a Christmas pageant for Christmas Eve. Hope, as the only baby in Sanctuary, would star as baby Jesus. Even Marley would be part of the show, starring as the donkey.

Emily had just finished getting Hope and Marley ready for their time on stage and was making her way to the church. Everyone in town was walking in the same direction, all eager for the show. Emily was happy to see Shawn waiting for her in front of the church.

"Well, now the show can start. Our stars have arrived," Shawn announced as he came towards Emily.

"That they have," Emily smiled.

"I wanted to let you know that I talked to Jessica," Shawn spoke as they walked inside. "She will take pictures, so you must enjoy the show."

"It's weird that I get to be worried about stuff like this with the dead walking just outside the walls."

"You have built something amazing," Shawn smiled. "You should be proud and just enjoy these moments."

"I'll try," Emily breathed. "Why don't you get us a seat, and I'll drop these two off?"

"I'll make sure you get front row," Shawn grinned.

Emily made her way upstairs and found Father Nathan doing a costume check on the other children.

"Everything going okay?" Emily asked.

"I'm managing," Father Nathan grinned. "We should be ready in just a few minutes. You can place Hope in the playpen and go get your seat."

Emily nodded and placed Hope in the playpen while Marley went around the room greeting all the children.

"Good luck," Emily smiled at Hope. "Mommy will be watching."

Hope grinned and seemed drawn into the excitement in the room. Emily forced herself to leave the room and make her way back downstairs. Emily quickly found Shawn in the front center pew. Emily sat down next to him and felt her nerves well up inside her. Emily felt Shawn reach over and grab her trembling hand.

"It's going to be fine," he assured her. "It's a simple pageant. She's not trying to take down her first zombie."

"I can't even think about that," Emily shuddered at the thought of Hope fighting a zombie.

Emily squeezed Shawn's hand as Father Nathan walked out and welcomed everyone. Emily held Shawn's hand throughout the entire production as she watched Hope and Marley. When the children lined up for their final bow,

Emily stood with Shawn and clapped with tears in her eyes. Once everything was done, Terra, who played Mary, brought Hope to Emily. Emily slowly made her way out of the church with Marley, Hope, and Shawn.

The cool air caused them to stand closer together once they stepped outside. Emily forgot about the troubles outside the walls as they all returned to Emily's house. Once inside, Emily took off Marley and Hope's costumes and placed Hope in the playpen. While it was Hope's bedtime, there was no way she was going to lie down just yet with all the excitement of the pageant. Emily walked over to Shawn, standing in front of the Christmas tree Emily had decorated.

"I take it the little one has some presents stashed somewhere," Shawn remarked.

"Yeah," Emily grinned. "I wanted to keep the magic of Santa for her."

"I slid one under here for her," Shawn said, motioning to a box. "I hope you don't mind."

"Of course not," Emily smiled. "I got you a little something."

"I got you something too, but I may have hidden it."

"Are you afraid I'll peak?" Emily teased.

"Maybe a little," Shawn smiled back.

Emily looked back at Hope to see that her energy was draining, and Hope was now lying in the playpen.

"I'd better get her to bed before she falls asleep."

"I'll wait," Shawn smiled at her.

Emily picked up Hope and quickly made her way upstairs. Emily got Hope dressed and into bed, grabbed Shawn's present, and headed back downstairs.

"I decided to give you yours early," Emily smiled as she handed Shawn the small box.

"Well, then you can have yours too," Shawn said as he took a box from behind the tree. Shawn handed the box to Emily and then turned his attention back to the one she had given him.

Emily grinned and watched while Shawn opened the box she had given him. Shawn smiled as he pulled out a handmade patch from the box that read "SANCTUARY."

"I thought you could add it to your vest. You said it was a symbol of your family."

"Did you make this yourself?" Shawn asked, holding it in his hands.

"I did," Emily grinned.

"I love it," Shawn said. "I will be putting it on as soon as I get home. Now, you open yours."

"Okay," Emily replied as she opened the box Shawn had given her.

Emily carefully pulled out a picture frame and turned it over. Emily felt tears in her eyes as she looked down at the picture.

"I had taken the pictures with a disposable camera I found. I made the frame, and Jessica helped me to develop the pictures."

Emily looked at pictures of her holding Hope, and they had to have been taken a few days after Hope was born.

"I love it," Emily smiled as she set the picture down and wrapped Shawn in a hug.

Emily slowly pulled back, but felt Shawn hold on to her. Emily looked up at him and watched as he slowly leaned down. Emily closed her eyes and felt his lips meet hers. Emily wanted to allow herself to fall into the moment, but immediately heard a voice in her head.

"Until death do us part," Chad's voice rang out.

Emily forced herself to pull out of Shawn's embrace and take a few steps back.
"I'm sorry," Shawn said, looking ashamed.

"No, I'm sorry," Emily replied.

"I should go," Shawn said while heading for the door.

"Shawn!" Emily called as she ran towards him and grabbed his arm. "I'm sorry," Emily began. "I have some pre-flash issues that I'm working through. I just have to finish before I can…." Emily couldn't finish her sentence.

Shawn turned towards her, and his face told her that he understood.

"I'm a patient man," he said. "I'm not going anywhere, and I'll be ready when you are." Emily allowed Shawn to pull her into another hug and stood there for a long time. Shawn eventually pulled away and smiled down at her.

"I will see you in the morning," Shawn said as he headed towards the door.

"I'll see you in the morning," Emily smiled back.

Once Shawn left, Emily picked up the picture of Hope he had given her. Emily looked down at the tiny baby in the photo and realized how much she had grown for the first time. Emily walked into the kitchen and grabbed the hammer and a nail. Once back in the living room, Emily hung the picture with the others on the wall.

Hope woke at her usual time on Christmas morning and made her way around the living room when Shawn arrived.

"Did you start without me?" Shawn asked as he entered.

"Nope," Emily smiled. "You got here just in time."

Shawn picked up Hope, who had walked over to him, and headed towards the Christmas tree. Marley lay by the tree, and Shawn set Hope, so she leaned against him. Emily and Shawn sat and helped Hope open her presents from "Santa." Hope had a new teddy bear, hairbows, a few small toys, and a new dress when everything was done. Emily laughed as Hope opened her present from Shawn, and it was a small jean vest. Marley was not forgotten as he received a new chew toy and collar.

Once all the presents were finished, Shawn stood on the floor and walked over to the front door. After looking out the window for a moment, he walked back to the center of the living room.

"If you say it's snowing, I'm going to have to call you a liar," Emily laughed. She could not remember the last time there had been snow on Christmas.

"No, there's no snow out there," Shawn laughed.

"Keeping an eye out for stray reindeer?" Emily joked.

"Not exactly," Shawn laughed back.

"Okay, I give up," Emily mused. "What the heck are you looking out the window for?"

"Let's get Hope's coat on, and I'll show you," Shawn grinned.

Emily eyed him carefully and slowly stood from the floor, picking up Hope as she went.

"I don't know if I should be scared or excited," Emily said cautiously.

"Proud," Shawn replied as he helped Hope into her coat and handed Emily hers.

"Yup," Emily smiled. "Now I'm scared."

"Just follow me," Shawn laughed as he headed for the door.

Emily held Hope in her arms as she and Marley followed Shawn outside. Emily's confusion grew as she saw everyone in Sanctuary gathered on the street in front of her house. Emily looked up at Shawn, who was still smiling from ear to ear.

"What's going on?" Emily asked as Shawn shut the front door behind her.

"It's officially been one year," Bobby said as he stepped forward. "One year since you found Sanctuary and made it your home."

Emily looked at everyone, still feeling very confused. While this was a special day for her, she figured the day she started letting people in would be a day for celebration for everyone else.

"If you hadn't found this place, then none of us would be here," Sam stepped forward beside Bobby. "We all just wanted to find a way to say thank you for giving us a home."

Emily looked at Hope, who seemed to enjoy what was happening even though she didn't understand it.

"We all celebrate different things and give different gifts on this day," Julia spoke. "But we as a community wanted to give you something together."

Emily looked up at Shawn, who continued to smile as he walked down the front steps and joined the crowd. Shawn and a few other men disappeared, and those who remained blocked Emily's view of what they were doing.

"I don't understand," Emily smiled.

Just as she finished, Shawn and the others walked back through the crowd carrying something. Emily watched as they set it up and turned it around for her to see. It was a large wooden sign with an inscription on it.

Welcome to Sanctuary

Designed by Robert
Built by Many

Made a Home by Emily

Emily looked at everyone and felt pride, just as Shawn said she should.

"We are going to put it outside the gate for everyone to see," Bobby said excitedly.

"Thank you all so much," Emily managed to say without crying.

Everyone began to clap as she walked toward them and took a closer look at the sign. Emily noticed that there were initials carved around the edge of the sign.

"Is this…?" Emily began.

"It's everyone who lives here," Terra chimed. "Derick says he can add the initials as people come to join us."

Emily looked and found Derick, who was nodding. She couldn't help but be surprised that he was part of this and agreed to future work.

"Do you like it?" Bobby asked.

"I love it," Emily grinned down at him.

"Why don't you all come inside, and I'll make us something warm to drink?"

"We don't want to trouble you," Isabelle said beside her. "Today is a day for the family."

"I know," Emily smiled. "That's why I want you all to come inside."

Everyone nodded as they understood what Emily was saying and began to make their way in.

"You guys can lean that against the house for now," Emily said to Shawn. "No one is getting out of this family celebration."

"Yes, ma'am," Shawn laughed.

Emily watched as they leaned the sign against the house and headed inside. Emily got Hope out of her coat and handed her to Margaret, who insisted on holding her. Emily made her way to the kitchen but found that it was already full.

"We are making cocoa for everyone," Terra smiled. "You go find a seat before they are all gone."

"Are you telling me I'm not allowed in my kitchen?" Emily looked at Terra sternly.

"I am," Terra said sternly back at her. "Are we going to have a problem?"

"I'll let you win this time," Emily laughed.

Terra nodded her head and seemed proud of her victory. Emily turned and headed back into the living room. The room was filled with people, and it was hard even to walk there. However, Emily found it surprisingly comfortable. The entire room was filled with laughter and love. Emily slowly walked through the room, talking to everyone she passed. Emily was even able to have a pleasant conversation with Derick.

Emily was surprised when a cup of cocoa was handed to her and saw that the cups were being passed throughout the room. Emily slowly drank her cocoa and enjoyed the atmosphere in the room.

"You have grown greatly from the woman who found this place a year ago."

Emily turned to see Father Nathan standing beside her.

"I've grown a lot from the woman I was before the flash," Emily smiled back at him.

"It's hard for me to see you as you described before the flash," Father Nathan grinned back.

"I'll never be her again." Emily felt confident in herself as she spoke.

"Well, that settles it," Father Nathan nodded. "Congratulations."

"I don't understand," Emily said.

"You are not the person you were. You are not the person who married Chad. I now pronounce you divorced."

Emily opened her mouth to protest, but no words came out. Emily instead felt herself smile. Father Nathan was right, and Emily felt free. "Thank you," Emily smiled.

"You've been free for a while," Father Nathan explained. "You just had to realize it for yourself."

Emily nodded and knew that what he said was correct. Father Nathan slowly made his way back into the crowd, leaving Emily with her newfound freedom. Emily continued to watch everyone enjoy themselves, none of them minding how crowded the room was.

"You look to be having a good time," Shawn spoke beside her.

"I am," Emily replied. "It's nice having a house full of family and love."

"Just remember when they all leave, and it's time to clean up," Shawn laughed.

"It will be worth it," Emily smiled.

"I expected to see Hope with you," Shawn remarked, noticing that Emily was standing alone.

"She got kidnapped as soon as we came in," Emily laughed. "I expect she will find her way back to me in time for a diaper change."

"I wouldn't be so sure," Shawn laughed.

"Everyone loves that girl, and not even her dirty diaper could get them to send her away."

"You're probably right," Emily laughed. "I will have to guard the door when they head home for dinner to ensure they don't take her."

"That sounds like the best plan to me," Shawn grinned.

"Are you planning on sticking around for dinner?" Emily asked.

"I thought it was a requirement."

"It is," Emily laughed. "I was just testing you."

"You are not going to get me with your tricks," Shawn laughed.

A few more hours passed, and Emily watched as people began to leave. They were heading home for their Christmas dinners and a little quiet time. Emily was thrilled when Isabelle brought Hope to her before leaving. Emily was even more excited to see Hope in a fresh diaper and happy. Once everyone was gone, Emily allowed Hope to play while she and Shawn made dinner and cleaned up the cocoa glasses.

Emily and Shawn sat at the table with Hope for their Christmas dinner. They even made sure to give Marley a plate of food. Once they all had eaten their fill, Shawn helped Emily clean up the dishes. The process went faster than expected, and they were all sitting on the couch while Marley lay on the floor. Emily grabbed the remote and watched as the television came to life. They all watched as "It's a Wonderful Life" played. Emily had promised to keep up this tradition her first Christmas here and was thrilled she could do it. Hope was showing signs of being ready for bed just as the credits began to play.

"I should be heading home," Shawn said as he stood. "I have the four am shift tomorrow."

"I should be getting her into bed," Emily replied as she stood and followed him to the door.

"Merry Christmas," Shawn said as he pulled Emily and Hope into a hug.

"Merry Christmas," Emily said back as she hugged him with her one free arm.

Emily shut the door behind Shawn as he left. Emily headed upstairs and got Hope ready for bed. Marley curled up under the crib as usual as Emily headed out. Emily returned downstairs, finished picking up the few things still out of place, and wrote in her journal. Emily found that the entry was longer than she had planned, but she didn't want to miss a detail of the day. Once Emily was finished, and the journal returned to the shelf, she headed upstairs and got herself ready for bed.

Emily headed to Hope's room once she was done, and after kissing Hope one more time, she and Marley headed back to her room and climbed into bed. Emily felt at peace as she lay down. She thought about the kiss the night before and pushed Shawn away. She knew she was free of her wedding vows before he had left that night, but didn't say anything. Emily didn't want to rush into something just because she felt she could. Emily would tell him, but for now, she just wanted to enjoy the freedom she felt. Emily wanted to see what would develop now that she no longer felt trapped by her vows. Emily allowed close her eyes and still kept seeing images from the day. Emily didn't lie awake long and slipped into a peaceful sleep next to Marley.

Chapter 18

Sanctuary moved into the new year with the same sense of peacefulness as it had on Christmas. Emily enjoyed January and watching everyone play in the freshly fallen snow. Hope and Marley were amusing to watch play together. Hope was sad when the last snow had melted, and spring began to sneak upon them. Sanctuary welcomed three new calves in early February, and Jacob was already hard at work getting the fields ready for the next season of crops.

Hope was walking strongly on her own and, at times, managed to outrun Emily. Emily was chasing Hope down the main street when a voice came over her walkie.

"Emily, we have someone wanting in!" Sarah was so excited that she was not speaking in her normal professional tone.

"I'm on my way," Emily replied.

Emily returned the walkie to her waist and scooped up Hope, who had stopped when Sarah's voice had come over the walkie. Emily quickly made her way to the COM room with Hope and Marley. Emily entered to see Margaret at the radio and Sarah standing behind her.

"What do we have?" Emily asked as she walked toward them.

"It's a large group, fifteen in total," Sarah replied.

"Wow," Emily said as she listened to Margaret continue to ask questions.

"There are only three children in the group, and two are teenagers," Sarah continued.

"Do we know where they are?" Emily asked.

"They are afraid to say," Sarah replied.

"They are trying to figure us out and have said they have met some bad people out there."

"Haven't we all," Emily half smiled.

"I don't know what else I can say to convince them that it's safe," Margaret said to them.

"Let me give it a try," Emily offered.

"Our town leader is here and is willing to speak with you if you would like," Margaret said into the radio.

"Yes, let me speak to him," a woman's voice said.

Emily handed Hope to Margaret and leaned closer to the radio.

"This is Emily, the leader of Sanctuary," Emily said after pressing the button.

"You are the leader?" the woman's voice spoke.

"Yes," Emily replied. "I understand that you have concerns about coming here."

"Of course, we do," the woman's voice rang out. "We want safety, but how do we know you're not going to try to make us slaves or try to eat us?"

"I would think the same if I were in your shoes," Emily replied. "And I'm thinking by your comment that you have encountered a man named Jeff."

"You know that rapist?" The woman sounded panicked in her reply.

"I know him," Emily replied. "He took me prisoner over a year ago. I managed to escape after stabbing him with a screwdriver. He tried to retake me last year, but my friends here helped to save me from him once again."

"Do you have a dog?" the woman asked cautiously.

"Yes," Emily replied. "His name is Marley."

"Jeff said he killed your dog," the woman said.

"He shot Marley, but our doctor was able to patch him up," Emily replied, trying to ignore the knot forming in her stomach.

"You have a doctor?" the woman asked.

"Yes, we do," Emily replied as she heard Shawn and Sam enter the COM building.

"It may help if we could see you," the woman said. "Can you meet us by the sign you set up?"

"You will have to tell me which one you're at," Emily replied, knowing that the woman was referring to the stations.

"There's more than one?" the woman asked.

"There are four," Emily replied.

"We are in a wooded area, and there is a dirt road of some kind," the woman explained. "Can you come alone?"

Emily turned to Shawn and instantly knew that something was wrong.

"How many people are in the group?" Shawn asked.

"Fifteen," Sarah replied.

"Why would they think you would come to meet fifteen of them alone?" Shawn asked, not hiding his concern.

"They knew about Marley getting shot and thought he was dead," Emily added.

"It's my opinion, but I don't think you should go. It sounds like it may be a trap," Shawn said with concern.

"I was thinking the same thing," Emily agreed, and she turned back to the radio.

"I won't be able to come personally," Emily replied. "I will send out our security team and will be waiting for you if you decide to come here."

"No!" The woman sounded agitated. "You need to meet us. Just you!"

"That's not going to be an option," Emily calmly replied.

"So, you are okay with killing us?!" The woman was screaming now.

"It's your choice," Emily remained calm as she spoke. "If you choose to come to Sanctuary, we will give you a hot meal and explain in detail how things work here. We then give you a choice to stay or leave."

"If you have nothing to hide, you should have no problem coming out to meet us." The woman was trying to make herself sound calmer. "I am willing to welcome you into my home," Emily replied. "This is the best I can do. Would you like me to send out my security team?"

"That's it?" The woman was raising her voice again. "We either say yes, or you are done with us?!"

"We will be here if you change your mind later," Emily replied. "The choice is yours."

The radio was silent for a few minutes, and Emily thought that the woman might be done talking.

"Fine, we will meet your security team," the woman replied.

"Can I have your name so they know who they are looking for?" Emily asked.

"Mariann," the woman replied.

Emily turned to Shawn and could see the concern on his face.

"Just to be clear, you agree to stay here?" Shawn asked.

"If it is a trap, it's for me."

"I agree," Sam spoke. "There are at least fifteen of them. It needs to be more than just you and me going out there."
"You're right," Shawn said. "Let's get Jose, Cole, Jacob…."

Emily could hear Shawn listing names, but couldn't focus on his words. This would be the first time she would send anyone outside the wall without going with them. Part of her wanted to tell them not to go. The chances of it being a trap were too high. However, if these people needed help, she could never forgive herself for being too scared to try.

"Emily, it's just up the road, so we shouldn't be gone more than an hour," Shawn said, pulling Emily back to the conversation. "If we are not back in an hour, it went wrong, and you have to remember not to come after us."

"I never agreed to that," Emily said.

"You have to," Shawn replied. "They know you will come after us, and you must stay safe for Sanctuary and our family to be safe."

"How about you all just come home, and then we don't need to have this conversation?"

Shawn breathed loudly, knowing that Emily was not going to agree. Shawn motioned for Sam to follow, and they left together. Emily picked up Hope from Margaret and followed them. Sam took off down the main street. Emily presumed it was to gather everyone that Shawn had listed. Emily followed Shawn to the gate and entered the code to open the inner gate. Shawn said nothing as the gate opened, and he walked through. Emily stood with Hope, watching as he got the trucks ready.

After a few minutes, Sam came through the gate and handed Shawn his weapons. Emily watched as they started to load up in the trucks and walked back outside the gate.

"Julia!" Emily called out after Julia returned to the gate after saying goodbye to Sam. "Would you mind watching Hope for a minute?"

"I'm going to take all the kids to my place until everyone's back," Julia replied as she took Hope. "I'll watch her until this is over if it's okay with you."

"That would be great." Emily tried to smile. "I'm sure it won't be for long."

"Let's pray everything goes smoothly," Julia replied as she headed down the street.

"Emily! Emily!" Shawn's voice rang out from inside the gate. Emily waited until Shawn walked through and spotted her waiting by the keypad.

"We're ready to go," Shawn said. "We just need you to open the gate."

"You're just going to leave without saying goodbye?" Emily asked.

"I'll be back in a little bit. No need to say goodbye," Shawn smiled at her.

"Well, at least a hug would have been nice," Emily sheepishly said.

"I can handle that," Shawn replied as he pulled her close to him. Emily hugged Shawn and knew she didn't want to let him go.

"I'll be back soon," Shawn whispered as he kissed her on top of the head and turned to head back through the gate.

Emily entered the code to open the outer gate and watched as three trucks pulled out. Once the last truck left, Emily closed both gates and watched until they were both closed. Once they were closed, Emily walked with Marley to the Armory and grabbed her weapons. Then they headed up the wall to keep an eye out until everyone returned. Emily was surprised that she would not be on the wall alone. Margaret and several others were already on the wall, armed and ready to go.

"We all stay here until they come home," Ben smiled.

"Thank you," Emily smiled back as she took her position over the gate.

Emily looked to see that the vehicles were already out of sight. Emily kept her eyes on the road as the minutes went by. It felt like it had been hours when Father Nathan approached her.

"It's been over an hour," Father Nathan was trying to sound comforting.

"I know," Emily didn't turn to look at him and kept her eyes on the road.

"Maybe you should try the radio?" Father Nathan suggested.

Emily nodded in agreement, pulled the walkie from her waist, and pressed the button. She prayed that the short didn't happen again, as it did last time outside the wall.

"Security team, report." Emily waited, but heard nothing in response. "Security team, report."

"Hello, Love," Jeff's voice replied. Emily stared at the walkie, feeling like she was in another nightmare. "Are you still there, Love?"

"I'm here," Emily replied. "Where is my team?"

"They were not much of a security team," Jeff replied. "Only one stayed to talk. The others disappeared into the woods."

"Are they…" Emily couldn't bring herself to finish the question.
"Dead?" Jeff finished for her. "They are all alive as far as I know. They took a good beating, especially the big guy."

Emily wanted to ask if Shawn was who Jeff still had, but knew she couldn't. If Jeff knew what Shawn meant to her, he would kill Shawn or use him to get Emily to surrender.
"If you want, I can bring the big guy home. We will just need you to open up that shiny gate, Love."

Emily went to reply, but caught movement on the road below. After a closer look, she saw Sam and the others running towards the gate. Emily ran to the control room and entered the code to open the outer gate. Once everyone was inside, Emily quickly closed the gate and opened the inner gate. Doc took off down the stairs to help those who had returned.

"I'll even help you find the ones who chose to run away." Jeff's voice rang out once again.

"And I'm just supposed to trust that you are honest, and it's not another trap," Emily replied.

"That hurts, Love," Jeff answered.

"What can I say, husband? I need you to prove to me that you're honest." Emily had made sure to call him husband because she knew it would make him feel in control.

"Anything for you, Love," Jeff replied.

Emily waited as the radio went silent.

"Talk!" Jeff yelled as the walkie came back to life. "Talk, you son of a bitch!"

"Is this supposed to prove something?" Emily spoke, hoping it would get Shawn to say something.

"No one worthy of Sanctuary," Shawn spoke with no emotion.

Emily knew what he was trying to tell her. He was saying there was no one there to save, just the trap by Jeff.

"Your daughter will be worried," Emily replied. "Do you have a message for her?" Emily was trying hard to hide who Shawn was to her.

"Tell her I'll find my way home as I promised."

"That's enough," Jeff interrupted. "I proved the big one is alive, and I'm willing to help you find the others instead of hunting them down and killing them."

Jeff was growing irritated that the attention was no longer on him.

"Are you going to let me in or not?" Jeff was growing impatient.

"No," Emily said with as much strength as she could muster.

"Even if this big guy means nothing to you, some of the cowards are worth saving." Jeff thought he would use the others to get her to open the gate.

"Doc is seeing to them now," Emily smiled as she answered. She knew that Shawn could hear her now and knew it would make him feel better to know they were safe.

"So, you are willing to let this guy die?" Jeff asked.

Emily fought the urge to scream no. She wanted to yell at Jeff that she would personally kill him slowly and painfully if he hurt Shawn.

"He knew the risk," Emily replied. "But perhaps we can reach another agreement."

"I'm listening," Jeff responded.

"You bring him back, and I will let you in," Emily said.

"You will let me and my people in if I bring him back?" Jeff asked.

"No," Emily replied. "I will let you in. Once I know, I can trust you. I will let the others in."

Emily knew that if Jeff came, he wouldn't survive the walk through the gate. She knew it was risky to use his trick against him, but she had no other choice.

"Sorry, Love," Jeff replied. "But now that the big guy knows you are willing to let him die, maybe I can get him to help me find a way in. I'll see you soon."

"Jeff?" Emily called into the radio, and silence was the only response she received.

"Shit!" Emily said as she slammed the walkie down on the control panel.

"We will get him back." Father Nathan tried to comfort her.

"Damn right I will," Emily replied. "Tell Sarah the walkies are not secure and to stop using them immediately."

Emily turned and left the control room before Father Nathan could respond. Emily made her way down the wall with Marley closely behind her. Emily walked through the open gate and couldn't help but be shocked as she looked at each of the men who returned. They were all hurt, some worse than others. Doc was making his way around to those who were shot first.

"Can I help, Doc?" Emily asked as she forced herself to move forward.

"I have them setting up the clinic to treat those needing stitches or surgery first," Doc said. "Cole seems to be the worst off. We need to get him there immediately, but I can't get him to try to walk."

"Come on, Cole," Emily said as she pulled Cole's arm over her shoulders.

Cole looked up at her, and Emily could see the pain on his face. "We have to get moving now," Emily said as she helped him to his feet.

Emily walked Cole to the clinic and helped him onto the surgery table. Time flew by as Emily helped Doc and the others get everyone patched up. The sun was down by the time they finished, and Emily had just finished making sure that Jacob made it home and was resting. Emily looked down at her hands, which were covered in blood. She tried to wipe it off on her jeans, but there was too much. Emily made her way home and went straight to study.

Emily grabbed a couple of pieces of paper from the desk and wrote quickly.

Julia,

I am so sorry for what happened to Sam. I'm sure you know that I can't leave Shawn out there. I wish I could tell you in person, but I know you would talk me out of going. They will take him back to their farm, and I must go after him. Please take care of Hope and give her the other letter if I don't make it back. And remember to tell Bobby that Hope needs a little luck. I know you will take care of Sanctuary. Thank you for everything.

Emily

Emily folded the first paper and moved on to the next one.

Hope,

I am so sorry that I am not here to see you today. Please know that I love you with all my heart. I left to save someone who saved you and me in more ways than I can count. I would love to stay with you and never leave these walls. But on the day you were born, I learned that wasn't an option. I have to go out and try to save an essential family member. Please remember, sweet girl, that the people inside these walls are our family. We must live for our families and do what we must to protect them. That is why I am leaving here today, to save a family member. Be brave, my little angel, and I will always love you.

Mom

Emily folded the paper and stacked it with the one for Julia. Emily headed upstairs and grabbed the duffel bag she carried when she first came to Sanctuary. Emily went to her bathroom and grabbed some basic first aid supplies. Once they were all in the bag, she headed downstairs to the kitchen. Emily quickly grabbed a few water bottles and filled them. Once they were in the bag, Emily added half a loaf of wrapped bread. Emily then grabbed the letters and headed out the door with Marley.

Emily saw that almost everyone was at home taking care of the wounded or watching on the wall. Emily walked to the clinic and left the letters at the front desk. She knew Doc would ensure they got to where they needed to go. Emily made her way through the dark with Marley through the inner gate. Once she entered the code, Emily knew everyone would hear the gate open and try to stop her.

Emily found her rifle and crowbar leaning where she had left them when she started helping Doc. Emily tossed her bag and weapons into one of the remaining trucks. Emily pulled the truck before the door to drive it out as quickly as possible. Emily returned to the keypad and entered the code to open the outer gate. Emily ran back to the truck with Marley and jumped inside. Emily drove the truck through as soon as the gate was open enough. Emily threw the truck into park and ran back to the external keypad. When she heard Sam yelling inside, Emily had just entered the code to close the gate.

"Emily! Emily, don't!"

Emily returned to the truck and looked back at Sam just as the gate closed in front of him.

"Sorry, Sam," Emily whispered as she climbed back into the truck and began the drive down the logging road.

Chapter 19

Emily was steering the truck down the roads leading to Jeff's farm. The drive was long, and Emily was surprised at how easily she remembered where it was. She had avoided the farm since she escaped, but avoiding it helped her remember precisely where it was. It was well after midnight when she arrived at the farm road that she knew led to Jeff's farm. Emily pulled the truck over to the side of the road and shut off the engine. Emily looked up the road and saw nothing but darkness. She had sworn she would never come back to this place. But she knew she had to get Shawn back. Emily straightened herself in the seat and prepared for what she was about to do.

"You ready for this, boy?" Emily asked Marley as she pulled the duffel bag strap over her head and her rifle.

Marley nudged at the crowbar, almost reminding Emily not to forget it.

"Let's go get him back," Emily smiled at Marley as she grabbed the crowbar.

Emily opened the truck door and climbed out. Once Marley was outside with her, Emily closed the door as quietly as she could. Emily then began to make her way up the country road, sticking as close to the tree line as she could. Marley seemed to agree with the plan as he walked right beside her. The walk took a long time, but Emily did not stop until she saw the farm equipment that made up the barrier around the farm.

Emily could see that Jeff and his group had been hard at work trying to make it more robust than the last time she was here. Emily could see torches of some kind burning inside the wall and hear the voices of people moving around. Emily jumped at the sound of branches breaking behind her. Emily turned quickly and swung her crowbar at the head of a zombie. She watched as the corpse of what was once a woman dropped to the ground. It was clear she couldn't hide here long, as the light and noise were going to keep drawing the dead in.

Emily moved quickly towards the barrier with Marley by her side. Emily ran close to the wall with Marley. Emily began looking for a way inside. Emily didn't stop until she found an old truck used as part of the barrier. A glance through the window showed her that she could see inside. Emily could see a woman walking around in ragged dresses that looked to be made out of old bags, while the men acted like animals. They yelled at the women while the women served them food and alcohol. Emily could see that Jeff had recruited children since she was last here. The boys were hanging out with the men and mimicking their behavior. The girls dressed like women and were waiting for the men. Emily hated to see that her fear for her child was precisely what was happening here.

Emily searched what she could see for any sign of Shawn. Emily felt her stomach drop as she spotted him sitting by the fire with Jeff. Shawn's face was bloody and swollen. His hands were tied in front of him. Jeff was laughing and eating while next to Shawn. Emily was too far away to hear what he said, but she was sure that Shawn was ready to explode with anger.

Emily pulled the pickup handle and was surprised to find it had opened. Emily slowly crawled through the truck, with Marley behind her, and opened the opposite door. Once she and Marley were both on the other side, Emily softly closed the door and moved her way through the shadows to a woodpile closer to where Shawn and Jeff were sitting.

"You don't talk much, and that's okay with me," Jeff said.

Shawn sat quietly, looking at the fire through swollen eyes.

"I'm sure you are excited to have a man in charge," Jeff continued. "All I need from you is help to get in."

"I can't open the gate," Shawn replied flatly.

"Sure, you can," Jeff laughed.

"No, I can't," Shawn repeated in the same flat tone. "What's your obsession with her anyway?"

"You know it is," Jeff said as he smacked Shawn on the chest. "Something about her fight makes her even more attractive."

"I guess I find it preferable to go after women who want me," Shawn replied, still staring at the flames.

"I like a fighter, and I know she wants it too," Jeff said.

"I think her stabbing you in the balls and shooting you, she's saying she doesn't," Shawn laughed as he finished his sentence.

"She doesn't know it yet, but she does." Jeff didn't seem phased at all by Shawn's comment.

"If you say so," Shawn continued to stare into the flames.

Emily pulled the rifle from her shoulder and lined the shot on Jeff's head. Emily was breathing out and preparing to fire.

"You're going to have to give me something if you want to join up," Jeff spoke again.

Emily pulled her face up from the sight and listened as Shawn spoke.

"I already told you everything I know. That bitch keeps everything to herself."

"But she trusted you," Jeff smiled. "Do you think she will come and try to save you?"

"Probably," Shawn laughed.

Emily lowered her rifle and fought hard to keep her rage under control. She had trusted Shawn, and now she was hiding in the dark to try to save him. Emily didn't want to believe what he was saying was true. Emily quickly looked around and realized she was going to get Shawn back tonight. Even if she did manage to take out Jeff, there was no way they would make it out of here.

Emily looked down at Marley, waiting for her to tell him what to do. Emily turned the rifle back over her shoulder and returned to the truck. Emily needed to come up with a better plan before she acted.

Emily made her way through the dark back to the truck. Emily opened the truck door. She had crawled through to get inside the camp and waited for Marley to make his way through. Emily began to crawl behind Marley when someone grabbed her leg and pulled her back out of the truck.

Emily hit the ground hard and looked up at the man who had grabbed her. Emily didn't recognize him, but could see movement behind him. She knew that he had already raised enough of a fuss that soon Jeff would be arriving any moment. Emily heard Marley growling and barking as he made his way back through the truck. Emily reached and slammed the truck door shut. Marley continued to bark and growl at the window that now stood between him and the strange man.

"Go home!" Emily yelled at Marley. "Go home!" Emily repeated as Marley continued to try to get through the window.

Emily breathed a sigh of relief as Marley went silent, and she was sure he was heading back to Sanctuary. The man who pulled her from the truck reached down, grabbed Emily by the arm, and dragged her to her feet.

"What is going on over here?" Jeff asked as he pushed through the crowd. A sickening smile spread across Jeff's face as he looked at Emily.

"We've been waiting for you, Love," Jeff said as he walked toward Emily.

Emily tried to pull her arm away from the man holding her, but couldn't get out of his grasp.

"I was just leaving," Emily said as casually as she could.

"We'll go with you," Jeff motioned to everyone around him. "We are eager to get inside those walls."

"Sorry," Emily smiled. "We are all full up, but I'll put you on the waiting list."

"I'm sure you can find the room." Jeff ran his hand down Emily's face, and she tried to turn away. "I am so eager to meet Charlie after all."

"Charlie?" Emily was confused and looked at Shawn, standing a short distance behind Jeff.

"Yes, Shawn has been filling us in on everything." Jeff motioned to Shawn as he spoke. "It's sweet that you named your son after your dad."

Emily felt guilty as she finally understood. Shawn had been acting and playing his part to stay alive.

"You son of a bitch!" Emily spat at Shawn. "I trusted you!"

"I know," Shawn replied. "But that's your problem."

"I like this guy!" Jeff exclaimed. "Let him loose."

Emily watched as one of the men stepped forward and untied Shawn's hands. Jeff stepped forward and took Emily's crowbar and rifle.

"Don't forget the knife," Shawn spoke as he stepped forward. Shawn walked to Emily and took the knife from her waist. "Don't want you trying to do something stupid."

"I'll leave that to you," Emily said as she pulled away from him.

"Let's get this lady to her room," Jeff laughed. "I'll show our newest member to his lodgings."

Emily felt the man holding her arm pull hard and begin leading her toward the farmhouse. Emily looked at the cellar doors and prepared herself to be locked down there once again. Emily was confused as the man led her through the front door. The farmhouse was surprisingly clean inside. The man continued to pull her up a staircase.

Emily struggled as the man led her to a bedroom
at the end of the hall.

The man didn't say a word as he forced
Emily into the room and closed the door behind
her. Emily ran to the door to open it, but found
that she was locked in.

Emily turned and began to survey the room
as she was trapped. Emily spotted a window and
made her way to it quickly. Emily opened it and
looked down. Emily cursed under her breath as
two men stood below on the ground. She closed
the window hard and looked around the room.
There was a large bed with red blankets and a tall
dresser. Emily made her way across the room to a
door beside the dresser. Emily opened the door to
find a bathroom.

Emily searched through the drawers and
cabinets for anything she could use as a weapon.
Emily found nothing and headed back to the
bedroom. Emily dug through the dresser and the
closet and still came up with nothing. She walked
back to the center of the room and felt like the
room was slowly closing in on her. She could have
handled being Jeff's prisoner better if he had put
her in the cellar. Emily couldn't stand being locked
in this bedroom.

Emily felt the energy draining from her and
made her way over to the bed. Emily sat down but
did not allow herself to relax. Emily sat for a long
time before she heard the door unlock and saw it
begin to open. Emily quickly stood from the bed.
She watched as another man she did not know
entered the room.

"Did Jeff change his mind and want me in
the cellar?" Emily asked as she stood still.

"You call him husband," the man sneered as he looked Emily up and down. "And he doesn't know I'm here."

"What do you want then?" Emily asked as the man stepped toward her.

"I'm here to collect what I have a right to," the man said as he stepped closer.

"Jeff said I wasn't to be shared," Emily said as she tried to find a way from the man.

"You call us all Husband!" the man yelled aggressively. "It's time for you to learn your place."

"You will not touch me!" Emily yelled as she tried to run for the door.

Emily cried out in pain as the man grabbed her by the hair and flung her back towards the bed.

"I can do rough," the man smiled as he quickly moved towards her.

"What the fuck is going on here?!" Emily never thought she would be relieved to hear Jeff's voice.

"I caught her trying to escape," the man said as he quickly turned around. "I was going to tie her down, so she didn't try again."

"He's lying!" Emily blurted out.

"I said no one was to enter this room," Jeff calmly said to the man, ignoring Emily completely. "It looks like you were trying to take what's mine."

"I would never," the man started with panic in his voice.

"I believe you," Jeff said as he patted the man on the back. "She can be a lot to handle."

Emily felt dumbfounded as she crawled to the other side of the bed. She knew that Jeff was an awful man, but she didn't think he was this much of an idiot.

"She is," the man laughed. "Would you like me to tie her down?"

"I don't think that will be necessary," Jeff smiled. "She's not going to try to run again. Are you, Love?"

Emily looked at them both in disbelief and didn't speak.

"I'll go check on the perimeter," the man said as he headed for the door.

"How did you find her escaping her room if you were on perimeter duty?" Jeff asked, still looking at Emily.

"I was just..." the man stuttered.

"I've also been wondering how she got into the camp." Jeff interrupted. "You were assigned that barrier section, weren't you?"

"I was, but I had to..." The man was trying to find a way to talk his way out of trouble.

"You went to take a moment with one of the women," Jeff said. "But all commotions interrupted, and you thought you would come up here and finish with what's mine."

The man stood still with a blank stare on his face. He knew he was caught and wouldn't be able to talk his way out of it.

"Is he standing there with a dumb look on his face?" Jeff smiled at Emily.

Emily nodded as she looked between the two men.

"I thought so," Jeff smiled. "You have lost your woman's privileges until I change my mind."

"Yes, boss," the man said with a sigh of relief. "It won't happen again."

"I know it won't," Jeff said as he looked back at the man. "You can go."

Emily watched as the man turned to flee from the room.

"Philip!" Jeff called out.

Philip stopped and began to turn back slowly. Before he had time to turn, Jeff pulled a gun and shot Philip in the head. Emily couldn't help but let out a slight scream as the gun fired. Emily watched as Philip's body fell to the ground and red blood began to pool around his head.

"I'll send someone up to take that out and clean up the mess," Jeff said casually.

Emily remained silent and tried not to move. She allowed her eyes to drift to the gun that remained in Jeff's hand.

"I'm not going to kill you, Love," Jeff smiled as he returned the gun to its holster.

"Why not?" Emily asked as she relaxed.

"I'm not done with you," Jeff smiled. "I've waited for months to get you back."

"I'm not yours," Emily glared at him. "I will never be yours!"

"You are mine," Jeff replied calmly. "You will learn that soon enough. You get some rest."

Jeff stepped over Philip's body, walked out the door, and locked it behind him. Emily sat on the bed, staring down at Philip's body. Emily knew he would stay dead, but she still felt uneasy about him being there. A few minutes passed, and Emily heard the door unlock once more. Emily looked up to see Shawn come through the door. Emily sat quietly as Shawn walked over to Philip's body.

"You knew I would come," Emily said as Shawn bent over to pick up the corpse.

"I did," Shawn said, not looking at her. "I knew you would come and most likely alone."

"You told him about Charlie," Emily spoke once more.

"Yes," Shawn said again, still not looking at her.

"So, you have this whole thing planned out?" Emily asked.

"No." Shawn's shoulders visibly sank. "But I'm figuring it out."

"You will pay for this," Emily said as she heard footsteps outside the door. "I will personally make sure of it."

Shawn said nothing, picked up Philip's corpse, and carried it out of the room over his shoulder. As he left, a young girl no more than sixteen entered with a bucket. The door remained open, but Emily was sure there was still a guard outside of it.

"I won't be long, miss," the girl said as she kneeled and began to clean up the pool of blood.

"Call me Emily," Emily said as she looked at the girl.

The girl looked half-starved and was wearing a plain brown dress. Emily could see bruises on the girl's arms and legs. Her long red hair was tied back with a string and looked as if to had not been brushed in months. The girl remained silent as she continued to clean the mess. "What's your name?" Emily asked.

"My husbands call me Love, miss," the girl replied.

"And it probably makes you sick to your stomach as it does me," Emily replied.

"What does your mother call you?"

"Bridgett," the girl replied as she stopped cleaning and looked up at Emily.

"That's a pretty name," Emily replied as she smiled at Bridgett. "You look exhausted. Why don't you rest, and I'll finish cleaning up?"

"No, thank you, miss," Bridgett said as she returned to cleaning. "I must do my job, or my husbands will be angry."

Emily knew that pushing Bridgett would not change her answer. Bridgett had been here a while and wasn't going to risk getting punished. Emily sat quietly and allowed Bridgett to finish her work.

"All clean, miss," Bridgett said as she stood to leave.

"Thank you," Emily smiled back.

Emily watched as Bridgett walked out the door. Emily saw a man reach and close the door behind her. Emily heard the door lock click and knew she was sleeping in for the night. Emily was exhausted from the day, but did not feel safe allowing herself to fall asleep. Emily rested on the bed and allowed herself to lean against the pillows. Emily thought about Hope and knew she would be in bed by now. Hope would be upset and not understand why Emily and Marley were not home. Emily prayed that Marley found his way back to Sanctuary. Julia should have found the gate code by now and would be able to let him in. Emily thought about Shawn, somewhere outside, playing his role in this perverted place. Emily felt like she should be crying, but no tears came. Emily sat on the bed and did not move even as the sun rose outside her window.

Chapter 20

Emily continued sitting on the bed and could hear movement outside her room. Emily forced herself to sit on the edge of the bed. Emily knew Jeff would be coming for her, and she didn't want to look weak when he did. Emily didn't have to wait long before she heard the door unlock. Emily stood as the door opened, and Jeff walked in.

"I was trying to let you sleep in," Jeff smiled as he entered the room.

Emily stared at him with hate in her eyes. Jeff came closer to her, unfazed by her stare. Jeff looked at her clothes and seemed displeased.

"Did you not find the clothes in the dresser?" Jeff asked.
"I'm fine," Emily replied. "I'll change when I go home."

"Have it your way," Jeff grinned. "We aren't planning on heading out until tomorrow."

"I'm not taking you with me," Emily glared at Jeff.
"Let's not get into this right now," Jeff grinned. "I simply came to invite you to breakfast." "I'm not hungry," Emily shot back.

"I said that wrong," Jeff said as he grabbed her arm. "I'm here to bring you breakfast."

Emily tried to pull her arm free. Jeff didn't let go and pushed her out of the bedroom and down the stairs. Jeff forced Emily into the kitchen and pushed her down into a chair. Emily sat still while Jeff sat in the chair next to hers.

"How do you want your eggs, ma'am?" a familiar female voice asked beside her.

Emily turned to see who the voice belonged to. The woman wore the same dress as Bridgett the night before. The woman's hair was also the same vibrant red, but was cut short. Emily studied the woman's face but was positive she had never seen her before.

"Your eggs, ma'am?" the woman asked once more.

Emily was positive that she knew the voice now, but couldn't find where.

"Oh," Jeff laughed. "This is Mariann. She's the one who made the call."

Emily looked back at the woman and could see the shame on her face. Emily could tell she had not made the radio call of her own free will.

"Scrambled is fine," Emily replied.

The woman rushed off and began cooking. Emily looked back at Jeff, who was leaning in his chair.

"She's Bridgett's mother," Emily said, pointing at the woman. "The bruises on Bridgett, your way of proving you would hurt her if her mother didn't do what you asked?"
"See, I knew you were smart," Jeff grinned.

"I figured you would know it was a trap, but you couldn't risk leaving people behind. I had planned for you to come out, but sometimes we don't get what we want."

"A lesson you refuse to learn," Emily sneered back at Jeff.

"Can we at least eat before we start again?" Jeff asked as Mariann set the plates down in front of them.

Emily refused to eat and sat in silence as Jeff stuffed his face. While Jeff ate his breakfast, a few men came into the kitchen. They would whisper something to Jeff, and Jeff would either nod yes or no. Then the men would leave without another word.

"You are going to need to eat at some point," Jeff remarked as he finished.
"I told you, I'm not hungry," Emily replied.

"If you don't eat, I'm going to have to assume it's Mariann's cooking," Jeff said, looking back at the woman who froze in fear.

"Her cooking is fine," Emily replied. "It's the company causing me to lose my appetite."

"You have an answer for everything, don't you?" Jeff grinned at her.

"Not everything," Emily replied.

Jeff laughed his sick laugh and stood from the table.

"Will you walk, or do I need to drag you around all day?" Jeff asked, looking down at her.

Emily stared back at him with anger. She knew she would have a bruise on her arm from everyone dragging her around. But she also knew that if she followed Jeff, he would take it as a sign that she was giving in to him. Jeff sighed and grabbed her hard by the arm. Emily was pulled out of her chair and dragged out the kitchen door. Jeff continued to drag her throughout the camp.

Emily focused on the women and girls wearing brown dresses. Each of them was severely underfed and had their fair share of bruises. Emily repeatedly looked behind her after Jeff continued talking with some men. She saw a man slipping the women and girls bits of food and looking at them with genuine concern.

"What do you do if you find a family?" Emily asked as Jeff was dragging her to his next meeting.

"Families don't exist in here," Jeff explained as he continued to watch. "Women belong to the community. If a man wants a woman to himself, he has to earn it."

"Has anyone ever earned it?" Emily asked, even though she already knew the answer.

"I have," Jeff grinned back at her.

Emily continued to look at the faces of everyone she passed, trying to make a note of the men who seemed to be playing a part, much like Shawn. Emily ignored what was happening before her until she heard Shawn's voice.

"Out for a walk?" Shawn asked as Jeff pulled her towards him.

"Just a little stroll with the misses." Jeff smiled back as he pulled Emily close and wrapped his arm around her waist. Emily tried to tear away, but she would not win in a battle of strength against Jeff.

"I finished fixing that truck, so the doors don't open," Shawn replied as if nothing was happening.

"And the body?" Jeff asked.

"Tied up by the gate like you asked," Shawn replied, glancing at Emily.

"Good," Jeff smiled. "That should remind everyone that no one touches her." Emily recoiled as Jeff pulled her even closer.

"What would you like me to do next?" Shawn asked.

"Get yourself some food, and I will check in on you later," Jeff smiled.

Emily watched as Shawn nodded and took off, walking in the opposite direction. Jeff released her waist and took her arm once again. Emily was dragged back into the order of the farmhouse. Jeff stopped far from the house and pulled Emily to face him.

"I know seeing him upsets you," Jeff said, trying to sound like he cared about her. "Don't worry. He will be gone soon."

"Are you sending him somewhere?" Emily asked.

"No," Jeff grinned. "I told you, those here must be loyal to me, or they are no good."

"And you don't think he's loyal to you?" Emily asked.

"I think his loyalty changes too easily," Jeff said as he pulled Emily closer. "I just wanted to tell you that we will have another gathering tonight."

"I think I'm busy tonight," Emily quickly replied.

"The gathering is for you," Jeff let his sick smile spread across his face. "You must prove to my guys that you are just as loyal as they are. You need to do what you were supposed to do the night you stabbed me with the screwdriver."

"I'd rather die," Emily spat back at him.

"You will, or we will make the display more intimate. It's your choice, Love."

Jeff turned and dragged Emily into the house and back to her room.

"I'll send Bridgett up to get you ready," Jeff said as he shoved Emily into the bedroom.

"I'm perfectly capable of getting myself ready," Emily said as she whipped around to face him.

"Fine," Jeff replied. Emily could tell that he was beginning to grow angry with her quips. "Just know that tonight is not optional."

With that, Jeff slammed the door shut and locked it. Emily punched the door as hard as she could. Emily held her hand afterward as the pain began to spread. She knew that hitting the door was pointless. She had to release some of the rage that was building inside her. Emily walked over and sat on the bed once more. She didn't plan to get out and knew Shawn didn't have one either.

Emily sat alone for hours, trying to find her way out of prison. Emily didn't see anyone until the sun began to set, and she heard the door unlock. Emily looked up to see Shawn entering the room.

"It's time to go," Shawn said flatly.

"I can't go out there," Emily said with more pleading in her voice than she intended.

"You know he's going to kill you, right?"

"I'll just have to prove myself too useful to kill," Shawn replied. "Please don't make me force you out there."

Emily crossed her arms and remained seated on the bed. Shawn sighed and walked across the room to her. Shawn was in front of her before Emily could react. Shawn quickly picked up Emily and tossed her over his shoulder.

"Put me down!" Emily yelled as she slammed her fist against Shawn's back.

Shawn said nothing as he carried her out of the room and downstairs. Emily struggled as they walked outside, and Shawn dropped her in the dirt. Emily looked up at Shawn with hate as he walked away. Jeff stood a short distance away, and Shawn walked to stand beside him. Emily could see everyone in the camp beginning to circle. There were more people here than there were last time.

"Some of you have been here before, but for a lot of you, this is new," Jeff spoke to the group. "After tonight, this lovely woman will lead us all to a place where we can grow and thrive. But first, she had to learn her place."

As he spoke, Emily remained sitting in the dirt, looking for a weak spot in the crowd.

"What will it be, Love?" Jeff asked as he looked down at her. "Are you going to give, or am I going to take?"

"You can go to hell!" Emily yelled at him.

"Take it then," Jeff grinned.

Emily braced herself as Jeff took a step forward. Jeff suddenly stopped and yelled out in pain. Jeff reached and touched his back. When he pulled his hand back around, Emily saw it covered in blood. Jeff turned and looked at Shawn. As he turned, Emily saw Shawn holding her knife with blood dripping from the tip.

"I'm going to kill you for that," Jeff said as he pulled his gun.

"Emily, get out of here!" Shawn yelled at her.

Emily stood as quickly as possible from the ground, but found that too many of Jeff's men were closing in on her. Emily looked back at Shawn and realized she couldn't leave even if she weren't blocked in.

"I'm not leaving you!" Emily yelled back at him.

Emily could see the anger boiling out of Jeff as she spoke. He now knew that not only was Shawn playing him but that Shawn and Emily were closer than he could have imagined.

"So, you two think you're going to take all of us down?" Jeff said, motioning to the group. "I think I'll add you both to the gate."

"You know the problem with having so many people and not getting to know any of them?" Shawn asked.

"What the hell does that have to do with anything?" Jeff asked out of frustration. Even Emily was confused by Shawn's question.

"The problem is that you don't notice when a large group of them is missing," Shawn grinned.

Just as Shawn finished talking, Emily heard a man scream towards the back of the group.

"What did you do!?" Jeff screamed at Shawn.

"Took out some pedophiles, but I may have forgotten to get the brain," Shawn laughed.

"Fuck you!" Jeff said as he began to pull the trigger on his gun.

Before Jeff could fire, gunshots began to rain all around the camp. Emily looked towards the barricade and saw the barrels flash as guns fired. Emily turned back to Shawn and could see the relief on his face. However, before either of them could move, Jeff fired his gun. Emily screamed as Shawn winced in pain and fell to the ground.

"No!!" Emily yelled as she ran towards Shawn.

Before she could reach him, Jeff grabbed her by the hair and began to pull her backward. Despite the pain, Emily forced herself to the ground and grabbed the knife that Shawn had dropped when he was shot. Jeff pulled her hair hard, and Emily was forced to her feet.

"I should have just killed both of you!" Jeff screamed at her.

Emily didn't say anything but thrust the knife into Jeff's stomach instead. Jeff released her hair and stumbled backward. Emily felt no remorse as Jeff fell to the ground, and a pool of ruby-red blood began to form on the ground around him. Emily turned and made her way to Shawn. Emily dropped to the ground beside him.

"Son of a bitch," Shawn breathed while holding his shoulder.

"You're alive," Emily smiled as she hugged him.

"Of course, I am," Shawn said. "I promised you I would come home."

"Damn right you did," Emily smiled down at him. Emily didn't think as she leaned down and kissed Shawn. Emily was pulled out of the kiss by a girl screaming.

"Go," Shawn smiled up at her.

Emily grabbed her knife and took off into the crowd toward the scream. Emily found Bridgett pinned to the ground with a zombie on top of her. The girl was struggling to keep from getting bitten. Emily rushed to Bridgett and sank her knife into the zombie's head. Once Emily removed the knife, she pushed the zombie off Bridget and helped her to her feet.

"Do you know how to open the gate?" Emily asked.

"Yes," Bridgett replied in a shaky voice.

"I need you to open it and let our reinforcements in."

"I have to find my mom," Bridgett said, looking around at the chaos unfolding.

"I will find your mom," Emily reassured Bridgett. "I need you to open the gate."

Bridgett looked at Emily and then took off running towards the gate. Emily began to make her way through the crowd, killing the zombies as she moved. Emily couldn't help but smile as she heard barking over the screams. Emily turned to see Marley run through the gate along with Sam and most of the people of Sanctuary.

Emily continued working through the crowd and saw some men and women helping in the fight. It wasn't long before Marley was by her side, and Emily could see that all of the zombies had found permanent death.

"Are you alright?" Howard asked as he approached her.

"Yeah," Emily sighed. "I'm fine, but Shawn was shot."

"We saw it," Howard said, looking toward Shawn.

Emily followed his eyes and saw that Sam was already with Shawn and helping him to his feet. Emily walked with Marley and Walter to Shawn and Sam.

"We need to get him back to Doc," Sam said as he helped Shawn stand.

"I've had worse," Shawn insisted.

Emily heard a coughing noise behind her before she could speak. Emily looked down at Jeff, who was still barely alive and was coughing up blood. Emily walked over to Jeff and knelt beside him.

"You fucking bitch," Jeff choked out. "You are going to get all these people killed."

"If you're right," Emily smiled. "Then I'll see you, Hell."

Emily watched as Jeff took his final breath and life left his body. Emily took her knife and stuck it in Jeff's eye. Emily pulled the knife out and slowly stood. Turning back, she saw that all her friends had been watching her. Emily wiped the knife on her jeans to clean the blade and walked back toward them.

"What do you want us to do with all of them?" Sam asked, nodding towards the remaining people of the camp.

"They come with us," Emily said.

"All of them?" Cole seemed shocked by Emily's reply.

"All of them," Emily said with confidence.

"All women and girls were slaves," Emily began to explain. "Some men played a part in keeping their families alive."

"What kind of person could pretend to be one of these bastards and not be a bad person?" Sam asked, looking at the group.

"I did," Shawn answered.

"We will interrogate them and ask the women what each man did. If they are innocent, we will give them a choice to join us."

"And if they weren't?" Howard asked, looking at her over his round glasses.

"For now, we will keep them locked up until a decision can be reached," Emily replied, looking back at him. "We will keep them in quarantine."

"I'll get them all loaded up, and we can head home," Howard said as he walked toward the survivors.

Emily wrapped her arm around Shawn and helped Sam lead him to one of the trucks outside the barrier. Once Shawn was in the truck, Emily shut the door and turned to see everyone loading into the different vehicles.

"I was told to give you a message," Sam spoke.

"I'm listening," Emily replied.

"First, Hope is fine but not happy," Sam started. "Second, Bobby brought Hope her little bit of luck, and third, if you do this again, Julia will probably kill you."

"I figured," Emily smiled. "Sam, how did you guys find this place? I never told anyone where it was."

"We were trying a road on a guess when we came across Marley. He led us all the way here. I have no idea where that dog finds the energy."

"He is exhausted," Emily responded as she petted Marley on the head. "He just wasn't ready to give up."

"I think we should get everyone back to Sanctuary right away," Sam said as the last of the people climbed into the vehicles. "If you want, I can bring a team back to scavenge anything useful."

"Let's go," Emily smiled.

Sam nodded and headed back to the car he drove. Emily walked around the truck and climbed inside while Marley jumped in the bed.

"You hanging in over there?" Emily asked as she started the truck.

"Never better," Shawn smiled back at her. "Let's go home."
"I'm sure Charlie misses us," Emily teased.

"Let's never tell Hope about that," Shawn laughed, even though Emily could tell it hurt him. "She may kill me as soon as she is old enough to reach the knives."

"Deal," Emily laughed as she drove the truck and began down the road.

Emily felt Shawn reach over and take her hand. Emily interlaced her fingers with his as she turned back onto the main road.

Chapter 21

Emily and Shawn drove back to Sanctuary in silence, still holding hands. Emily prepared to put the truck in the park as they approached the gate to enter the code. She was surprised as the gates began to open upon her approach. Emily pulled through and drove the truck straight in front of the clinic. Emily let go of Shawn's hand as she climbed out of the truck, and Doc walked out of the clinic.

"Is everyone all right?" he asked, looking at Emily with concern.

"Shawn's been shot in the shoulder," Emily explained as she walked around the truck. "Everyone else is fine and is settling the new arrivals into the quarantine zone."

"New arrivals?" Doc questioned. "I thought this was a rescue mission?"

"It was," Emily said as she opened the truck door and helped Shawn to his feet. "More people needed to be rescued than just me and Shawn."

"I see," Doc said, still confused.

"If you fix him up first, we can talk about the others," Emily said as she helped Shawn around the truck.

"Of course." Doc seemed to realize what was happening and came to help Emily with Shawn.

Emily walked Shawn to the surgery room and helped him to the table.

"I'll be back to check on you in a little bit," Emily said to Shawn.

"Give her a kiss for me," Shawn smiled.

Emily left the surgical room and walked out of the clinic to the street. Emily could see Sam trying to organize everyone in the quarantine area and knew that she should help, but she had to do something first. Emily looked across the street to the bakery and saw Julia with Hope. Emily took off at a run as Marley jumped out of the truck and joined her. Emily scooped up Hope and wrapped her in a hug.

"I missed you so much," Emily said as she held Hope.

"She missed you, too," Julia smiled at her. "I tried to get her to lie down, but she refuses."

"Thank you, Julia," Emily said as she looked at her friend. "For everything."

"Next time, don't just take off and leave me a note," Julia said sternly.

"I'm sorry," Emily replied. "I was afraid you would try to stop me."

"Damn right, I would have!" Julia replied. "I understand why you had to go. I was afraid we lost you when I told Bobby Hope needed a little luck."

"I knew you could handle it," Emily smiled.

"This was a one-time thing. I need you to change that code right away," Julia was back to sounding stern.

"I will, I promise," Emily said as she moved Hope to her hip. "I have to help get everyone we brought back settled first."

"You brought people back?!" Julia did not try to hide her shock as she spoke.

"Most of them were prisoners just like I was," Emily explained. "They deserve a chance."

"What about the ones that weren't prisoners?" Julia asked, concerned. "How do we keep them from getting in?"

"We will be careful," Emily smiled. "There will be a trial-type interview for each person. I'm still working on the details, but none of them will come in until we are sure they are safe."

"What about the ones that have been discovered were willing participants? What will we do with them?"

"I don't have all the answers," Emily admitted. "But we will figure it out together."

"I trust you," Julia replied after a moment.

"I'll follow your lead. Let me take her a bit longer while you take care of things there. It's not a place for a baby."

"I owe you big time, Julia," Emily said as she handed Hope back. "I'll be back. I promise," Emily said to Hope before leaving for the gate.

Emily walked towards the gate with Marley and heard that some men were unhappy with Sam's directions. Emily picked up her pace to get inside.

"I'm staying with my family!" a man shouted at Sam. "You are not taking them away from me again!"

"I'm not taking them away from you, but we have to take precautions to keep everyone safe," Sam explained, trying to remain calm.

"Then just let us go!" the man yelled. "No one asked for your help!"

"Do we have a problem here?" Emily asked as she approached them.

"This gentleman is upset that we are separating the men from the women and children. I thought it best until we know which men were playing a part and which weren't."

"I agree," Emily said, looking at the man.

"I'm not letting anyone take them away from me again!" the man continued to yell at Sam.

"What's your name?" Emily asked.

"Steve," the man answered. "I just want to be with Mariann and Bridgett."

"Let me ask you, Steve," Emily began. "If I agree to let you stay with the women, then I have to let all men. I'm sure you know some of the guys here don't want to give up their ways. Do you want them to access where your wife and daughter sleep?"

"Of course not," Steve said as he visibly calmed down.

"This is the best way for us to keep them safe until we can figure things out."

"Fine," Steve said, looking over at Bridgett and Mariann.

"We are putting all the men in the back cabin," Sam spoke. "We will bring cots and tents if needed."

Steve turned and walked to join the other men as Cole led them to the back cabin.

"Is Doc going to come to do the exams?" Sam asked.

"He's patching up Shawn right now," Emily replied. "Depending on what time he finishes, it may have to wait until morning."

"I'll go ahead and tell them he'll be doing it in the morning," Sam nodded. "I've got this under control if you want to go check on Shawn."

"Please ensure they all get something to eat," Emily requested.

"It won't be fancy, but we will get them something," Sam agreed.

"Thank you," Emily smiled at him.

"We will take care of them," Sam replied, not looking at her.

"I meant for coming after us," Emily said, looking at Sam.

"We're family," Sam turned to look at her as he spoke.

"But if you run away like that again, I will personally lock you in a cell."

"I understand," Emily nodded as she turned and headed back out into town with Marley.

Emily walked through the gate and took a deep breath. She had never been so happy to be home. Emily looked at the clinic but knew that Doc would not be finished yet. Instead, Emily headed to the bakery and picked up Hope from Julia. Hope fell asleep in Emily's arms as she walked home. Emily decided to skip the bath tonight and let Hope sleep. Once Hope was in bed, and Marley was in his usual position under the crib, Emily walked out and shut the door. Emily grabbed the baby monitor from her room and headed back into town.

"Sam had me carry this while you were gone," Howard said as he handed Emily her walkie. "It doesn't go with any of my outfits, so I thought it best to give it back to you."

"Thanks," Emily smiled as she took the walkie and put it on her waist.

"Doc radioed," Howard continued. "He said that Shawn is out of surgery and awake if you want to see him."

"Thank you, Howard," Emily said as she took off for the clinic.

Emily jogged through the door of the clinic and to the patient rooms.

"I told you she would be here," Doc said to Shawn.

Shawn turned towards the door and smiled at Emily.

"How's he doing, Doc?" Emily asked as she walked toward Shawn.

"He will be fine if I can convince him to rest," Doc said, exhausted.

"I have work to do," Shawn said as he tried to sit up.

"No, you don't," Emily said as she put her hand on his chest and pushed him back down.

"Normally, I would say he could go home and rest, but we both know he won't," Doc continued. "Someone is going to have to watch him to ensure he doesn't push it."

"You have a lot of work to do in the morning, Doc," Emily started. "You go get some rest, and I'll take Mr. Stubborn to my place for the night."

"Are you sure?" Doc asked, looking at Emily.

"Yeah," Emily replied. "I owe him for dropping me on my ass."

"You can explain that later," Doc said, rubbing his eyes. "Here's his pain medication. He can walk around tomorrow, but no lifting or using that arm."

"You got it, Doc," Emily said as she took the medication.

"Alright, let's get you home," Emily said to Shawn.

"I'm not sure I feel safe sleeping there," Shawn smiled at her. "You may kill me in my sleep for that whole dropping thing."

"Get up," Emily laughed as she grabbed Shawn's good arm and helped him sit up.

"I'll see you in the morning, Doc."

"I'll wait for you before I start," Doc said as he turned to make his way upstairs.

"Are you sure about this?" Shawn said as he stood up.

"I am," Emily replied as she took his good arm and led him out of the clinic.

Emily walked with Shawn to the house and closed the door behind them once they were inside.

"I'll lie on the couch," Shawn said as he started crossing the living room.

"I don't think so," Emily said as she grabbed his arm and led him towards the stairs. "The moment I fall asleep, you will sneak out and do everything Doc told you not to."

"You don't know that," Shawn said in the tone of a pouty three-year-old.

"Look me in the eye and promise you weren't planning on sneaking out," Emily said to Shawn as they reached the stairs.

"Well, I could still do the same thing if I sleep in the guest bedroom."

"Come on," Emily said as she led him up the stairs. "And I never said you were sleeping in the guest room."

"I'm not going to fit in the crib," Shawn joked.

"You are going to sleep in my room," Emily replied as they reached the top of the stairs.

"Now listen," Shawn said, laughing. "I am supposed to be resting. So, if this is your trick to get me into bed…."

"Oh, shut up," Emily replied as she hit him in the stomach. "You get in there and lie down while I check on Hope. I'll be right back, so don't try to run off."

"Yes, ma'am," Shawn pouted as he walked into the bedroom.

Emily made her way to Hope's room and peeked in. Hope was still fast asleep, and Marley stood up as she entered. Emily tried to get him to stay with Hope since his spot was taken in the bed, but Marley pushed past her and headed for her room. Emily looked one more time at Hope and saw that the bandana was back to hanging above the crib. Emily quietly closed the door and headed to her room. Shawn was lying down on the far side of the bed, and Marley had lain across the foot of the bed.

"He started to lie on the floor, but I called him up," Shawn explained. "I hope that's okay."

"It's perfectly fine," Emily smiled. "I'm just going to clean up a little first. Not all of us got a sponge bath tonight."

"Don't remind me," Shawn shuddered.

Emily grabbed her pajamas and headed into the bathroom. After a quick shower, she brushed her hair and teeth. Emily walked back into the bedroom and was surprised to find Shawn was still awake.

"I thought you would be asleep by now," Emily commented as she sat on the bed.

"I haven't gone to bed by ten since I was a kid," Shawn laughed. "It just feels wrong somehow."

"Most days, I'm lucky to make it until then," Emily admitted as she slid into the bed.

"You are amazing," Shawn said as she lay down.

"Well, I know the painkillers are working," Emily laughed.

"No, really," Shawn insisted. "It killed me to treat you like I did at that place."

"It's okay," Emily tried her best to sound reassuring. "I knew it was an act."

"I hope you don't mind me using your dad's name. I didn't want to tell him anything true about Hope."

"It's fine," Emily insisted. "I appreciate everything you did to protect her."

"I may not be her dad, but I love that little girl," Shawn said with sincerity in his voice.

"I know you do," Emily smiled.

"So, I kissed you on Christmas Eve, and you said you needed more time."

"Yes," Emily replied with hesitation.

"But I get shot, and you don't need time anymore?"

"Not exactly," Emily laughed. "It just didn't feel right to come running up to you saying, 'I'm ready now.'"

"Just so you know, I would have been okay with that approach," Shawn said in a groggy voice.

"I'll keep that in mind moving forward," Emily smiled as she grabbed his hand. "You need to get some rest."

"I don't want to," Shawn said, half asleep.

"Why not?" Emily asked.

"If I sleep, this will all be a dream."

"I'll be here when you wake up," Emily reassured him. "I promise."

Emily held Shawn's hand as she listened to him fall asleep. Emily slowly slid out of bed and motioned for Marley to stay. Emily tiptoed out of the bedroom and downstairs. Emily didn't stop trying to sneak until she was in the study. Emily made her way over to the desk and turned the chair around. Emily revealed the computer and worked through the process of changing the gate codes. She knew Julia would be checking in the morning. Emily did not want to feel Julia's wrath in the morning for procrastinating.

Once Emily had finished, she took a small slip of paper and wrote down the gate codes. Emily then made her way back upstairs to Hope's room. Hope was still fast asleep and didn't stir as Emily made her way over to the crib. Emily reached up and pulled the bandana down from the nail. Emily carefully tucked the paper into the folds of the bandana and returned it to the wall.

Emily had considered changing her hiding place for the fail-safe, but decided against it. Even if anyone had seen Bobby with the bandana, it was unlikely they knew what was in it. They probably wouldn't count on Emily putting the codes in the same hiding spot if they did. Emily kissed Hope on the head one more time before leaving the room.

Emily opened her bedroom door and slowly tiptoed her way back to the bed. Emily slid into the bed carefully.

"Where did you go?" Shawn asked beside her.

"I had to take care of something downstairs," Emily replied as she rolled over to face him.

"So, I can't work, but you can?" Shawn replied.

"That's right," Emily said in her most comforting voice.

"I think I should be able to work if you are," Shawn said, still half asleep.
Emily knew that he was out of it because of the pain medication. She also knew that there was a good chance that he would not remember any of this conversation in the morning. Emily reached over and found Shawn's hand on top of the comforter. Emily wrapped her fingers with his and lay silent.

"You promise you won't leave again?" Shawn asked, barely loud enough for Emily to hear.

"I promise," Emily whispered back. "I need you to go to sleep now."

"I will, but only for you," Shawn replied.

Emily lay in the dark for a while. She was almost afraid to move until she was sure Shawn was deep asleep. Even as Shawn began to lightly snore, Emily continued to lie and look at him in the dark. While she couldn't see him clearly, her eyes had adjusted enough to make out his general features.

Emily couldn't help but realize that Shawn was the polar opposite of Chad. He didn't care about looking a certain way or his status. The only thing he cared about was taking care of his family. He didn't care what sacrifices he made to do it or if it cost him his own life.

Emily focused once again on the man who was lying beside her. Shawn was not only the type of man she needed but also the type she wanted in her life. However, they had fought and disagreed on some issues. But those issues boiled down to them caring so much for each other.

Marley readjusted at the foot of the bed, trying to adjust to his new sleeping position. Shawn was a tall man, and there wasn't much room for Marley to lie below him. Emily moved herself to the center of the bed, closer to Shawn. Emily felt Marley move as he noticed the change in her position. Marley stretched himself out behind Emily and seemed to be much more comfortable.

Emily finally settled in between Shawn and Marley. She could tell it didn't take long for Marley to fall asleep behind her, and Shawn would not be waking up anytime soon. Emily closed her eyes, and for the first time in months, she did not fear she would have a nightmare. Instead, she focused on the kiss she shared with Shawn on Christmas Eve and that day, his arm around her as she took care of him, and the feeling of his hand in hers as she lay in bed. It didn't take long before Emily was fast asleep herself.

Chapter 22

Emily woke the following day and was happy to find Shawn was still asleep next to her. Emily slid her hand out of his and rolled over to see that Marley was still behind her. Emily gently ran her hand through his fur, and Marley opened his eyes. Seeming to know she was trying to be quiet, Marley climbed off the bed gently, and Emily followed. Emily grabbed some clothes and made her way to the bathroom. Emily got dressed and put up her hair. Emily opened the bathroom door and saw Shawn holding his shoulder.

"I'll get you some water so you can take your medicine," Emily grinned at him.

"I should head home and at least get some clean clothes," Shawn said as he began to stand.

"At least wait and take your medicine, and then we can go together," Emily said as she walked to the bedroom door.

"You are not going to let me out of your sight, are you?" Shawn asked as he walked toward her.

"Nope," Emily replied as she opened the door and walked to Hope's room.
Hope was awake and ready to start her day as Emily opened the door. Emily made her way to Hope and quickly got her dressed for the day. Once Hope was ready, Emily headed downstairs and noticed that Marley was not with her. Emily walked to the kitchen and saw that the back door was open, and Shawn was standing outside of it smoking.

"Did you take your medication yet?" Emily asked as she sat Hope in the highchair and began getting her breakfast ready.

"I decided to wait so you could see me do it," Shawn said as he finished his cigarette and walked back in with Marley.

"Glasses are in the cabinet," Emily nodded as she walked over to Hope and began feeding her breakfast.

Shawn grabbed a glass and filled it with water. Emily watched out of the corner of her eye as Shawn took two of the pills that Doc had given him. Shawn sat down and waited while Hope finished her breakfast. The four of them walked out into the early morning together and saw that Sanctuary was already awake, and people were busy everywhere. Emily walked up the road towards Shawn's apartment with Shawn, Hope, and Marley.

"Good morning," Doc greeted them as he came out of the clinic. "I was hoping that you would be coming out soon. How is the patient this morning?"

"I was forced to sleep and take my medication," Shawn said, rolling his eyes.

"Oh, poor baby," Doc replied in a mocking tone. "Emily, I wanted to talk to you about how you want me to handle the newcomers. Normally, if they show no signs of infection, we bring them in, but I feel that won't be happening this time."

"No," Emily replied. "For now, let's get their exams done. Anyone who is infected, we will find a way to separate from the others, but for now, they are all going to stay in quarantine."

"I'll meet you there then," Doc smiled as he made his way to the open inner gate.

"Was that open all night?" Shawn asked with concern in his voice.

"Sam made sure there was a guard on it," Emily calmly replied.

"Have you decided what you will do with all of them?" Shawn asked as they continued up the street.

"I think it's time I put together that council I talked about," Emily began. "I don't think I can make these decisions alone."

"The final decision will be yours," Shawn said as they reached the door.

"I know, but I still want help reaching that decision," Emily smiled.

"I understand that," Shawn nodded as he stopped. "I promise, I'm just going up to change, and then I'll meet you at the gate."

"Alright," Emily said with suspicion.

Emily turned to the gate as Shawn opened the door and headed to his apartment. Emily reached the gate and saw that Doc was already taking people into the small clinic. Emily pulled the walkie from her waist and pressed the button.

"Sam, are you available?" Emily asked.

"I'm on my way to the gate," Sam replied.

"I'll see you in a few minutes then," Emily said, returning the walkie to her waist.

Emily watched as Doc led several women back to quarantine and brought a few more out.

"Doc working his way through?" Sam asked as he walked up beside her.

"He is," Emily replied as she turned to face him. "We have some big decisions to make."

"You mean you have some big decisions to make?" Sam corrected.

"I've thought it's time to set up that council I talked about when you first arrived."

"Do you want them to help with the trials you talked to Julia about?" Sam asked.

"To start with," Emily smiled. "I wanted to ask you to be part of it."

"I would be honored," Sam replied. "Who else do you want to ask?"

"Julia, Shawn, Howard, Cole, Jaycob, Sarah, Jessica, and Doc," Emily listed. "What do you think?"

"I assume you have a reason for each of them?" Sam asked.

"Of course," Emily laughed. "Do you want me to list them?"

"Nope," Sam laughed. "Do you want me to gather everyone so we can talk when Doc is done?"

"If you wouldn't mind," Emily nodded.

"Well, he made it easier," Sam said, looking behind her. Emily turned and saw Shawn walking through the gate.

"I'll make sure he doesn't run off," Emily laughed. "Let's all meet at my house."

"We'll meet you there in a little bit," Sam said as he walked out the gate.

"You put him to work already?" Shawn asked as Sam passed him.

"He's going to gather everyone I want on the council," Emily replied. "I'm in charge of you and Doc."

"Lucky me," Shawn smiled back at her and wrapped his arm over her shoulder.

Emily and Shawn stood together and watched as Doc continued to walk the women to the clinic. After returning a woman and a young girl to quarantine, Doc returned alone.

"That's all the women and children," Doc said as he walked toward Emily and Shawn.

"How are they?" Emily asked.

"The boys are well-fed, but all the girls and women are severely malnourished. All the girls and women have been beaten, and many of them have been raped. The mental abuse they suffered will last long past the physical."

"I wish I were surprised, but it's about what I expected," Emily replied.

"I know I need to examine the men, but I need to take a moment," Doc said, looking exhausted. "I know some of them did this, and I'm not sure I have the strength to be gentle right now." "Tell me about it," Shawn said through his teeth.

"Let's all head back to my house, and we can figure things out there," Emily said.

"One other thing, six of the women were surprisingly healthy. They didn't have any bruises or marks on them. They claimed to have been raped, but it was like they were reading from a script when they said it."

"That is strange," Emily agreed. "We will get to the bottom of it."

Doc nodded in agreement as Emily turned and started back through the gate with Marley. Shawn and Doc followed Emily to the house, where the others were already waiting. Emily opened the door, and they walked inside. Emily ushered them to gather around the dining room table and then sat.

"So, you want to know our opinions?" Cole asked, not being shy.

"Yes," Emily replied. "There are people out there, and whether we allow them in or not will have an impact on everyone."

"You said something about a trial-type process," Julia spoke up, leaning forward.
"Yes, but I am unsure how to do it," Emily continued.

"I think some of us are wondering why you want us involved," Howard said.

"Some of you have expertise that will be useful," Emily looked around the table as she spoke. "But I have come to trust all your opinions, and that's what I need for this council."

"Well said," Howard grinned back.
"Well, we'd best get started," Sam spoke.

They all sat around for hours talking about the best way to learn about each person who had returned and the trial process. Everything went smoothly except for how to handle those found to have been willing participants in the rapes.

"We should line them up and shoot them," Sam asserted.

"You want your son to know that we just shoot unarmed people?" Julia argued.

"No, I want him growing up knowing he's safe from people like that," Sam continued.

"I can't say I disagree with him," Jacob spoke.

"Why don't we just put them in a cell?"
Howard offered.

"We only have three, and then we all
would be responsible for taking care of them,"
Sam replied.

"If they are not contributing and still get
our supplies, it defeats the purpose of the credit
system," Jessica spoke up.

"We could let them go," Julia suggested.

"So, they can set up a new camp and start
doing it again!" Cole spoke in disbelief.

"Cole's right," Emily spoke up. "Letting
them go is not an option, and I agree with
Jessica that it wouldn't work keeping them as
prisoners."

"So, we kill them," Julia spoke. "But what
if we get it wrong and they are innocent?!"

"We will just have to take our time and be
positive that they are not," Emily said.

"I can't live with that blood on my
hands," Julia said, looking away from Emily.

"I'm not asking you to," Emily replied. "I
would like you all to sit in on the interviews
with me and let me know what your opinion is.
I will decide, and the blood will be on my
hands."

"That's a lot of responsibility," Howard
said, looking at Emily over his glasses.

"I'm willing to take it," Emily replied. "I
just want to know what each of you thinks so I
can feel confident that I made the best decision
possible."

"How will they be killed then?" Sarah asked.

"Will it be by firing squad or hanging?"

"To conserve ammo, I suggest hanging," Shawn spoke with no emotion.

"From a medical standpoint, I would suggest using the bullets. It would be more humane," Doc said, rubbing his temples.

"I don't want them to suffer, so we will take the loss of ammo," Emily said, agreeing with Doc. "I also think it would not be good for morale to set up gallows."

"That I can agree with," Julia said.

"We don't have to rush this," Emily said to them all. "We can take our time and repeat interviews if needed. We just need to ensure we do this as best we can."

Everyone nodded in agreement as she finished.

"Doc, are you up to finishing the medical exams today?" Emily asked.

"I can," Doc nodded. "I will then put a list together of everyone, and we can begin the interviews."

"You want to start them today?" Emily asked in shock.

"I think we all would," Howard spoke. "It's making everyone uneasy having them in a holding pattern."

"We do have one more thing to decide," Shawn spoke. "I know all newcomers were supposed to stay with Emily, but there are just too many. I think we need to decide on temporary housing inside for them."

"I'm not sure that housing is the way to go until they sign the ledger," Jessica said.

"We could ask for volunteers to take in some," Sarah offered. "It would give us a way to get to know them outside the interviews and report what we find."

"I think that is the best way to go," Emily smiled. "Does anyone have any objections?"

Everyone remained silent, and Emily took that as they agreed.

"I'll get us all some notebooks from the store," Jessica said as she stood. "I want to keep notes as we do this, and I'm sure everyone else does as well."

"Yes," Julia agreed. "I would hate for us to pronounce someone guilty because we mixed up their names. There are thirty-four souls out there."

"I agree," Emily nodded.

"I also want to talk to Jose about turning one of the old office buildings into a town halltype building," Sam said. "Doing all of this business where you live just seems wrong."

"I'm fine with that," Emily agreed.

"We can use the conference room in one of them for the interviews to start with," Jessica said. "It's large enough."

"While Doc finishes his exam, we can all head over to get it set up," Shawn said as he stood.

"Doc, is he allowed to clean?" Emily asked and could feel Shawn glaring at her.

"I would rather he come with me to finish the exams," Doc spoke. "Just having him there would keep the men from wanting to kill me." "Alright," Shawn sighed. "One-armed bodyguard coming up."

Everyone laughed, and the tension was finally released in the room. Emily stood as everyone got up and headed for the door.

"I'll meet you at the conference room," Shawn said as he wrapped her in a hug.

Emily hugged him and watched as he headed out the door with Doc. Emily made her way to the kitchen and fed Hope her lunch. Marley followed her, ate what was left of his breakfast, and then lay on the floor. Once she was finished, Emily walked with Hope and Marley out into the town.

"Howard said you may need someone to watch Hope," June greeted her.

"It may not be best to take her into the interviews," Emily smiled back.

"She can hang out with me for the rest of the afternoon," June said as she took Hope from Emily's arms.

"I appreciate it," Emily said as she let go of Hope.
"With everything going on," June began,
"I was wondering if you needed help with the plans for her birthday?"

Emily stood with a blank expression on her face for a few minutes. Emily then remembered that Hope's first birthday was the following week.

"I completely forgot," Emily admitted. "I should be able to handle it. It will just be a small celebration here at the house."

"I don't think so," June said as she shook her head. "Everyone will want to celebrate, and your house is not nearly large enough for that."

"I just thought…." Emily began.

"Hope's birthday is not just the day you gained your daughter, but the day that gave us all hope. It's the day you opened those gates and let us all in," June smiled. "Why don't you let us handle the plans, and you just worry about getting the birthday girl there on time?"

"Okay, but nothing too crazy," Emily said as June walked away.

June didn't reply and simply waved as she walked with Hope towards the school.

"She's going to go crazy, isn't she?" Emily asked, looking down at Marley.

Marley stared up with a puzzled look on his face and started to walk up the road. Emily took that as a yes and followed. Emily made her way to the conference room and took a seat at the table. Everyone except for Shawn and Sam had already arrived and were sitting. Marley lay down under the table, but Emily knew he would not be sleeping.

"How was the last of the exams?" Emily asked Doc.

"I separated three," Doc responded. "No clear bites, but they had a fever and were pretty scratched up. I'll watch them for 24 hours, and if their fever breaks, we can start their interviews."

"Please keep me informed," Emily said as she looked down at a list that Doc slid in front of her.

"I thought we would start with the women and children," Doc said. "Sam and Shawn are escorting the first of them here now."

"Did the men all behave during their exams?" Emily asked.

"One took a swing at me," Doc replied. "He missed, and Shawn warned him that if he did it again, he wouldn't be walking out of my office."

"I take it he didn't do it again?" Emily asked, laughing.

"No, he didn't," Doc laughed.

Sam and Shawn entered the room as he finished with a woman, about fourteen years old, and an eight-year-old boy. Emily could see that the kids were clinging to the woman, who was probably their mother. All of them looked terrified, and Emily could not blame them. Sam shut the door behind them and followed Sam to the table to take their seats.

"I know it won't help," Emily began. "But there is no need to be scared. We are just talking and trying to get to know each other better."

"You want to make sure we are not crazy like Husband Jeff was," the woman said, looking down at the children.

"Well, yes," Emily replied, looking at the others.

"Ask your questions," the woman said, looking Emily in the eye.

"Just to make sure we have things correct, let's start with your names," Emily said.

"My name is Clair, my daughter is Jenny, and my son is Christopher," Clair answered, looking up.

"How long have you been with Jeff?" Emily asked as she wrote down their names.

"He captured us in the early spring," Clair answered, still not looking up.

"Did Doc go over the findings of your medical exam with you?" Emily asked as she glanced at Doc.

"He told us we would live and told us what happened to us like we didn't already know," Clair responded shortly.

"The mother was sexually abused, but neither child showed any signs," Doc spoke, and everyone continued to write.

"Are you able to identify if any of the men we returned with are the ones who assaulted you?" Sam asked.

"Does it matter?" Clair laughed.

"We don't want to invite them to stay if they are guilty of such things," Emily explained.

"Invite?" Clair laughed again. "You took us all prisoner just like he did, but sit here like you're better."

"I understand why you would feel that way," Emily said, trying to sound comforting.

"Right now, we want to ensure you are all healthy and remove the men who did those evil things."

"And then what?" Clair asked sharply. "You tell us what we are expected to do and the consequences if we don't."

"Not at all," Emily smiled. "We will invite those who were prisoners inside to see what we have. We will explain how things work here and then give you a choice. You are welcome to join us, or you are free to leave. If you choose to leave, we will give you supplies and let you go on your way."

"You expect us to believe that crap?" Clair spat at her.

"It's the truth whether you believe it or not," Emily remained calm in her tone. "We will prove it as soon as this process is finished."

"Are you able to give the names of the men here who assaulted you?" Sam asked in a professional tone.

"No," Clair said. "I only knew them by Husband."

"Are you willing to identify them if you could see them?" Julia asked.

"You planning on a lineup?" Clair asked in a mocking tone.
"We could do pictures," Jessica suggested.
"If it would make you more comfortable."

"You all are serious," Clair said with disbelief."

"We are," Emily smiled back. "Are there any of them you feel comfortable saying are innocent?"

"There were some that were kind and never touched us," Clair stated. "They would even help us when no one was looking, but I don't know their names."

"Is there anything we can get you to make you more comfortable while we work through this process?" Emily asked.

"A pregnancy test?" Clair asked, looking at the floor. "I just need to be sure."

"I took a blood sample," Doc stated. "I will be checking all the women for pregnancy. I will have all of the results in the morning."

"Thank you," Clair said, looking back at Doc.

"Shawn and Sam will take you back for now, and we will talk again once we have the pictures," Emily smiled.

Sam and Shawn stood right away and led them out the door. Shawn closed the door as they left, leaving Emily and the rest of the council alone.

"I don't know if we will learn much until we have the photos," Cole said.

"I agree," Emily replied. "I think we should hold off on the interviews until we have them."

"I will get the camera and get them right away," Jessica said as she stood. "I should have them ready first thing in the morning."

"We will meet back here in the morning then," Emily stated. "Let's try to get photos of everyone. I'm not sure we should assume that all women are innocent. Some may want to continue living in that type of society."

"You think some of them will want to return to living that way?" Jacob asked in disbelief.

"The human mind is complicated," Howard replied. "I agree that we should be suspicious of everyone until we know for sure."

"I'll go with Jessica to keep her safe while she takes the photos," Cole said as he stood and followed Jessica.

Everyone filed out of the room, leaving Emily sitting at the table, looking at what she wrote.

"I heard you want a building converted," Jose said as he entered the room.

"Yes," Emily said as she looked up. "We were thinking a town hall-type of building."

"I'll work on drawing up some plans tonight and bring them to you for approval," Jose said, looking around the room. "I will need the original blueprints to decide which will work best."

"Of course," Emily smiled back. "They are in my office. Please, help yourself."

Jose left without another word, passing Shawn as he went.

"We should get out of here," Shawn said. "There's nothing more that we can do today."

"It just feels wrong to stop after the first interview," Emily said as she closed her notebook.

"I know, but you said it yourself; we must take our time."

Emily stood and walked to Shawn, who wrapped her in a hug. Emily allowed Shawn to lead her out of the building and back onto the street. Shawn walked Emily and Marley to their front door.

"I'll go pick up Hope," Shawn said as he let go of Emily. "I assume she is with June."

"Yeah," Emily said, feeling exhausted. "But you are not supposed to lift anything." "Then I will let her walk," Shawn smiled. "This could take a while."

Shawn turned to leave, laughing. Emily opened the door and headed inside with Marley. Emily walked straight to the couch and allowed herself to collapse. Marley jumped on the sofa beside her and lay his head on her lap. Emily petted his head as she leaned back and closed her eyes. Emily and Marley remained this way until the front door opened.

"Mama!" Hope yelled as Shawn closed the door.

Emily's eyes shot open, and she leaned up.

"Hope?" Emily called back.

"Mama!" Hope yelled as she ran towards Emily.

"Why didn't you tell me she started talking?" Shawn asked as Emily picked up Hope.

"Was she talking the whole way home?" Emily asked.

"No, silent as a mouse until we came in the door. Is this the first time she's talked?" Shawn asked, realizing Emily had happy tears in her eyes.

"Yes," Emily said.

"Now, that's a way to end a long day." Shawn smiled as he sat down next to her.

Chapter 23

Everyone had gathered in the meeting room the next day, eager to start the interviews. Jessica had arranged all of the photos on top of the table.

"Rumor around town is that Hope is talking," Howard smiled at her.

"Yes, she said Mama last night." Emily smiled with pride.

"Did she call you Mama or Shawn?" Doc teased. "I joke, of course, most babies who learn to talk don't know what the words mean."

"Well, she seems to," Emily laughed. "She called it out when she got home. I called her name out of surprise, and she yelled it again while running to me."

"That's a smart little girl," Howard smiled at them.

Shawn and Sam came in with Clair and her children once more. Clair seemed calmer today, and the children were visibly more relaxed.

"You stopped the interviews yesterday," Clair said as she looked at Emily.

"You helped us realize that names may not be something people could give, so we wanted to get these pictures ready," Emily replied.

Clair stepped forward and looked at the photos. Emily and the rest of the council sat quietly as Clair and her children looked at them.

"He's the one," Jenny said, pointing at a picture of a man.

"What did he do, sweetie?" Emily asked as she held up the photo.

"He hid me when the bad man came for me," Jenny said, looking at her mom. "He took me back to my mommy after the sun went down."

"Do you recognize anyone else?" Emily asked them all as they continued to look at the pictures.

Clair pointed at three of them and said they had all raped her. Christopher said that he saw two of the men kill a woman who wouldn't follow the rules.

"What about the women?" Emily asked, noticing that they all stared at the photos of the women but didn't say anything.

The family, along with the council, seemed confused by the question.

"What about this one?" Emily asked as she picked up a photo of a brunette woman that she saw them all look at with just as much fear as they had the men they claimed assaulted them.

"She was a wife leader," Jenny spoke.
"What's a wife leader?" Julia asked.

"She was one of the high-ranking women," Clair began. "She received better food and clothing. She was in charge of keeping the young girls in line and training them to keep the men happy."

Emily set the picture back down and looked around at everyone. She could see that they were all just as disgusted as she was.

"Were there others?" Howard asked.

"Yes," Clair replied as she pointed at five more pictures.

"Thank you," Emily said, and motioned to Shawn and Sam that the interview was over.

"Do you have my test results?" Clair asked.

"Yes," Doc replied. "All of the pregnancy tests were negative."

Emily watched as Clair breathed a sigh of relief. Shawn and Sam walked them to quarantine and brought in the next person. Emily continued to ask the same questions and identify who they could be in the pictures. Emily learned during Bridgett's interview that one of the men whom everyone kept saying helped them was her father. They interviewed everyone except the six accused women and all the men.

"I don't know if I can talk to anyone else," Sarah said as Shawn and Sam left with the last woman.

"We have to try," Julia said.

"She's right," Emily agreed. "We must at least get through the first interviews today."

"I'm trying," Sarah sighed as Shawn and Sam returned.

Emily conducted the interviews with the remaining people just as she had with all the others. If a man had been accused of rape, she would ask them if they had anything to say to defend themselves. It surprised her that every man accused would begin pointing at the pictures of the woman who accused them, calling them crazy when Emily was careful not to tell them who accused them. The ones who hadn't always been accused demanded to know if their families, wives, or children were safe as soon as they came in.

"That's everyone," Jacob said as he leaned back. "What do we do now?"

"Do we just vote or…" Cole started.

"We should at least talk about them," Julia said. "Just to make sure no one missed anything."

"I agree," Emily sighed. "I know we are all mentally exhausted, but I think we need to talk about it while it's fresh in our minds."

Emily sat with the council and talked about the thirty-four people they had met that day. Emily listened as they talked back and forth about how best to handle a particular person and things they thought a person was lying or hiding. Emily remained quiet as they spoke and simply listened to them.

"I believe we all have a lot to think about," Emily said as they finished. "We will meet again in the morning for a vote."

"We can take a break, but I think we should vote today," Sam replied. "They are crammed in like cattle in the quarantine area. It was not meant for that many people at once.

With the six women being accused, we don't have the room to separate them."

"That's not going to work," Emily agreed.

"How many do we have that everyone agrees are safe to invite in?" Shawn asked.

"Twenty-two," Emily replied without hesitation.

"Those we believe we can trust, we will find volunteers to house them and get them out of quarantine. The others will remain there to give us more time," Emily explained. "I can't decide that someone deserves to die after just one day."

"Alright," Sam said, sliding back. "Do you have a list of those you want to bring in and give a choice?"

Emily ripped a paper out of her notebook and handed it to him.

"I will start talking to everyone and see if they would like to volunteer."

"I'll take Bridgett and her family," Emily said to him. "Unless you don't think I have enough room for a family of three?"

Sam looked at Shawn awkwardly and wrote on the paper.

"If there are any for which you can't find volunteers, just let me know," Emily said as she spoke. "I'm excited to see what Jose has come up with for a town hall."

Everyone stood and followed Emily outside. Emily could see that Jose and his team had worked hard on the building next door.

"I'm supposed to go do a follow-up with Doc," Shawn said beside her. "Am I trustworthy to do this one alone?"

"Okay," Emily teased. "But you better not give him any trouble."

"Yes, ma'am," Shawn smiled as he began the walk toward the clinic.

Emily walked to the building and, after making sure it was safe, went to find Jose. Jose was giving the men directions as she approached. Most of the walls had been knocked down, and only the studs remained.

"It doesn't look like much right now," Jose stated, "But it will look amazing when it's done."

"I trust you," Emily said as she looked around.

"I even put you in an office for you. I thought you would like a space to work that wasn't your home."

"That would be nice," Emily smiled back at him. "I'll let you get back to work."

Emily waved goodbye to Jose as she left. Emily spent the next few hours making her way through the town. She had not been able to make her rounds in days and missed checking in with everyone. Emily was surprised at the number of people who told her they were volunteering to take in some new arrivals. It wasn't long before Emily saw Shawn pairing up the new arrivals with their host families.

Emily returned to the gate just as Sam brought Bridgett and her family.

"All of you will be staying with Emily," Sam said as he walked them in. "She's our leader."

"We need a better title for me," Emily laughed. "Leader makes it sound like we're aliens."

"It kind of does," Bridgett agreed.

"We'll work on it," Sam laughed.

"If you guys want to follow me, we'll get you some clothes, and then I'll show you the house," Emily said as she motioned for them to follow.

Marley fell back and walked with Bridgett. Emily felt more confident in her decision to allow them to stay with her. If Marley felt comfortable enough to relax around them, there was nothing to worry about. Emily led them to the clothing store. Emily waited by the door while they each grabbed a couple of outfits and allowed Jessica to note what they had taken. Once they were done, Emily led them all back to her house.

"You all are welcome to the showers," Emily said. "There are two extra rooms upstairs that you are welcome to use tonight."

"Why would you do this?" Steve asked, looking around the living room. "If I were you, I would have sealed this place up and never opened the door."

"That was my first plan," Emily admitted.

"But when I went into labor, I quickly realized I couldn't do this alone. I opened the gate, and the first group I let in saved me and my daughter's lives."

"You have a baby?" Bridgett asked excitedly.
"I do," Emily smiled. "She will be home in time for dinner."

"How old is she?" Mariann asked.

"She will be one next week," Emily said, still having difficulty believing it herself.

"Can I go take a shower now?" Bridgett asked, looking at her parents.

"There's one down here and two upstairs," Emily answered as they all looked around.

"I'll be in the office if you need me."

Emily turned and walked into the study as the family began to make their way to the bathrooms. She had done this enough to know they needed some time without anyone hovering over them. Emily took the time to sit and update her journal on the events that had taken place. Marley took his customary position on the floor. Emily had just finished writing when Steve appeared in the doorway.

"You find everything you need?" Emily asked as she closed the journal.

"We did," Steve replied. "I just wanted to say thank you."

"It's my pleasure," Emily said as she stood.

"Almost every child we talked to told us you saved them at some point."

"I did the best I could," Steve stated. " I didn't tell anyone that Mariann and Bridgett were my wife and daughter. I was out scavenging when they got picked up. When Jeff took me in, I saw how men's families were treated and thought it safer for them. It also kept them safe if I got caught helping the women."

"It makes sense," Emily agreed.

"You said there were rules to staying, and we got a choice," Steve continued.

"Yes, I thought I would give you a moment before we went over all that," Emily said.

"No offense," Steve said. "But with everything, I think everyone would like to know now."

"We can go find the others and see if they are ready," Emily said as she stood.

Steve walked back into the living room to get Martha and Bridgett. Emily and Marley led them outside and found everyone with new arrivals walking toward her.
"I take it everyone is eager to learn about Sanctuary?" Emily asked Isabelle who was the first to reach her.

"Can you blame them?" Isabelle smiled.

"They've been wondering about this place since they were brought here days ago."

"That's fair," Emily smiled.

"Alright, everyone," Emily spoke loudly to all the new arrivals. "If you want to follow me, I'll give you a tour and explain how we do things here."

Emily walked with Marley and began the tour. Emily had done this enough that she went through the tour with little thought. They eventually found their way back to the main street, where she ended the tour.

"Do you guys have any questions?" Emily asked the group.

"What is going to happen to the ones you didn't bring in?" a female voice asked.

"We are still looking into them, but no final decisions have been made," Emily replied.

"So, there is still a chance that you will invite them in, too?" the same voice asked.

"If we can prove they didn't hurt or rape anyone, yes," Emily tried to remain calm as she spoke.

"And the ones that did? What are you going to do with them?" Steve asked.

"The council and I are working on that. We want to ensure that everyone is safe," Emily reassured everyone.

"You said we would sign a ledger and get a house and job once we decided to stay," Bridgett said. "When can we do that?"

"I prefer everyone to sit with the information for a while before they sign," Emily explained. "However, if you all would like, we can meet after breakfast to allow everyone to make that choice."

Emily watched as everyone nodded, and the crowd began to break up as the hosts guided everyone back to their homes.

"You guys are welcome to go inside, or you can walk with me. I need to pick up my daughter. It's just a few blocks away," Emily said to Clair, Steve, and Bridgett.

"I think we would like to go with you," Steve said, looking at his wife and daughter.

"It's just this way," Emily said as she walked towards June's house.

Emily knocked on the door when they arrived.

"Mama!" Hope exclaimed as June opened the door.

"I tried to get her to talk all day, but nothing. She sees you and talks immediately," June laughed.

"She just loves her mama," Emily said as she took Hope's hand.

"That she does," June laughed. "She's welcome here anytime."

"I appreciate it," Emily said as she allowed Hope to begin to pull her towards the street.

"Have fun," June smiled as she closed the door.

Hope led Emily to the street, but stopped when she saw people she didn't know.

"Steve, Mariann, Bridgett. This is my daughter, Hope."

"Hi, Hope," Bridgett waved as she kneeled.

Hope smiled and waved back at Bridgett.

Steve and Mariann both looked shocked to see that Hope was real. Hope went back to leading them all back to the house. Once inside, Emily placed Hope in her playpen.

"I'm going to start dinner," Emily said to everyone. "Are you guys allergic to anything?"

"No," Mariann spoke. "Would it be okay if I held her?"

"As long as she's okay with it," Emily smiled. "Be careful. She's fast and will disappear if you don't keep an eye on her."

Emily made her way to the kitchen and began cooking. Once dinner was nearly ready, Emily set the table and moved everything in as it finished. Emily had just put the chicken on the table when she heard the front door open. Emily entered the living room to see Shawn come in and rub his shoulder.

"Just wanted to make sure everything was okay here," Shawn said, looking at Emily as she came in.

"You're just in time for dinner," Emily replied. "What did Doc say?"

"That depends," Shawn said timidly. "Are you going to hit me if I lie?"
"There's a good chance of it," Emily said as she crossed her arms.

"He says it's healing, but it will be a few more days before the stitches come out," Shawn said. "He wants me to avoid lifting until then and then light duty for a few weeks."

"Did you take your pills today?" Emily asked as he rubbed his shoulder again.

"I'm fine," Shawn said. "We can save them for someone who's hurt."

"You are hurt," Emily replied. "Please, take them for me?"

"That's low," Shawn said. "I'll take them after dinner."

"Well, the food's ready," Emily smiled. "Come on, everyone," Emily called to the rest of the room.

Emily took Hope from Mariann and led the way into the dining room. Emily set Hope in her high chair and put her dinner on the tray. She knew Hope would be a mess by the end of the meal, but decided to give her some independence and let her feed herself. Emily realized quickly that there would be no leftovers as the new arrivals began to eat like they hadn't eaten in months.

"I've left my medicine upstairs," Shawn said as he stood.

"I'll walk up with you," Emily said as she lifted Hope out of the high chair. "It's time for someone to get ready for bed."

"We will handle clean-up," Mariann said as she started grabbing plates.

"You don't have to," Emily replied. "I can take care of it once Hope is in bed."

"We insist," Steve said as he stood to help his wife.

"Well, I appreciate it," Emily smiled as she left the room with Shawn.

"I think they are on the nightstand," Emily said as they walked past her room. "I'm going to get her cleaned up, and I'll meet you in a bit."

"Good night," Shawn said to Hope before he walked through the door.

Emily cleaned up Hope and got her into bed.

"Good night, beautiful," Emily whispered as she kissed Hope.

Emily walked to the door and looked back to see that Marley was under the crib. Emily turned off the light and closed the door. Emily returned to the hall to her room and found Shawn waiting for her.

"Did you find them?" Emily asked.

"I did," Shawn held up the bottle. "I took two like I'm supposed to."

"Good," Emily said as she sat down beside him.

"I was hoping to talk to you for a minute," Shawn said as he took her hand.

"What's going on?" Emily asked as she intertwined her fingers with his.

"We haven't gotten to talk since we got back," Shawn said as he looked at her.

"Is something wrong?" Emily asked with a sick feeling in her stomach.

"No," Shawn responded right away. "Things just happened fast, and I want to make sure you are okay with this." Shawn motioned with their hands.

"What would make you think I wasn't?" Emily asked.

"At Christmas, you said you had to work through stuff, and then I got shot. I just want to ensure you are ready for this, and it wasn't just a reaction at the moment."

"You don't remember talking before you fell asleep the first night we were back, do you?" Emily asked.

"Not really," Shawn admitted.

"I pushed you away at Christmas because of my ex-husband," Emily explained. "I still felt bound by my vows and needed to work through that before allowing myself to move on. I had been working with Father Nathan to do just that."

"I don't want to let something that happened in the heat of the moment put that off track," Shawn said as he tried to pull his hand away.

"You're not," Emily insisted as she pulled him back. "I've been free of it for months and was just looking for the right way to tell you."

"Really?" Shawn asked her.

"Really," Emily reassured. "I think we should still take it slow, especially with Hope involved, but I am ready for this. That is, if you are?"

"Oh, I'm ready," Shawn laughed.

"Ms. Emily," Bridget spoke from the doorway. "I just wanted to say goodnight before we head to bed."

"Good night," Emily responded.

Bridget headed down the hall with her parents to the spare rooms.

"I assume that you are staying again tonight?" Emily turned back to Shawn.

"There are strangers in the house," Shawn replied. "Do you want me to go to the couch?"

"Do you want to sleep on the couch?" Emily asked, smiling.

"Not really," Shawn smiled at her.

Emily grabbed her pajamas and quickly dressed in the bathroom. When she returned, Shawn was walking back into the bedroom with Marley.

"She's out like a light," Shawn said as he walked around opposite the bed.

Emily crawled into bed and turned off the light. Soon, all three were fast asleep.

Chapter 24

Emily met with all the new arrivals early the following day and was pleased that they had decided to stay. Emily assigned them each a place to live and a job. Once they were settled in, Emily headed over to check on the progress of the town hall. Jose and his team had finished tearing out most of the interior walls and were framing the new rooms. Jose insisted that it would be done in a few days.

"The people still in quarantine are starting to get out of control," Sam said as she came out of the town hall.

"What do you mean?" Emily asked.

"They are demanding to come in," Sam explained.

"That's not going to happen," Emily said as she walked towards the gate.

"Shouldn't we wait for backup?" Sam asked as he followed her. "They are pretty riled up."

"I think you two can handle it," Emily said as she looked down at Marley and continued walking.

Emily opened the door to the quarantine and was greeted by a group of angry women. Emily watched as the door to where the men were opened, and they joined the women.

"Why are we still here!" one of the women shouted at Emily.

"We are evaluating each of you to make sure letting you inside won't put my people in danger," Emily explained.

"We don't want in!" one of the men yelled.

"Just open the gate and let us out!"

"That's not an option until we determine you are not a danger to others," Emily said aggressively.

"What would make you think we are dangerous to anyone!?" another woman yelled.

"We told you we were abused, but you still left us trapped here!"

"We will conduct another round of interviews today," Emily replied. "You will each have your chance to speak then."

"That's not good enough!" one of the men yelled.

"That's the best I can do," Emily said. "Sam, please escort the men back to their section."

"You think he's going to force us all through that door?!" a different man yelled.

Marley had grown tired of how the men were talking to Emily. Marley stepped forward and bared his teeth at the men. Emily watched as Marley continued to snap and herded the men back through the door. Sam closed and locked the door once they were through.

Emily then walked with Sam and Marley out and locked the door to the women's area behind them. Marley didn't relax until they had walked back through the gate.

"I'm going to meet with the new arrivals," Emily said to Sam. "Once that is done, I will meet with the council to do the final set of interviews."

"Good luck," Sam said as Emily continued up the street with Marley.

Emily could see a group forming on the street in front of her house. First, Emily pulled the host families aside and talked to them about the new arrivals. The host families had seen nothing that concerned them and expressed that they would feel comfortable with the latest arrivals joining Sanctuary. Emily approached the new arrivals and waited as they each told her their decision. All of them had decided to stay, and soon the ledger was being passed around. Emily had assigned them a place to live, but didn't have time to walk them all to their homes with the remaining interviews. Instead, she handed the list to Isabelle and asked her to show them to their homes. Emily told everyone she would meet with them as soon as possible to assign them a job.

Emily returned to the conference room just as Shawn and Sam walked through the door with one of the women. The woman was still agitated and glared at Emily while Shawn and Sam took their seats.

"So, what makes me a possible threat?" the woman asked.

"Several individuals have identified you as a 'wife leader," Emily replied. "Tell us about that."

"I did what I had to do to survive," the woman replied casually. "You see me as a threat because I'm a survivor?"

"Is it true that you prepared and coached young girls on how to please their husbands?" Julia spoke next.

"Yes," the woman replied without hesitation. "Better them than me."

Everyone turned to look at Julia as her pencil snapping filled the room. Emily could tell that Julia wanted to do more than break her pencil at that moment.

"You would do the same thing," the woman smiled. "I don't regret what I did and would gladly do it again."

"That's enough," Shawn said as he stood and took the woman by the arm.

Sam stood and followed Shawn out to get the next person. The interviews only got worse. Some women claimed that what they did was a talent and tried to see if they could do the same work in Sanctuary. The men were worse as they admitted what they did and even requested access to the girls. Shawn grew rougher and rougher as he escorted each of the men from the room.

"These people are sick!" Julia exclaimed as soon as the interviews were over.

"Sick implies that I could help," Doc replied. "There is no helping these people."

"Does anyone think that any of these people can be saved?" Emily asked the table.

Everyone remained silent, and Emily

knew that they all agreed with her.

"They can't stay here," Julia said.

"You know what that means?" Emily asked.

"Yes," Julia replied.

Emily looked around to see everyone nodding.

"You all agree that these people can not continue to live in this world?" Emily asked to be sure.

"My daughter is not growing up with those sick fucks," Cole spoke through his clenched teeth.

"We will take them outside the wall tonight and carry out their sentence," Emily said as she closed her notebook. "I will carry it out personally."

"We all agree and will help you," Shawn said, looking around the table.

"I can't ask you to do that," Emily replied, shaking her head.

"You didn't," Doc spoke. "Don't get me wrong, I don't think I can help, but if others can, it would be best. Imagine being the last in line waiting while eleven other people are shot in the head for your turn. That makes us just as cruel as them."

"I won't ask anyone to help," Emily said.

"But those who want to volunteer can meet me at the gate after dark."

Emily stood without looking back and left the room. Emily made her way to June's house and picked up Hope. Emily spoke to no one as she returned to the house and fed Hope dinner. They had just finished eating when Emily heard the front door open and close.

"Ladies?" Shawn's voice bellowed through the house.

"Kitchen!" Emily called back to him.

Emily was finishing the dishes as Shawn entered.

"I just wanted to talk to you a little bit more about tonight," Shawn said as he sat by Hope.

"Not in front of her," Emily smiled at Hope.

Shawn picked up Hope from the high chair and held her in his lap.

"Is she going to a babysitter tonight?" Shawn asked.

"It won't take long. She can sleep in her bed, and I will take the monitor with me," Emily replied.

"Are you sure that's a good idea?" Shawn asked with concern. "We have quite a few new people, and I'm not sure they can be trusted that much."

"I thought you agreed they were innocent?" Emily said as she dried her hands with a towel.

"I did, but…." Shawn tickled Hope and didn't finish his sentence.

"I will ask Doc to sit with her while we are gone," Emily smiled.

"Would it be bad if I already did?" Shawn slunk down like he was afraid Emily would hit him. "He should be here in a few minutes."

"Good," Emily smiled. "You can explain to him how you pick up Hope when you are still lifting a restriction."

"Shit!" Shawn exclaimed as he realized what he had done. "I didn't think!"

"Give me the baby," Emily said as she took Hope from Shawn. "Please don't learn to say that word."

"Great, now I'm teaching a baby to cuss," Shawn said, covering his mouth.

"I do it sometimes, too," Emily smiled. "Don't worry about it."

"Are you still going to tell Doc on me?" Shawn asked.

"Not this time, but I will sing like a canary next time!" Emily laughed.

"Deal," Shawn smiled.

"I'd better get her laid down before he gets here," Emily said as she turned and headed upstairs.

Emily found Doc and Shawn waiting for her when she returned downstairs with Marley.

"I'm sorry I can't help tonight," Doc said as soon as he saw Emily.

"There's nothing to be sorry for," Emily replied with a smile.

"I tried to tell him," Shawn said from behind Doc.

"Thank you for sitting with Hope while we do this."

"It's my pleasure," Doc said.

Emily walked out the door with Shawn and felt the reality of what they were about to do hanging heavy in the air. Shawn grabbed Emily by the hand and led her to the armory. Emily stopped to look at everyone who had gathered. Cole, Sam, Howard, and Jacob were waiting for them.

"Are you all sure you are up to this?" Emily asked as they handed her a handgun.

"Let's get this done," Jacob said as he slid his handgun into the waistband of his jeans.

Emily turned and walked with all of them to the quarantine area. Emily helped the men as they secured the remaining people in zip-ties and escorted them outside the wall.

"Are you letting us go?" one of the women looked up with pleading eyes.

"You all have been convicted of unforgivable crimes against the living," Emily said as professionally as she could.

"For these crimes, you have been sentenced to death."

Emily pulled her handgun from her waist and saw that the others did the same.

"You can't do this!" one of the men yelled. "We are people, not zombies!"

"Which means you had no excuse," Jacob said as he aimed his gun at the men.

"May God have mercy on your souls," Emily said.

Immediately, each of them fired two rounds, and the twelve people dropped to the ground lifeless. Emily lowered her weapon and tried hard to keep her composure. While she had killed many zombies and Jeff, this felt different. The guys lowered their guns, immediately dragged the corpses up the road, and put them in a pile. Emily felt herself move and help. Once all of the bodies were stacked, they burned them.

Emily walked back through the gate with everyone and back to the armory once the gate was shut. No one spoke as they returned their weapons and headed back into town. They walked up the road together and broke apart in silence as each of them headed home. Emily walked into her house with Shawn and shut the door.

"Is it done?" Doc asked as he stood up.

"It is," Emily replied, feeling exhausted.

"She didn't make a noise," Doc said, trying to change the topic.

"Thanks, Doc," Emily smiled. "I'll see you tomorrow."

Doc took the opportunity to leave without hesitation. Emily made her way upstairs and could hear Shawn behind her.

"Would you like me to get Marley?" Shawn asked as they reached the top.

"Not yet," Emily replied as she turned and headed into the bedroom.

Emily sat down on the edge of the bed and dropped her head into her hands. Shawn sat down beside her and wrapped his arm around her. Emily expected herself to cry, but no tears came. Instead, she felt exhausted.

"I don't want to ask if you are okay," Shawn said.

"I appreciate that," Emily said as she lifted her head. "I'm not so that you know."

"I know," Shawn replied as he pulled her closer. "That's part of what makes you amazing."

"The fact that I feel like shit for killing child molesters, rapists, and essentially pimps makes me an amazing person?" Emily looked up at Shawn with confusion.

"Yes," Shawn smiled down at her. "You did what you had to do to keep everyone safe. But you still allow yourself to feel the emotion of taking a human life."

"I still don't understand," Emily stared back at him.

"Taking a life shouldn't be easy," Shawn explained. "It's the fact that you manage to hang on to your humanity in this world that makes you amazing."

Emily leaned her head against Shawn and closed her eyes. He held her tight and allowed her to sit silently for a long time.

"We should get to bed," Shawn finally spoke.

Emily nodded as she stood and grabbed her pajamas. Emily came out of the bathroom to see that Shawn and Marley were waiting for her. Emily crawled into the bed and Shawn's arms. Emily lay her head on Shawn's chest as he held

her. Emily felt Marley jump up on the bed
behind her and lie down. Emily closed her eyes
and saw an image of each person's face who
died that night.

Chapter 25

It had been a week since everything had happened with Jeff, and things were beginning to feel normal at Sanctuary. Everyone contributed, and Hope's birthday party was planned. June was right that no one wanted a small event. All the new arrivals had settled into their new jobs and blended into Sanctuary seamlessly. Shawn had continued to stay at Emily's every night, and it had not gone unnoticed. While they only slept, it didn't stop the rumors from flying.

Emily and Shawn walked down the main street, hand in hand, while Marley and Hope walked ahead of them. It seemed like Hope was growing more every day. Her steps were steady, and she was saying new words daily. Emily smiled as Hope walked up the street like she owned the place.

"Are you ready for her party tonight?" Shawn asked beside her.

"I was thinking about postponing," Emily replied as she waved at Hope, who had turned to look at them.

"Postponing the party won't keep her from growing up, you know?" Shawn smiled at her.

"You just have to kill my dreams, don't you?" Emily pretended to be flustered.

"That's me," Shawn laughed. "Killer of dreams."

"Good morning, you two," Julia said as she walked toward them. "I was wondering if I could steal away Emily and Hope to get their opinion on the cake for tonight?"

"I need to go get a report on the wall for last night," Shawn smiled as he let go of her hand. "I will catch up with you guys later."

"Hope, do you want to see your birthday cake?" Emily asked Hope as Shawn walked away.

"Cake!" Hope squealed. "Yes, cake!"

Julia laughed as she turned towards the bakery with Hope running behind her. Emily shook her head and followed Marley. Emily walked into the bakery and could not help but gasp at the cake sitting out. It was four tiers with pink and white trim.

"You don't think it's a bit much?" Emily asked as she picked up Hope.
"Not at all," Julia smiled. "We have a lot of people to feed tonight."

"You're the expert," Emily laughed.

"Cake!" Hope clapped next to her.

"I also made a small cake just for her," Julia smiled.

"It looks amazing," Emily smiled. "It's more than I could have imagined."

"Speaking of imagination," Julia looked at her slyly. "You two are living together now?"

"Not exactly," Emily replied shyly. "We are taking it slow."

"I don't think you know how slow it works," Julia teased.

"It's not like that," Emily insisted. "I had to make sure he would rest and ...."

"Yeah..." Julia encouraged her to continue.

"I honestly didn't want to be alone after everything," Emily admitted.

"So... you're telling me that you just sleep?" Julia asked.

"Yes," Emily laughed.

"If you say so," Julia smiled. "Oh, don't forget we have the town picture at noon. Jessica asked me to remind you."

"Well, I think we can make it," Emily replied, looking at Hope.

Emily waved goodbye to Julia and headed back out to the street with Hope.

"Do you have a moment?" Jose asked as the door to the bakery closed behind her.

"Of course," Emily replied as she turned to him.

"We officially have the town hall done, and I wanted to get your approval."

"Lead the way," Emily said as she motioned up the street.

Emily followed Jose into what used to be a building with nothing but offices; what they were for, she wasn't sure. Now a sign hung above the door that read "Town Hall." Emily walked through the door and gasped at the sight around her. The area was opened up in the front. There was a long table on a small raised portion of the floor at the far end with enough tables for everyone in the council. There were several rows of chairs between the table and the door. Emily followed Jose through a door on the left and looked around at a large office.

"Sarah says she can set you up a computer terminal here so that you can work," Jose explained.

"This is perfect," Emily said as she looked around. "It is exactly what we needed."

"I'm glad you like it," Jose smiled. "I did have a suggestion for what we should do next."

"I would be glad to hear it," Emily smiled.

"Cole is still working out of that one-car makeshift garage. I want to recycle one of the houses, just framed it into a full garage."

"I agree," Emily smiled. "He needs an official workspace, especially with me assigning him another mechanic to help."

"We will get started on it right away," Jose nodded. "It will take us quite a bit longer than this, but we can do it."

"We will also work on getting him more supplies to ensure he has everything he needs." "I'm sure he will be thrilled," Jose smiled.

"I'm going to get ready for the picture. I think Derick is hovering to talk to you."

Emily looked back and could see Derick peeking through the open door. Emily knew he probably wanted to make sure she would keep her promise. On Halloween, she had told him that if he didn't break any rules, she would allow him a small drink on Hope's birthday. Emily watched as Jose headed out and motioned for Derick to come in.

"I didn't mean to interrupt," Derick said as he walked toward her.

"You didn't," Emily smiled. "What can I do for you?"

"I have done as you asked," Derick started.

"I wondered if I could ask you one thing in return."

"What were you thinking?" Emily asked, feeling that she already knew the answer. "Don't give me the drink tonight?" "What?" Emily asked, confused.

"I've been sober for a while now, and I know if I have that drink, I won't be able to stop," Derick explained. "I want you to keep the law in place to protect me from myself if I slip." "Consider it done," Emily smiled at him.

Derick nodded and left the office without another word.

"I just got this office, and I'm already working," Emily said to Hope.

Hope smiled at her and looked around the room. Emily sat Hope on the ground and held her hand as they walked out of the office. Emily closed the door as soon as Marley followed them out. Emily walked outside and saw everyone gathering in front of her house. Emily walked with Hope and Marley up the street.

Jessica was already putting everyone in position for the picture. Jessica led Emily to her place next to Shawn. Once everyone was in position, Jessica took the picture. As soon as Jessica announced they were done, everyone began to scatter. Emily knew that they were off to start setting up for the party.

"I would like to get a few of you guys," Jessica said to Emily. "To mark Hope's birthday."

"That would be great," Emily replied.

Jessica worked for the next little bit, taking various pictures of Hope. Hope had no problems with all of the extra attention. By the time they were finished, the rest of the town had most of the party set up for that night.

"I'd better get the guest of honor to bed," Emily said as she picked up Hope.

"I'll give you a hand," Shawn replied as he followed them inside.

Hope put up a bit of a fight, and it took quite a while for Emily to get her to lie down for her nap. Hope eventually gave up and fell asleep. Emily and Shawn returned downstairs, leaving Marley to nap with Hope.

"Can you believe she's one already?" Emily asked as she and Shawn sat on the couch. "No," Shawn laughed.

Emily laughed as she leaned back against the couch.

"I wanted to talk to you," Shawn said, turning towards her.

"You should never start a conversation with a woman like that," Emily said as she turned towards him. "Are we breaking up already?"

"What!? No, of course not!" Shawn exclaimed. "I just wanted to let you know that I think it's best if I start staying at my apartment again."

"Do I snore or something?" Emily asked.

"No," Shawn laughed. "I know that you wanted to take it slow, and my moving in right now is not taking it slow."

"I don't think you've quite moved in," Emily said, trying to think of an argument but knowing she didn't have one.

"Really?" Shawn asked, looking at her with a half-smile.

"No," Emily said, ashamed. "I guess we don't want Hope growing up thinking you move in with a guy as soon as you start dating."

"Exactly," Shawn agreed. "Not to say we can't have sleepovers now and then."

Emily knew that Shawn was teasing and winked at him.

"I'd better get going," Shawn said as he stood.

"I was roped into helping with the lights."

"You have fun with that," Emily grinned as she stood to walk Shawn to the door.

Once Shawn was gone, Emily went upstairs to wrap Hope's birthday present. Emily pulled the book from the top of her closet and sat on the bed with the wrapping paper. Emily opened the book and began to flip through the pages. Emily had worked with Jessica to make Hope a storybook about her family. The story read like a fairy tale and started with pictures of

Emily as a kid. Emily had pulled the photos from the album she had brought with her. Emily even included a few pages about Chad, but had to be very careful in choosing the words for that part of the story. The end of the book was about their family in Sanctuary. Emily made sure to add to the book as Hope grew to make the story more about Hope's life.

Emily closed the book and carefully wrapped it with the pink paper. Just as she finished, Hope announced over the monitor that she was done with her nap. Emily left the present on her bed, went to Hope's room, and got her ready for the party. Once Hope was changed and dressed, Emily grabbed the present from the bed and headed outside with Hope and Marley.

Emily gasped as she looked at the street where the party would take place. Shawn had gotten the lights set up, but so much more had been done. Jacob had brought up some farm animals, and a petting zoo was set up for the kids. Buttercup was there with a saddle on, ready to give the kids rides up and down the street. The amount of pink that covered the street almost made Emily dizzy.

"I think we could have done more," June said as Emily walked down the steps.

"Probably, but I don't think getting the circus here is an option," Emily laughed. "We have a chair for you two over there," June said. "We are ready to start if you are."

"Is there a way to postpone this?" Emily replied, looking down at Hope.

"She's going to grow up if you are ready or not," June laughed.

"Well, might as well let her have fun then," Emily sighed as she walked towards the chairs that June had pointed to.

Soon, everyone in Sanctuary who was not on wall duty was gathered, and the music was turned on. Emily allowed Hope to walk around and smiled, watching her interact with everyone.

"Is it okay if we let Hope ride Buttercup?" Jacob asked as he walked towards Emily, holding Hope's hand.

"Is she big enough?" Emily asked, feeling concerned.

"She is," Jacob smiled. "If you would prefer, we could have an adult ride with her."

"I'll do it," Emily said as she quickly stood up.

Emily followed Jacob and Hope over to Buttercup and climbed into the saddle. Jacob handed Hope to Emily, and Emily sat Hope on the saddle in front of her. Emily signaled Buttercup to walk and smiled at Hope's excitement. Hope squealed and clapped as Emily led Buttercup up the street. Emily led Buttercup to the gate and turned her around to head back to Jacob. Jacob helped Hope down, and Emily climbed down after.

"I think she had fun," Jacob said as he set Hope on the ground.

"She did," Emily smiled back.

"You may want to make your way to the cake. Julia seemed eager to start it since presents will take a while."

"Cake!" Hope yelled as she took Emily by the hand and started leading her towards where Julia was waiting.

Emily sat Hope in the highchair, and Julia set the small cake in front of her. Emily joined the rest of Sanctuary as they sang Happy Birthday to Hope. Hope smiled and blushed at the song. Once they finished, Emily helped Hope blow out the candle on top. Julia quickly removed the candle as Hope dove into the cake with her hands. Emily tried to help Julia distribute the cake to everyone else, but Julia insisted that Emily relax and enjoy watching Hope.

Once the cake was finished and Hope was cleaned up, Bobby and Terra began to bring Hope her presents one at a time. Emily sat with Hope, reading each of the cards and helping her open her gifts. Most of them were homemade, but Emily just felt that it made each of them more memorable. After the first couple, Hope seemed to realize that Emily said "thank you" and began to say it herself. Hope took nearly an hour to open all the presents, and Emily felt it would take her that long to carry everything inside after the party.

Emily placed Hope on the ground and allowed her to run around with the other children when she was done with the presents.

Emily prayed that all this running would help
Hope lie down more easily for bed than she had
for a nap.

"You know, she may be old enough to
convert her crib to a toddler bed," Julia said as
she sat beside Emily.
"Are you trying to kill me?" Emily asked.
"I remember feeling like that," Julia
smiled.

"I thought I would offer some mom
advice."

"I appreciate it," Emily smiled. "It's hard
for me to accept she's growing up already."

"I wish I could tell you it gets easier,"
Julia smiled.

"I know it would be a lie," Emily
laughed.

The sun was starting to set, and Emily
could see that Hope was beginning to wear
down. Hope kept sitting down and rubbing her
eyes. Emily picked up Hope and decided to put
the princess to bed before she turned into a
demon. Emily returned to the party after Hope
and Marley were tucked in with the baby
monitor.

The other parents seemed to have taken
her lead and taken the other children to bed.
Cole was handing out glasses of a clear liquid
that she knew was moonshine. Emily quickly
made her way over to inform Cole that Derick
did not get his drink that night. Cole seemed
confused but accepted what she said. Emily

declined the glass Cole offered her, deciding she wasn't in the mood that night.

"Rumor has it that Derick is being denied his promised drink," Shawn said as he walked up beside her and wrapped his arm around her.

"It's by his request," Emily smiled up at him.

"He said he couldn't handle it."

"Well, that does it," Shawn laughed. "The world is officially over."

"My thoughts exactly," Emily smiled.

Emily stuck close to Shawn for the remainder of the party. Once everyone was celebrated, Shawn walked Emily back to her house, but stopped at the front door.

"So, I may be regretting what I said now," Shawn said as he pulled her into a hug.

"Why don't you come over for breakfast?" Emily offered as he finally let her go.

"I'll see you bright and early," Shawn replied as he headed down the stairs.

Emily and Shawn began a routine of meeting for breakfast each morning over the next couple of weeks. Shawn helped Emily convert Hope's crib into a toddler bed, and Hope seemed thrilled with the situation. Emily was a preschool teacher, one of the new arrivals from Jeff's camp.

After much discussion, it was decided that while Hope was younger than a typical preschool student, it was best for her to join the class. Hope continued to show signs of advanced mental and physical development, and Emily had finally conceded to let her attend. There was only one other student in the preschool class, and Emily thought it best for Hope to have more interaction with a child close to her age.

Emily had just finished dropping Hope off at school and headed towards the wall for her morning check-in. Hope had no problems heading into school, and it turned out that Emily was the only one crying.

"Emily, report to the COM building."

"Everything alright?" Emily replied on her walkie.

"New group," Sarah replied.

Emily returned the walkie to her waist and made her way up the main street. She met with Shawn and Sam, who had heard the radio as she reached the building.

"How many do we have?" Emily asked as she walked in.

"Eleven," Margaret answered. "Four of them are children."

"How far out are they?" Shawn asked before Emily could.

"They are on foot and just passed the SUV," Margaret answered as she turned back to the radio.

"Let me know when you see the wall, Charles. Our leader will open it once you are closer."

Emily felt all color drain from her face, and all of the oxygen leave the room.

"Did you say, Charles?" Emily finally asked.

"Yes," Margaret replied. "It's Charles and his family, children, and grandchildren."

"Wasn't your dad's name Charlie?" Shawn asked, realizing what she was thinking.

"Everyone called him Charlie," Emily said as she turned to head out of the COM building.

Emily ran up the wall stairs two at a time. Emily looked into the distance just as a group walked into view. They were still too far away for Emily to see, but she couldn't help but pray it was them. Emily made her way to the control room and entered the code to open the outer gate.

Emily returned to the wall to see that Shawn and Marley were waiting for her. Emily walked up beside them and looked back at the group drawing closer. Emily strained her eyes, trying to make out their faces.

✳✳✳

Joe walked with J.R. down the road in front of the rest of their family.

"Uncle Joe, when can we go home?" J.R. asked.

Joe looked down at J.R. and could tell that he was exhausted.

"We have to find somewhere safe, and we will make that our home," Joe responded as he tussled J.R.'s hair.

"Maybe Sanctuary is safe," J.R. said, looking ahead.

"What's Sanctuary?" Joe asked as he followed J.R.'s gaze.

Joe could see a weathered wooden sign ahead. The sign read "Sanctuary – A Place to Live Among the Living."

"Dad!" Joe called to Charlie, who ran up to join him and J.R. "What do you think?" Joe asked.

"It's worth a try," Charlie replied as he patted Joe on the back and walked towards the sign.

Author's Note

Thank you for joining Emily and Marley on their journey. I hope you enjoyed their story as much as I did. If you could please review it, it would be greatly appreciated.

Are you looking for more? Please check out my other books.

Scan the QR code below for links to my social media, mailing list, and other books.

www.ingramcontent.com/pod-product-compliance
Lightning Source LLC
Chambersburg PA
CBHW011925300726
48970CB00008B/2572